FLOWERS IN A DUMPSTER

MARK ALLAN GUNNELLS

Crystal Lake Publishing
www.CrystalLakePub.com

ISBN: 978-0-9946793-2-1

Cover Design:
Ben Baldwin—www.benbaldwin.co.uk

Interior Layout:
Lori Michelle—www.theauthorsalley.com

Editor:
Monique-Cherié Snyman

Proofread By:
Jason L. Hood, Paula Limbaugh, and Sue Jackson

COPYRIGHT ACKNOWLEDGEMENTS

"The Support Group" was originally published on the site deviantart.com as the 1st runner up in Clive Barker's "Men of the City Contest" in December of 2014. "Transformations" appeared in the now defunct online e-zine The Harrow Vol 11, No 9 (2008). "The Last Men on Earth" was self-published as a digital short in December of 2011. "Welcome" appeared in The Harrow Vol 9, No 2 (2006). "Welcome Back" also appeared in The Harrow Vol 10, No 7 (2007). All the rights for these stories have reverted back to the author. All the rest are original to the collection.

PRAISE FOR MARK ALLAN GUNNELLS

"An interpretation so left of field that its concept alone must be celebrated. The Men of the City as human stains is not a new notion, to be sure, but the idea that the very cities themselves are in revolt against them, doing what must be done in the name of peace, is at once hilarious and horrifying, as all great satire must be."

—Clive Barker

"What I love about Mark Allan Gunnells' stories isn't just the chill factor, or the wit, or the dramatic turns —although those things are all present —but the compassion inherent in the storytelling. Whether it's a couple touching hands as they approach an ominous house or a gruff husband giving in to his wife's kindness, the rich humanity is what makes these stories so effective and memorable."
—Lisa Morton, Bram Stoker Award-winning author
of *Ghosts: A Haunted History*

"Mark Allan Gunnells is an under-rated writer. He's been that since long ago when I first discovered some of his early writing for Sideshow Press. He should be better known just on the basis of the output of high quality fiction. Part of the problem (and really the strength of Mark's writing), I think, is well demonstrated in this present collection. The stories are

very diverse, each told in a distinctly different voice. These pieces are stylistically and thematically different. None have predictable endings. Often the stories end with the reader left with an unsettling moral ambiguity. Rather than relating his work to a more well-known horror writer, I think his stories may be closer in tone/feel to the work of Raymond Carver, a mainstream writer, who wrote a lot of dark fiction. The present collection contains surprises from story to story, rewarding the good reader. All a joy to read."
—Gene O'Neill, *The Hitchhiking Effect*, and *The Cal Wild Chronicles*

"*Flowers in the Dumpster* is filled with solid stories from an author who knows his craft. I was thrilled to find surprising gems sprinkled throughout. Highly recommended."
—Kate Jonez, Bram Stoker (R) and Shirley Jackson Award nominated author of *Ceremony of Flies* and *Candy House.*

"Mark Allan Gunnells's writing on the first page of the first story was so attention-grabbing that I was immediately hooked. It's rare these days to find a new writer (to me) that not only can tell a story but actually knows how to paint pictures with words so effectively."
—Mass Movement Magazine

TABLE OF CONTENTS

PAST LIVES

SADIE SPOTTED THE stranger first. Miguel, there's someone coming!"

A dark-skinned man, wearing dusty jeans, bolted out of the doublewide mobile home shotgun in hand. "Where?"

Sadie pointed down the dirt road to the approaching figure. Dust billowed around the distant stranger, a tall, emaciated white man dressed in rags. He moved quickly, weaving slightly.

"Sadie, get inside."

"But Miguel—"

"Get inside and watch Zeke." Reluctantly, Sadie did as she was told and disappeared inside with their son. As the silver-haired stranger drew closer, Miguel lifted the shotgun and pointed it at the man. "Just keep walking, amigo."

The stranger held out two empty, bleeding hands. "Please . . . if you could just spare a drop of water."

"Got nothing for you here expect some buckshot. Just keep moving. We don't want any trouble."

"I don't either. Trust me, I've had enough trouble."

The stranger turned, exposing the left side of his face. Miguel gasped at the sight of those ugly red burn scars. The left ear was singed off completely, and so much scar tissue surrounded the left eye Miguel was certain the stranger couldn't see out of it. "What happened to you?"

"A year and a half ago I was in what used to be New York, roasting a rat I managed to catch over a fire I built in an old trash barrel. A gang of guys ambushed me. It wasn't enough just to take my meal and shoes, they stuck the side of my head in the flames."

"Well, we've all got sob stories," Miguel said in a neutral tone.

"Just . . . please! I haven't had anything to drink in over a day, nothing to eat in almost a week. Just *anything* . . . a drop, a crumb. I'm begging you to show a little mercy."

"We're all out of mercy here."

"Miguel," a voice hissed from behind. He turned to see his wife standing in the doorway.

"Woman, I told you to stay inside."

"*Woman*? Don't go all alpha male on me. We have enough to share a meal with someone in need."

"Sadie, you're too trusting."

"I'm not a fool, Miguel. Look at him. It's obvious he doesn't have weapons, and he's so frail. Even Zeke could take him in a fight."

Miguel turned back to the stranger, the gun never wavering. "What are you doing so far off the beaten path?"

"The cities aren't safe. I learned that the hard way. Scavengers and thugs have taken over. I figured 'off the beaten path' would be safer."

"That's why we're out here, but it's not without its dangers. Still have to protect what's yours."

The stranger held out his hands again. "I'm not a

threat. I know you've got no reason to trust me, but keep the gun on me the whole time. I'm fine with that. Please, just a bit of sustenance, a place to rest for a while, then I'll be on my way."

Sadie made the decision by walking past Miguel and taking the stranger's arm. The man stumbled, and fell against her. "Miguel, put that damn gun down. Get over here and help me get him inside."

He growled in frustration but leaned the gun against the side of the mobile home. He took the other man's shockingly frail arm. The stranger kept thanking them as they helped him up the steps and through the door. He collapsed into a torn recliner that bled stuffing from several rips. Even though his skin was hot to the touch, he shivered.

Miguel stepped back outside and retrieved the shotgun, training it on the stranger once more.

Sadie shot him a venomous glare. "Is that really necessary?"

"He said I could keep the gun on him."

"It's fine," the stranger said in a quavering voice. "I'm just grateful to be out of that sun, even for a minute."

He was out of the sun, true, but without electricity to run air conditioning or a fan, it was just as hot inside as out. Miguel found it even more stifling in the mobile home, which was why he spent most of the day outdoors, working in the garden or down at the lake.

"Zeke," Sadie called, "come out here."

"Woman, leave the boy out of it."

"Stop calling me *Woman* like that or I'm going to slap your face, *Man*. If we can't show a little kindness and charity then we've truly ceased to be human. Is that what you want for our son, to lose his humanity?"

Miguel didn't have an answer, so he stepped back and let Sadie take over. But he did not lower the gun.

Zeke came out of his room and entered the living room cautiously, keeping his distance from the stranger. He looked afraid but also curious. It's been years since he'd seen anyone other than his parents. He was only twelve, but in many ways he was already a man. This new world was not a place for children.

Sadie said the boy's name three times before he tore his eyes away from the stranger and looked at her. "Run down and fetch some water for our guest."

"Guest?" Miguel said, raising an eyebrow.

Sadie ignored him and clapped her hands, causing Zeke to jump. "Hurry." Zeke nodded then disappeared out the door. Turning to the stranger, Sadie said, "I'm going to fix you a little something to put in your belly. If you really haven't eaten in a week, it's best not to gorge yourself. You'll only make yourself sick. We do have some fresh veggies from the garden, though. I'll make you a small salad." She turned her eyes to her husband. "You, behave yourself."

After Sadie left through the archway, heading into the kitchen area, Miguel took a seat on the sagging sofa directly opposite the stranger. He placed the gun across his lap, but his grip remained firm.

The stranger had closed his eyes. Miguel assumed he was asleep until the man suddenly said, "I am sorry for intruding on your family this way." Miguel grunted in response. Opening his one good eye, the stranger lifted his head slightly but allowed it to drop back against the cushion for lack of strength. "So are you folks from this area originally . . . I mean, before everything went to hell?"

At first Miguel didn't answer, but finally he said, "Look, Mister—"

"Edwin, my name is Edwin."

"I don't really care. Let's just get something straight here. We're going to give you some water, some grub, then you hit the road. This is a rest stop for you, nothing more. We're not buddies."

"We're both from Texas, though Miguel's family is from Mexico originally," Sadie said, returning with a plate of sliced cucumber, tomato, carrot, and onion. "Sorry, we don't have anything in the way of salad dressing."

Edwin smiled only for a second—the effort to raise the corners of his lips seemed monumental. "That's quite alright, ma'am."

"Sadie."

"Thank you, Sadie. You're a true Christian lady."

Edwin speared a slice of cucumber with the fork and tried to bring it to his mouth. His hand shook violently, making it difficult for him to hit his mark. Without a word, Sadie sat on one of the chair's arms, took the plate from Edwin and proceeded to feed him as if he were a young child.

Zeke returned at that moment, carrying a slightly crumpled plastic water bottle. Sadie motioned the boy over. At first he seemed reluctant and glanced at his father. Miguel begrudgingly nodded. He walked slowly over to the recliner and held the bottle out.

With another of those faint, transitory smiles, Edwin took the bottle. "My God, it's actually cool."

"Miguel came up with a system," Sadie said with such genuine pride Miguel smiled despite himself. "We get the water from the lake about a half mile behind the house, boil it, then we bottle the water and keep it in a net that's submerged in the lake itself. It doesn't keep it ice cold or anything, but keeps it cool."

Edwin took a deep swallow of the water. He coughed and sputtered, prompting Sadie to pat him on the back a few times. When the fit passed, he took a few more tentative sips. "This is like a little bit of Heaven in a bottle."

Zeke sat next to his father, his eyes glued to the stranger. Miguel couldn't really blame him. Not only was it someone new, the scaring on the left side of the man's face made it hard to look away.

"So where are you from, Edwin?" Sadie asked as she continued to feed him the vegetables.

He chewed methodically, swallowing with some trouble and washing it all down with the water. "Well, I was born and raised in Ohio, but I was living in the North East when everything went down."

"And what brought you down south?"

"I spent last winter in what had once been a Buddhist monastery in West Virginia. It was rough. I figured a warmer climate would do me better this year."

Sadie nodded and continued feeding him until the plate was clean, after which she stood and looked over at her husband. "Come help me in the kitchen."

"I really think I should—"

"You should really come help me in the kitchen."

Before Miguel could say anything more, Sadie turned and headed through the archway.

Miguel sighed and handed the gun to Zeke. They'd started teaching the boy how to use firearms three years ago. In the distant past Miguel had abhorred guns, been a proponent of gun control legislation. He would have considered allowing a twelve year old to handle a weapon akin to child abuse, but he lived in a different world now. Being able to defend yourself was an unfortunate reality they all had to accept.

Leaving Zeke to watch over Edwin, Miguel followed after his wife. She leaned against the counter with her arms folded across her chest. He recognized the look on her face. "No, Sadie. Don't even think about it."

"You don't know what I'm going to say."

"I most certainly do, and we're not keeping him. He's not a stray cat."

"I think we should at least let him stay the night."

"I already said no."

"The man can barely stand. He couldn't even feed himself."

"That could just be an act to get us to let our guard down."

Now Sadie put her hands on her hips and tilted her head. "You can see the man as well as I can, and I know you don't believe that."

She knew him better than anyone ever had. There was little he could hide from her. "Be that as it may, he's not staying here."

"Just one night, Miguel. That's all. Let him have dinner with us, sleep in an actual bed, get rested up before he continues on. One night."

Miguel chewed this over for a couple of minutes, his eyes darting between his wife and the archway, through which he could see the frail man in the living room. Finally he said, "Okay, but only one night. And I mean that. Not one night that turns into two that turns into a week that turns into a month. He's out the door bright and early tomorrow morning."

Sadie smiled and reached up on tiptoes to deliver a kiss to Miguel's cheek. "Thank you. It's nice to know the compassionate man I fell in love with all those years ago is still in there."

"You keep him alive," Miguel said then gave her a real kiss.

As the sun slipped below the horizon, Miguel lit the torch lamps in the backyard and started to cook dinner on the grill. He had no charcoal, but his crude fire, made from twigs and paper scraps, got the job done. The sizzling meat caused Miguel's mouth to water and his stomach to growl.

Behind him, the family sat at the wooden picnic table, Zeke on one side, Sadie and Edwin on the other. The stranger seemed to be regaining some of his strength. He was still weak and shaky, but he'd managed to walk out to the picnic table by himself and stumbled only once.

"So this is possum meat, you said?" Edwin asked.

Miguel nodded, flipping over a hunk of meat with a bent barbeque fork. "I set up a few traps down by the lake. I catch a few from time to time."

Sadie laughed, and even without looking over his shoulder, he could tell from the sound that she was embarrassed. "I know it might seem a little gross, eating possum . . ."

"Oh, not at all," Edwin assured with a flip of his hand. "When I was in New York, I practically survived on rat. And it has been so long since I've had meat of any kind, I'm grateful that you are willing to share."

"Think nothing of it. You know, it tastes pretty good. I even dry some of the meat and make it into a jerky."

"Really? Possum jerky?"

"Yeah," Miguel affirmed. "We'll give you some for the road when you leave tomorrow."

"Don't be rude," Sadie said.

Edwin laughed. "It's okay. I promise I won't overstay my welcome. I hope to make it to Florida by winter. I'm thankful for the hospitality you have shown me, but I'll be moving on tomorrow."

Miguel said, "Good," and started transferring the meat to a chipped plate. On the grill, he tossed some large hunks of potato and carrot to roast. That didn't take long. He brought everything to the table, dividing up the food equally among the four of them, and took a seat next to Zeke.

Before anyone started eating, Sadie insisted everyone hold hands, bow their heads and say grace. She offered up the prayer, as usual: "Dear Lord, I just want to thank you for protecting this family and keeping us safe even in these crazy times. Thank you for providing this food we are about to consume, and use it to nourish our bodies and keep us healthy and strong. And Lord, I also want to thank you for guiding Edwin to our door. We will treat him with the kindness and generosity with which you treat us. Amen."

Everyone muttered an "Amen" in response then dug in.

At first they ate in silence, but then Edwin moaned low and said, "This is absolutely delicious. Miguel, were you a cook in your former life?"

Miguel snorted a laugh but didn't answer.

"Actually, Miguel was a kindergarten teacher," Sadie answered for him.

Edwin chortled. "Really?"

"That surprise you?" Miguel asked, chewing on a rather tough piece of possum.

"Honestly . . . yeah. A little."

Miguel shrugged. "Well, I was different back then. The world was different back then."

"No argument there."

Sadie said, "What about you, Edwin?"

"What about me?"

"What did you do back when the world was different?"

"Oh, I was a lawyer, um, once upon a time. Not much use for those now."

"Wasn't much use for them then, either," Miguel muttered.

"Again, no argument there."

"I was a nurse," Sadie said.

Edwin smiled at her. "Now that I have no trouble seeing." Then he looked across the table at Zeke. "And what about you, young man? What were you before the world went and fell apart on us? A doctor? An astronaut?"

Zeke stuffed a hunk of potato in his mouth and shrugged.

"Zeke was only seven when the sickness started," Sadie whispered, picking up a piece of carrot then putting it back down, as if this topic had robbed her of her appetite. "Which means it has only been five years. Feels like a hundred. Sometimes I think I can barely remember what life was like . . . *before*."

Edwin nodded. "When the sickness hit, it swept through the world pretty fast. Who would have thought that life as we knew it could collapse so completely, so quickly?"

"I'll tell you what I do remember," Sadie said. "The news reports. We'd gather around as a family and watch. I mean, we were scared enough just seeing what was happening in our own city. At first it seemed like a simple case of the flu, but the sick people didn't get better, and many were dead within a week of contracting the illness. The news gave us conflicting reports about the cause, how to treat it, how to prevent it, but one thing was clear—it was happening *everywhere*."

"And the damn President on the airwaves almost every night telling us everything was A-Okay," Miguel grumbled, bitterness dripping from his words like acid. "I mean, people were dropping like flies, the hospitals were overrun, similar reports were coming in from across the globe, but still that pompous prick with his fat face and jet-black hair just smiled and said there was nothing to worry about."

Sadie smiled apologetically at Edwin. "You'll have to excuse my husband. He gets a little, shall we say, passionate on the subject of President Kane."

Edwin chewed on a piece of meat, swallowed, and then asked Miguel, "You don't think the government had something to do with the disease, do you?"

"Would you put it past them? It could have been some kind of biological warfare project gone horribly awry. Regardless of how the sickness started, though, there's no way the President didn't know how serious it was."

"Maybe he just didn't want to create a nationwide panic," Edwin said.

Miguel pushed his almost empty plate aside. "Panic? Maybe people could have protected themselves better if they were a little more panicked? By lying to the public about the seriousness of the outbreak, it made people complacent. Even when they saw the evidence with their own eyes, they believed the President because surely he wouldn't lie to his citizens, right? It doesn't matter if he had a hand in creating the virus or not, his actions doomed this country. I consider the man a murderer. He should be put to death."

"He's probably dead already," Sadie said quietly, but her words were corrosive, too. "Or at least, he is if there's any divine justice left in the world."

Miguel shook his head. "If that man turned out to be one of the two percent with a natural immunity . . . Well, that would be enough to make me question my faith."

"Don't blaspheme," Sadie said, but she wore a faint smile. Edwin now pushed his own plate away. He looked uncomfortable, his face twisted in a grimace. "Please forgive us. This is terrible dinner conversation. It's been so long since we've had a guest, we've forgotten our manners."

"No, it's not the conversation. I think my exhaustion is finally catching up to me. Would you mind terribly if I retired for the night?"

"Of course not. I'll warn you, the pull-out sofa bed isn't the most comfortable thing in the world."

"The last few nights I've slept on the ground, so it'll be like sleeping on a cloud, I'm sure."

Edwin rose from the bench when Miguel said, "Stick around and have breakfast with us in the morning. If you're going to be setting off, might as well do it on a full stomach."

Sadie graced her husband with such a brilliant smile he suspected he would get a little something extra in the bedroom. Edwin smiled at him, too. "That's very kind of you. I'll see you good folks in the morning."

"Do you need any help?" Sadie asked.

"I think I can manage. Good night and bless you all." With that, Edwin hobbled back to the mobile home and disappeared inside.

Miguel and Sadie exchanged smiles over the table. Miguel turned to his son . . .

. . . and gasped. Zeke had gone pale.

Edwin expected he would have no trouble falling asleep, but sleep eluded him like a slippery eel. He tossed and turned on the mattress, which was in fact less comfortable than the hard ground, but his troubled mind was what kept him awake. He could hear the family talking quietly outside, though he couldn't make out their words.

They were such a lovely family, and one of the few fully intact families he'd run across in the last few years. What were the chances all three would be immune to the virus? Of course, if both parents had a natural immunity, it would definitely increase the chances of their offspring being immune as well.

He would never be able to fully express his

appreciation at the generosity they had extended to him. Miguel's initial hostility and mistrust were understandable, but it was obvious these were good people.

This was why he thought it might be best to sneak out early in the morning before they awoke. They had a nice setup here and he wouldn't mind staying for a while, but he couldn't risk them finding out the truth.

Still listening to the family's murmured conversation out back, Edwin finally fell asleep.***He awoke sometime in the night to the sound of creaking floorboards and heavy breathing. Edwin cracked open his right eye and scanned the room, but the overwhelming darkness kept him from seeing enough. As his vision adjusted, he thought he detected a hulking figure standing right next to the bed.

"Miguel?"

There was no answer, but then the figure raised something into the air. Edwin tried to move, but he wasn't fast enough. Pain exploded along the right side of his head and he plunged back into even deeper darkness.

When Edwin came to the next time, he found it much easier to see his surroundings, thanks to the torch lamps' flickering flames. He lay outside on the surface of the hard, splintering picnic table. Edwin tried to rise, despite the intense pounding in his head, but found himself strapped to the table with sturdy ropes. He craned his neck to look back toward the mobile home and saw Miguel standing there. "Hello, Mr.

President."

Edwin could only make a hoarse croak when he tried to speak. He licked his lips and tried again. "What are you talking about?"

"I'll admit, you're pretty unrecognizable," Miguel said, raising a baseball bat and propping it casually over his shoulder. Edwin saw the blood on the end of it. "You've all but wasted away, your hair has gone silver, and what with half your face looking like Freddy Krueger there is a good chance that we would never have realized who you really are. Believe it or not, Zeke was the one that put it together."

"Miguel, I don't know what Zeke thinks—"

"He was only a boy when the sickness hit, so I doubt he even remembers what President Kane looked like, but it was something you said that struck a nerve with him. After spewing lies and misinformation at the public in your press conferences, you'd always conclude with, 'Good night and bless you all.' Funny, Sadie and I had forgotten that, but Zeke remembered. And once he said something to us, it all fell into place. President Stephen E. Kane. Let me guess . . . the 'E' stands for Edwin, right?"

Edwin thought about denying it, but he didn't have the strength. "What happened was not my fault. I didn't do anything."

"Except deceive the entire nation."

"At first I honestly didn't know the severity of the situation."

"And after you did?"

"Well, my advisors kept telling me it was best not to come clean with all the frightening details, that it was better to keep the public calm."

Miguel snorted a laugh. "So the Leader of the Free World was just following orders, just like the Gestapo."

"Please, you don't understand. I was just trying to—"

"And not only did you lie your ass off to us all back then," Miguel said, paying no heed to Edwin's words, "but then you came into my home and lied to my family."

"I did not lie."

"You didn't give us your real name and you said you were a lawyer before the world ended."

"As you already deduced, Edwin *is* my real name, my middle name, and before I went into politics, I was a lawyer."

Miguel smiled. In the flickering light it was frightening, predatory. "It's pretty slippery maneuvering, deception without any outright lies. Typical politician."

Edwin looked past Miguel toward the open back door of the mobile home. It was obvious to him that he was not going to be able to reason with this man, so he figured his only hope was Sadie. She seemed the more rational and compassionate of the two. "Sadie!" he yelled. "Sadie, please come out here!"

"I'm right here, Mr. President."

The voice startled him, causing him to yelp. He craned his neck to look in the opposite direction, the far side of the yard that led to the lake. A figure stood just outside the torches' reach, but then Sadie stepped forward and her face was painted with shifting light and shadow. She looked sad and weary.

"Sadie, thank God. You've got to help me. Your husband is out of control."

Sadie walked forward slowly and took a seat on the picnic table's bench. She stared off into the distance, her eyes unfocused as if she were seeing another place, another time. When she spoke, her voice was flat. "When my mother first got sick—just a case of the sniffles, that's how it started—I begged her to go to one of those emergency clinics that sprung up around town, after the hospitals became overcrowded. I heard on the news they had specialists there that could help. I was down on my knees, in tears, pleading with her. She wouldn't go, though. She'd always been a stubborn woman. She kept saying, 'The President says there's nothing to worry about, that people are freaking out for no good reason, like with the Bird Flu.'"

Here Sadie paused and turned her gaze on Edwin. He suddenly wished she'd look away again. "My mother died in agony, choking on phlegm, spitting up blood, struggling for each breath, cursing God and screaming for me to kill her."

Edwin shook his head, still hoping to get through to her. "That's not my fault. If she was showing *any* symptoms it means she was already infected. There was no cure, no treatment, so she was a dead woman regardless of whether or not she went to a clinic."

Sadie's expression became so cold and emotionless it terrified Edwin. He turned his head back toward Miguel, who suddenly seemed to be the lesser of the two evils.

Miguel laughed softly. "That was probably the wrong thing to say to her."

Sadie pushed herself up from the picnic table and walked around it, joining her husband. The two stared down at Edwin as if he were a pesky insect that needed to be squashed. These two good Christian people, a former kindergarten teacher and nurse, now looked like monsters.

"So what are you going to do?" Edwin asked, not really wanting to know the answer. "Beat me to death with that bat?"

Miguel glanced over at the bat on his shoulder as if he'd forgotten it was there. Then he tossed it off to the side, where it landed in the high grass with a faint *thud*. "No, amigo. That would be too good for you."

"What then, the shotgun?"

Sadie shook her head. "All that buckshot in your flesh would be too wasteful."

"Wasteful? What are you talking about?"

Miguel reached to his waist where he pulled a serrated hunting knife, lethal and nasty looking, from a leather sheath. "Looks like we're going to be having steaks for dinner tomorrow night."

Sadie's lips spread into a wicked grin. "With plenty left over for enough jerky to last us through next winter."

Edwin screamed long before the knife was used, but there was no one left in the dead world to hear or care.

THE SUPPORT GROUP

NEW YORK ARRIVED late, but New York was *always* late. He took his usual seat next to Los Angeles, who despite her caked-on makeup and hair extensions looked haggard and frail. Across the way, London nodded, sucking on his pipe so that an amorphous cloud of smoke enveloped his head. Paris was also in attendance, perched on the edge of one of the uncomfortable folding chairs that made up the circle. Her pointy hat looked rather ridiculous.

The group was packed today, almost all the seats taken.

"So what'd I miss?" New York asked then doubled over as a violent fit of coughing tore through him. He hacked up black sludge into a handkerchief.

Los Angeles had her chin tucked down against her chest, and she flicked her eyes toward him as if she hadn't the strength to actually lift and turn her head. "I was telling everyone how I tried to shake the little buggers off again, but they just hold on for dear life and keep going like nothing happened."

All around the circle, everyone nodded soberly. They were all inflicted with the same disease. Little parasites had infested them and were slowly killing them. They came to the group for mutual support but also to hear stories of possible treatments and cures.

"I tried washing them away," Miami said, reaching up and scratching at her head. "I mean, I really doused the fuckers. Got rid of some of them, but not enough, and it seems more just came to take the place of those I washed away."

Next to Miami, New Orleans laughed, the sound deep and resonant. "Tell me about it. Several years back I really thought I'd managed to wash myself clean of the things, but now they're all back. I can feel them crawling all over my skin."

New York squirmed in his seat. He too felt the parasites all over him, polluting his body with their foul sickness. It had been so long since he had felt anything but tired and weak and contaminated. He didn't even know what it was to be healthy anymore.

"What are we going to do?" he asked, his voice breaking. The question, familiar to the group, summed up why they came back week after week.

"You could do what I did."

All eyes turned at the sound of Chernobyl's thick accent. She was the only person any of them knew that had actually beaten the disease. But the radiation treatment had taken a lot out of her, leaving her a withered husk of her former self. Her hair had fallen out except for a few matted clumps, and she seemed lost in her clothes, as if she were nothing more than a stick figure held together by twine and parchment.

Everyone was impressed by Chernobyl's success at eradicating the parasites, but no one was willing to pay such a steep price to be free of them.

And yet, New York thought as he coughed up more

black sludge mixed with his own blood, he might just be getting to the point that he'd try anything.

WELCOME

STRANDED IN THE middle of somewhere.

The thought entered Steve's mind as he stepped out onto the asphalt. Al exited the passenger's side and joined him in front of the car. They raised the hood and stared down at the Toyota's innards for some time.

"So," Al said, breaking the silence, "how long are we going to look before we finally acknowledge that neither of us knows the first thing about cars?"

Steve closed the hood. "I think this is about long enough. I can't figure out what could be wrong with it."

They'd had the Toyota Celica only four months, the first new car either of them had ever owned. If the two men had not pooled their resources, they would never have been able to afford the automobile. It had been running smoothly up until a few minutes ago. Al noticed a low sound, like playing cards in bicycle spokes, and then everything shut down. No lurching or sputtering. The engine simply ceased, and Steve had guided the car to the right where it coasted to a gentle stop on the grassy curb.

"Well, looks like we're stuck here," Steve said. "Better pull out your phone and call a tow truck."

"Oh yeah, my phone."

"Don't tell me you didn't bring your cell."

"No, I brought it, it's right here." Al pulled the compact black phone from his pocket and held it up. "But I'm out of minutes."

"Well, that's great," Steve said, but there was no harshness in his voice. While he was more than a bit irritated by their brand new car's refusal to go, he found the situation more amusing than anything else. This whole scenario—a young couple's car breaking down in a remote area—was straight out of one of those cheap horror flicks Al always dragged him to. With one significant deviation, though. In those movies, the car always broke down in some backwater hillbilly town where the residents wanted to rape you or eat you or sacrifice you to some corn god. The area in which Steve and Al now found themselves was nothing like that.

"I guess we should go ask someone if we can use their phone," Al said, leaning over and bumping his shoulder into Steve's.

Steve planted a quick kiss on Al's lips. "Guess so. I just hope the people in this neighborhood can afford phones."

Al laughed and the two headed across the street.

Ever since Steve and Al moved in together, they had developed a fondness for taking drives. It started out as a game. They would pick a road that neither of them had ever been down and see where it led. This soon evolved into routine drives through the more affluent neighborhoods of town. Steve and Al shared a studio apartment, a tiny box of a place that reminded both of them of a motel room. They couldn't afford anything bigger yet, Steve worked as a waiter and Al with mentally handicapped children, but they could dream of something bigger. They would drive through the rich neighborhoods and pick out their favorite houses, speculating on how it would be to live in such domestic palaces.

It was toward one of those domestic palaces that Steve and Al now walked.

The house was large, two stories, of multi-colored brick. The downstairs boasted large bay windows under which beautifully landscaped shrubbery grew. On either side of the front door, a large oak slab with a polished brass knocker, were old-fashioned gas lanterns. Even now low flames flickered, though darkness had not yet fallen. The house was expansive without being cold and foreboding like some other large homes. There was a certain coziness to this house. In fact, Steve had been about to pronounce this home his favorite of the evening when the Celica had stopped running.

In the front of the house was a paved drive that curved in a semi-circle, bordered by a row of knee-high bushes. Steve and Al walked down one side of the drive, fingers intertwined, and a gentle breeze ruffled their hair. Al glanced at his watch. 06:47 PM. The sky was the deep purple of a fresh bruise, stars flickering like the flames of the gas lanterns. It was a gorgeous spring evening, the kind of evening romance novelists wrote about in their saccharine fiction.

"Think we'll be invited in for tea?" Al asked. "Get a firsthand glance at how the other half lives?"

"Who knows? Maybe they'll be looking for a couple of young house-boys to do the cleaning in nothing but a pair of bikini briefs."

"Look no further then, we're the fellas for the job."

"Damn straight," Steve said.

There were four steps leading up to the door, the brass knocker shaped like a Chinese dragon. Steve pressed the doorbell and he and Al waited for a glimpse into the type of house in which they'd always dreamed of living.

Several seconds ticked by with no response. They were beginning to wonder if anyone was home, whether they should walk down the street to the next house, when footsteps sounded from inside. Hurried, frantic footsteps, as if someone was running down the hallway to answer the door.

"Sounds like someone's glad to have visitors," Steve said.

The door was wrenched open, hard enough that it swung wide and banged into the wall inside the house. A young woman stood framed in the doorway, blonde hair swept up in a sloppy bun, her eyes wide and wild, her breathing ragged. She wore faded jeans that came a few inches short of her ankles and a T-shirt with the word 'Superstar' printed on the front in silver spangles. The shirt was too small for her, exposing her midriff and stretching the word across her chest.

"Oh my God," she said in a hoarse whisper. "You're here. Someone's really here."

Steve and Al cut sideways glances at one another, not sure how to reply. Finally Steve held out his hand. "Hi, my name is Steve, and this is my friend, Al. Our car broke down across the street and—"

"Fred!" the woman shouted over her shoulder. "Fred, hurry. Someone's here. Get Gracie."

A man appeared beside the woman. He wore

corduroy overalls that were at least three sizes too large for him and a pair of glasses that slid down his nose to perch on the tip like a gargoyle on the side of a building. "I can't believe it. Linda, are we dreaming? After all this time, it's too good to be true."

Al tugged on the sleeve of Steve's shirt and began to back away. "If this is a bad time, we don't want to bother you. We'll just be on our way."

"No!" the couple in the doorway shouted in unison. The woman, Linda, spoke quickly, "Your car broke down, right? You're stranded, you need help."

Fred stepped aside. "You can use our phone. Please come in, the phone is in the living room."

Steve and Al hesitated on the doorstep, a welcome mat with silly cat designs at their feet. Linda and Fred seemed like one seriously disturbed couple, their eagerness to have Steve and Al in their home on par with that of the witch's to get Hansel and Gretel into her oven.

"Oh, I'm sorry," Linda said with a smile that dimpled her cheeks in the most delightful way. "I know we're acting peculiar, you'll have to forgive us. We've been having an argument and you interrupted us."

"Yes, yes, that's right," Fred said. "But we're not going to turn away two gentlemen in need of help. Please, feel free to use our phone."

Al looked at Steve. Steve was the stronger personality of the couple and Al usually followed his lead. Steve considered for a moment then nodded once. "If you don't mind, we'll only be a minute. Call for a tow and get out of your hair."

Fred and Linda stepped back, and Steve and Al stepped over the threshold and into the house.

They stood in a large foyer, a crystal chandelier overhead. The floor consisted of maroon tiles, an oval-shaped oriental rug covering a large section of it. A curving staircase stood to the right, as well as an archway leading into the living room. A hallway stretched ahead. Steve and Al looked around them, drinking in the luxury with their eyes. Linda and Fred smiled at one another, idiot smiles like those worn by the children Al worked with at the Center. They seemed to be in the grips of a euphoric joy that sprang from nowhere.

"So, your phone?" Steve asked, rocking on the balls of his feet. "Where is it?"

Fred backpedaled down the hall. "I'll get Gracie. She's in the library."

"I'll go get our stuff from upstairs," Linda said, rushing toward the stairs. She paused halfway up, glanced back at the stranded men and said, "Sorry," then hurried to the second floor, leaving Steve and Al alone in the foyer.

"What the fuck have we walked into?" Steve asked, not bothering to keep his voice low.

"*Twilight Zone* would be my first guess, or *Tales from the Crypt*."

"Oh, Jesus, let's find the phone before that cackling Crypt Keeper shows up."

They walked through the archway into the living room. The beige carpet was thick, the furniture antique. A cordless phone sat on an end table by a wooden rocker. Steve picked it up and punched some buttons, listened for a few seconds, punched a few more buttons, grunted, then hung the phone up with some force.

"Let me guess," Al said, a slight tremor of unease coloring his voice. "Doesn't work."

"Dead as Elvis. I suggest we get the hell out of here before Linda and Fred have us for dinner, and I do mean *have us* for dinner."

"Right behind you."

Steve and Al walked through the archway into the foyer as Fred came rushing down the hallway carrying a young girl in his arms. She couldn't have been more than five years old—pale and hollow-eyed, with a mop of curly strawberry-blonde hair on her head. She wore nothing but an adult T-shirt that hung far below her legs. She had two fingers stuck in her mouth and she chewed on them as she examined Steve and Al with her blank eyes.

"Linda!" Fred shouted up the stairs. "What are you doing? We don't need everything. Leave it, leave it! Let's go, for Christ's sake!"

A second later, Linda bounded down the stairs, two large duffel bags slung over her shoulders. Her bun had come loose and her hair trailed behind her like a comet's tail. She tripped near the bottom of the stairs. She almost fell down, but steadied herself with a well-placed hand on the banister. "Ready. Let's get the hell out of here."

"Would you two mind telling me what's going on?" Steve asked. "I mean, you two are crazier than shithouse rats, if you ask me."

Even in the bizarreness of the situation, Al couldn't help but smile. One of the things he loved most about Steve was his ability to call a spade a spade in the bluntest of terms and to never take shit from anyone.

In this instance, however, his directness was

ignored. Linda and Fred, with Gracie in tow, pushed past the two men and headed for the door. They hesitated at the threshold, staring through the doorway, as if through a portal into another dimension. Finally, with great sighs, they bolted forward, through the door and onto the steps. Here they paused again, their faces slack with shock.

Steve and Al started to follow, but they stopped when Linda and Fred burst into hysterical laughter. Loud, high-pitched guffaws that shook their bodies and caused them to lean against each other for support. Tears mixed in with the laughter, and Gracie clung to her father with the fierceness of someone clinging to a life preserver.

"They are crazy," Al said. "Not weird, not eccentric. These people are certifiably insane."

Linda turned her head and considered the men through the open door, as if only now reminded of their presence. "I'm sorry. I wish it didn't have to be like this, but it's the only way."

"Come on," Fred said, grabbing his wife by the arm and pulling her down the steps.

"Wait a goddam minute," Steve said and walked through the door.

Or tried.

When he reached the threshold, Steve stopped suddenly, cried out, and stumbled back. To Al, it looked like one of those comical scenes where someone walks into a glass door cleaned so thoroughly as to be invisible.

"What in the name of Jesus," Steve muttered, rubbing at his forehead.

Outside, Linda pulled free of Fred's hold and

started back up the steps.

"Linda, what the hell are you doing?" Fred asked. "Are you nuts?"

Linda turned back to her husband. "It's only fair. The folks before us explained things. They gave us some idea what was going on. I wouldn't be able to live with myself if we didn't do the same for these guys. It's the most we can do considering what we're sentencing them to."

Fred said nothing for a moment, merely hugged Gracie to his chest and rocked on his feet. "Fine, but don't go back in. Tell them from out here."

"I'm not an idiot."

"Are you sure about that?" Al said, standing close by Steve. "This whole situation seems pretty idiotic to me."

Linda stopped on the top step and said in a voice that was soft and full of sympathy, "I know this must all seem strange to you, and it's about to get a hell of a lot stranger. I wish I could tell you what was really going on, but there is a limit to what we know."

"Lady, what kind of drugs are you taking?" Steve asked, walking back to the threshold but not attempting to cross it.

"This house," Linda said, ignoring Steve's comment, "this is not our house. It does not belong to Fred and me. For the past two and a half years, it has been our prison."

Steve made as if to walk through the door again, but instead he shuffled back a few steps. It appeared as if he *bounced* back. "What the hell is this?"

"Two and a half years ago, the three of us—Fred, Gracie, and I—were invited to a birthday party for one of Gracie's friends from pre-school, held on this street. We got the address wrong, unfortunately, and we came to the door of this house instead of the house where the party was being held. An elderly man came to the door, and when we explained what had happened, he graciously invited us in to use his phone.

"Once we were inside, he began running around frantically, packing and calling out to the others in the house, much the same scene that you experienced with us. There were two others, another elderly man and an elderly woman. We were dumbfounded, and they fed us some preposterous story before running out the door and leaving us alone in the house. Soon after they were gone, we discovered that the story was true."

"What are you talking about?" Al asked, approaching the doorway with the wariness of one approaching a lion's den.

Linda sighed. "We were unable to leave the house. When we would try to walk through the door, we were stopped by some invisible force, which I believe you have had a taste of yourself. The windows would not open nor break, and believe me we tried. The phones did not work. We would stand at the open door and yell at the top of our lungs, and no one heard or saw us. We were trapped in the house. The next morning, we discovered that our car—which had been parked in the drive out front—was gone. It simply vanished.

"We've been here ever since; for two and a half years we have not set foot outside this house. Until today. Everyday fresh food would be in the refrigerator and cupboards, appearing as mysteriously as our car disappeared. No new clothes appeared, though. We had to make do with what was already in the closets here."

"Okay, I see," Steve said. "You've been trapped in the house for two and a half years. Why are you suddenly able to leave now?"

Fred stepped up next to his wife. "Are you dense or what? Can't you figure that one out? The three people who were here when we first set foot inside the house told us that we would be stuck here until someone else came along and entered the house of his own free will. Once that happened, we would be free to go and the new arrivals would be the prisoners, at least until someone else came along and walked through the door."

Steve and Al were silent for some time.

Steve, as usual, was the first to speak. "So you're saying—"

"I'm sorry," Linda said for the third time. "By simply stepping through the door, you've freed us, but you have inadvertently imprisoned yourselves. Like I said, I wish it didn't have to be like this, but the house demands its prisoners."

"Help us then," Steve said. "You know what's going on here, so get help."

"We can't."

Fred hugged his wife and said, "We were told that if we tried to rescue those who came after us, great misfortune would befall us."

"Great misfortune," Steve repeated. "That's a vague pronouncement."

"We can't risk it," Fred said, his wife and daughter both crying in his arms. "We've had enough misfortune for one lifetime."

"And us?" Al said.

"Your misfortune is only beginning."

Without another word, Fred led his wife down the steps and toward the street. Steve called out to them, but they did not stop and they did not look back. They turned right at the street, and walked on until they were out of sight.

"Is this some kind of sick joke?" Al asked in a strained voice. "They're fucking with us, right?"

Steve held his hand out to the open doorway. "I don't know. Feel this."

Al reached out. His fingers reached the doorway but would go no farther. Steve knew what he felt. Some force, not hard like a wall, but solid and spongy, like the feel of one of those gel wrist pads that came with some mouse pads. There was some give but no penetrating it.

"What is this?" Al asked.

Instead of answering, Steve placed both hands open-palmed against the invisible blockade and pressed as hard as he could.

"This is crazy," Steve said, panting. "I can't get through it."

Al strode into the living room. "This can't be. It can't be."

Al picked up the wooden rocker and swung it into the bay window. It shattered into a thousand fragments—the rocker, not the window. The window remained intact, not even a crack.

Steve placed a hand on Al's shoulder.

"The backdoor," Al said, shrugging off his lover's hand and running through the archway and down the hall. At the end of the hall was a large kitchen, bright yellow walls with a rabbit theme. Rabbit salt-and-pepper shakers, rabbit-shaped oven mitts, a large rabbit cookie jar. On the far side of the kitchen was a door, a sheer curtain covering glass panels at its top.

"Al, wait," Steve called out, right behind him. "You're panicking."

Paying Steve no heed, Al threw open the door and ran headlong toward the backyard. He collided with the invisible blockade and rebounded into the house, his feet slipping out from under him, tumbling to the linoleum with a soft *thud*.

"Al, are you okay?" Steve asked, kneeling next to his lover.

"This isn't real. It can't be real. I refuse to believe it's real."

"Come on now," Steve said, placing his hands under Al's arms and raising him to his feet. "Have a seat." He positioned Al on one of the wooden stools aligned beneath a counter by the refrigerator.

Al leaned forward, burying his head in his hands, and muttered repeatedly, "Isn't real, can't be real, isn't real, can't be real."

Steve opened several cabinets until he found the glasses. He filled one with water at the sink and took it over to Al. "Drink this. I'm going to go look around."

Without looking up, Al took the glass and sipped the water, still repeating his mantra like a prayer.

Steve left his lover in the kitchen and walked down the hall, checking all the rooms. Besides the living room and kitchen, the downstairs also contained a full bath, a spacious walk-in closet full of coats and shoes, a large room filled with wall-to-wall bookshelves and a huge roll-top desk in the center, and a dining room with one of those exaggeratedly long tables that Steve only ever saw in movies. All the windows were sealed shut, and although Steve banged on the glass until his knuckles bled, the panes remained whole and unbroken.

Steve ascended the curving stairwell to the second floor. Here were four bedrooms, the master bedroom with the four-poster bed, larger than Steve and Al's entire apartment, and another full bath. Same story with the windows. A narrow flight of stairs led up to a musty smelling attic. The circular window that looked out onto the street was as impenetrable as the rest. Steve noticed as he tried the window that the Celica was no longer across the street.

As Steve turned to leave, he caught sight of something from the corner of his eye. At first, in the failing light, he couldn't make sense of what he saw, but when he stepped closer it became clear. "Holy shit," he said under his breath.

Deflated, Steve made his way back to the kitchen. Al stood by the open backdoor, glass of water clutched in his hands so tightly Steve was afraid it would shatter.

"It's real," Al said, looking into his lover's eyes. "We're trapped in this house like they said."

"It would appear so. I don't know how, but there doesn't seem to be any way out of here."

Al lowered his head and began to cry, soft but powerful sobs that racked his body. Steve hugged him close, kissing him on the forehead and whispering meaningless assurances that everything would be all right. Steve was wryly amused by the way he and Al were reacting to this impossible situation. Al was the one who thrived on tales of the absurd and impossible, yet it was Steve who had managed to maintain his wits in the face of their otherworldly predicament.

"What are we going to do?" Al asked, his well of tears finally running dry. "I mean, what can we do?"

"I guess there's nothing we can do right now. We need to think this through, figure a way to get out of here."

"Did you find anything upstairs?" Al asked.

"Um, no. Nothing useful."

Al studied his lover's face for a moment. "Steve, what's up there?"

"I told you, nothing."

"Bullshit, there's something you're not telling me."

"You don't want to know, Al. Trust me on this one."

"Tell me what it is or you know I'll go look for myself."

Now it was Steve who studied Al's face, examining the resolve he saw there. "Come on, I'll show you."

Steve led Al up to the attic, his feet shuffling slowly. Once they reached the attic, Al followed Steve over to one corner of the darkened room. Steve had hoped it would be gone, like the car, but it was still there. Magic-marker scribbled on the wall. Three names—Linda, Fred, Gracie—and several hatch marks, four in a row with a fifth slashed through. Al seemed to be counting under his breath, but Steve had already done the calculations.

"Thirty-one," he said aloud. "Must be months. Thirty-one to be exact, that's two years and seven months. I saw no calendars in this place, so this was the only way they had to keep track of how long they were prisoners here."

"Well, we already knew that. Why didn't you want me to see this?"

"It wasn't this I didn't want you to see."

Al hesitated. Finally he said, "Show me."

Without speaking, Steve turned his attention to the far corner. Al walked over, getting his eyes close to the wall. When his vision adjusted, Al gasped and backpedaled quickly.

Here were three other names—Macey, Teddy, and Ralph. And more hatch marks; too many to count. They covered the entire wall on this side of the attic, from floor to ceiling.

"This must be more than twenty years," Al said softly, reverently.

"I'd say that's a conservative estimate. To fill up the entire wall, I'd say that was much more than twenty years."

"Should we count them?"

"Do we dare?" Steve asked hollowly. "Do we really want to know? I mean, *really*?"

Al lowered himself slowly to his knees and began to cry again. Silent tears that rolled fat and copiously down his cheeks. Steve joined his lover on the floor, cradling and rocking him.

"Fred, Linda and Gracie got out in two and a half years," Steve said, a tremor in his voice that might have been hope or desperation. "We could get lucky. Someone could happen along tomorrow."

Al's eyes never left the hatch marks. "Yeah, tomorrow."

They stayed in that position, kneeling on the floor in each other's arms, for some time. Full dark had fallen outside before Steve noticed that Al had fallen asleep. Steve gently lifted his lover in his arms and carried him to the master bedroom on the second floor. He laid Al on the four-poster bed beneath the billowy canopy, kissing him softly on his sweaty brow.

Steve left the room, closing the door behind him. He stopped in the second-floor bathroom and washed his bloody knuckles, bandaging them with some gauze he found in the medicine cabinet. He made his way down the curving staircase to the foyer and stared at a world of which he was no longer a part.

The universe certainly had a sense of irony. He and Al had always wanted to live in a house like this.

He finally understood the old cliché, *be careful what you wish for.*

Steve glanced down at the front stoop, the welcome mat with the silly cat designs mocking him with its cheeriness. With a sigh that embodied all the weariness one could bear, Steve closed the door.

TRANSFORMATIONS

JASON FIRST DISCOVERED a reference to *Transformations* on a message board dedicated to people like himself; those inflicted with the curse of homosexuality and seeking a way out.

A recovering lesbian from Utah fleetingly mentioned a book as being instrumental in her conversion. She'd gone into no further detail, but Jason was left with the impression of it being some kind of self-help book.

A Google search yielded only minimal results, but he'd learned enough to discover *Transformations* was no self-help book. Instead, it was a book of spells. Spells that could, reputedly, change a person into something they were not. Change a person's appearance, attitudes, even gender. And yes, sexual orientation.

Normally, Jason would have laughed off such claims as ludicrous, but he'd already tried therapy, religion, even hypnotism. Nothing worked. He was desperate.

Tracking down a copy to purchase proved a difficult enough task. The book was rare, dating back to the early 1900s. It wasn't the sort of thing one could pop into Borders and pick up. Jason found a few on eBay going for as much as one thousand dollars, much too steep for a social worker's salary. Finally, he had contacted the recovering lesbian from the message board, the one from whom he had first heard of the book. She still had her copy and offered to part with it for the bargain price of four hundred dollars. This put quite a strain on Jason's wallet, but his desperation had grown into an obsession.

The spell to change one's sexual orientation proved to be surprisingly simple. Jason had expected something complicated, requiring ingredients such as 'eye of newt' while sitting in the center of a pentagram. Instead, all he needed to do was recite a short incantation to invoke an elemental demon with sway over the powers of identity and sexual desires, at the stroke of midnight during a full moon. Being an educated man, of course Jason did not believe in demons. However, he hoped performing the spell would act as some sort of psychosomatic panacea, and he would awaken in the morning craving female companionship, like a lifelong vegetarian who suddenly discovers he loves the taste of meat.

So as the witching hour approached at the next full moon, Jason turned out the lights in his apartment, took a seat on his bedroom floor, and lit a variety of black candles surrounding him. Not because the spell required it, but because he felt the circle of candlelight lent the proceedings a certain needed ambiance.

Then, at the moment when it was neither today nor tomorrow, Jason recited the invocation.

"I call on you, Lord of Desire. I call on you to come to me, to make me that which I am not, but that which

I so long to be. Reveal yourself to me, my Lord. Wield your power like a mace. Reach your hands deep inside me, to my most secret inner place. Mold my soul as if it's clay and you a potter at the wheel. Transform my desires, my very essence, change the way I think and feel. I call on you, Lord of Desire. I beseech you to bestow your help on this poor soul whose body is a traitor. Please make me into someone else."

As his voice faded into silence, Jason tensed. His hands curled into tight fists in his lap, and waited for . . . he wasn't exactly sure what he was waiting for. Perhaps a flash of fire and smoke? An elaborate light show? A phantom draft that would blow out the candles and plunge him into unrelenting darkness? There was nothing, though. The candles' flames did not even flicker. Even though he had not actually expected anything otherworldly to occur, he had to admit his disappointment.

The sound of someone rather pointedly clearing his throat caused Jason to jump, knocking over one of the candles and singeing the carpet before he was able to douse the flame. His eyes darted about the room, seeking out the source of the sound. His gaze finally trained on a man standing in the doorway of the open closet, leaning casually against the jamb with his arms folded across his chest. His expression, mild interest bordering on all-out boredom, seemed out of place in Jason's bedroom.

Jason opened his mouth to speak but found his voice locked away inside.

A smile curled one corner of the stranger's lips and he said in a deep baritone voice, "In the immortal words of Lurch . . . *you rang*?"

Jason tried to speak again but couldn't get past the blockage in his throat. He swallowed hard and made another attempt, squeaking out the words, "Who are you?" in a breathless rush.

"I'm the one you called for, of course." The stranger stepped farther into the room, moving with a lithe grace. He was tall with a muscular physique, black wavy hair and a neat mustache and goatee. Jason felt himself stiffening in his pants, which made him cry.

"Dry your tears, mortal," the stranger said, squatting down in front of Jason. "I'm here to end your suffering."

A few sniffles and a swipe of his arm across his eyes later, and Jason had himself back under control. "So you're the Lord of Desire?"

"I am, but you may call me Andros."

"I didn't really believe you existed."

"Luckily, belief isn't needed in order to summon me, only desperation. And you seem to have that in spades."

"Can you help me?" Jason asked, reaching out to touch the man but pulled back before making contact. "Can you take away these wicked desires and make me normal?"

Andros' smile was easy and inviting. Funny, he didn't look or act like a demon at all. "I can. For a price."

Jason frowned; *Transformations* hadn't mentioned anything about a price. "I don't have much money, I'm afraid. I paid what little savings I had for the book I used to summon you."

"Demons have no need for mortal currency," Andros said with a booming laugh. "We trade in souls."

"You want a soul?"

"Don't sell me short, my friend. I am much greedier than that. I don't want *a* soul. I want thirteen."

Jason's mouth fell open. "Thirteen souls? How am I supposed to provide you with thirteen souls?"

"That I do not know," Andros said with a shrug of his shoulders. "But that is the payment I require to grant your request. Specifically, the souls of thirteen homosexual men, sacrificed to me."

"I have to . . . kill them?"

"No, that won't be necessary. Just bring them here and get them into the closet. I will do the rest."

"The closet?"

That half-smile touched Andros's lips once more, a look of wry amusement. "Rather appropriate irony, wouldn't you say? Just get them inside the closet and close the door. I will take them."

"Will I have to . . . will there be any clean-up involved?"

"There will be nothing left. I will devour their flesh as well as their souls. No fuss, no muss."

Jason stared into Andros's handsome face for a moment then glanced at the closet. The space was cramped with no light inside. He didn't like the idea of committing murder, let alone multiple murders, but as Andros said, Jason wouldn't have to *kill* anyone. Not directly, at least. He knew he was arguing semantics with himself, but it was the price Andros demanded. "I suppose if it's the only way."

"It is. But you must act quickly, mortal. You have only until the next full moon to fulfill the terms of this pact. If you fail, you will never receive what you desire."

Jason waffled for only a moment, before he made up his mind. "I'll do it," he said and held out his hand. Andros's grip when he shook was firm and warm.

"It is a deal then," Andros said, backing up until he was inside the closet, surrounded by sweatshirts and jeans. "The souls of thirteen homosexual men, and then I will grant your request."

With that, the closet door slammed shut of its own accord, and the candles blew out.

Jason delivered the first soul the very next night. He found the man—he refused to think of him as a *victim*—at the town's only gay club, a place called Liaisons. Jason had always secretly wanted to visit the establishment, but this was the first time he had ever actually stepped foot inside. It looked like any other bar. No naked men, no leather, no sex in shadowy corners. There were a few drag queens walking around and couples of the same sex swayed in one another's arms on the dance floor, but those were the only signs of the bar being a haven for homosexuals.

He took a seat at the bar, ordered a beer, and scanned the crowd. He wasn't sure what to do next. Having fought his homosexuality his entire life, he was clueless as to the ins and outs of gay courtship, so to speak. Should he pick someone and offer to buy him a drink, engage in a little chitchat? Or should he just cut right to the chase and invite someone back to his apartment?

While Jason debated the best way to snag a man, he himself got snagged.

He was older, mid-forties at least, with a receding

hairline and a paunch that poked out the front of his shirt. His eyes were bleary with drink and his smile somewhat predatory. Although there were several empty stools nearby, he took the one right next to Jason, leaning close until their thighs rubbed together.

"Haven't seen you here before," the man said, his words only slightly slurred.

Jason forced a smile. "This is my first time."

"Oh! A virgin, how delightful."

A blush spread up from Jason's collar and swallowed his entire face. He stared down at his drink and began peeling the label away from the bottle. "So, you come here a lot?"

"Every weekend," the man said, leaning even closer so that his alcohol-laced breath washed over Jason's face. "Some weeknights, too. I guess you could say I'm always on the prowl."

Sweat trickled down the sides of Jason's face and his hands shook, causing the beer bottle to tap a staccato against the bar.

"It's okay, son." The man placed a hand high on Jason's thigh and squeezed firmly. "No need to be nervous. I ain't gonna bite ya. Might *nibble* you a bit, but only if you ask me to."

The man quested higher, closer to the crotch, and Jason felt his body respond. He fought to hold back the tears that threatened, managing another forced smile. The smile turned into a gasp of surprise and pleasure when the man's fingers brushed the bulge between his legs, briefly stroking the hardness there before moving back down the thigh.

"So little virgin, what brings you out to Liaisons tonight?"

Jason took a fortifying drink of beer and said, "Looking for somebody."

"That so? Anybody in particular?"

Jason met the man's eyes with a boldness he didn't really feel. "You."

The man's smile widened, becoming grotesque, almost as if his face were splitting in two. "Looks like it's my lucky night. You wanna dance?"

"I'd rather just go back to my place and fuck," Jason said, afraid he was being too forward.

His fear was unfounded. The man laughed and said, "Gotta love a man who cuts right through all the bullshit. By the way, I'm—"

"No names," Jason said abruptly. It would be so much more difficult if he knew the man's name. "I don't want to exchange names."

"Cool with me. I understand the need to be discreet; nobody knows about me either."

Jason nodded and fumbled some bills out of his wallet to pay for his drink, but the man waved his hand and said, "I got it."

After the man paid for their drinks, they went out to the gravel parking lot. Jason's car was near the back of the lot, but the man stopped at a pickup two rows from the club. "I'll follow you back to your place."

"Why don't I drive you over?" Jason asked. Since the man would never leave Jason's apartment, he didn't want the truck parked in front of the building. "You look like you may have had a bit more to drink than I have."

"Friends don't let friends drink and drive," the man said and laughed loudly. "You sure you won't mind driving me back to my truck after?"

"Not at all." Jason led the man toward his car and opened the passenger's side door for him. As he crossed to the driver's side, hand on the door handle, he knew this was his last chance to turn back.

Taking a deep breath, he opened the door, got inside the car, and crossed the point of no return.

Jason lived on Chestnut Street, in a rambling three-story house that had been converted into several apartments. Jason lived on the top story, accessible around back by a flight of thirty-five steps. By the time they reached the top, Jason's companion was winded and a bit damp around the forehead.

"That's quite a workout," he said.

Jason fumbled his key into the lock. "Hope it didn't wear you out."

"Oh, I think I'm getting a second wind," the man said, stepping up close and pressing his groin against Jason's backside. Jason could feel the erection poking at him. For just a moment he leaned back into it, before he quickly opened the door and led the man into the small kitchen.

The kitchen opened into the small living room, which opened into the small bedroom, which opened into the even smaller bathroom. Four rooms, running straight back from the rear of the house to the front. It wasn't much, but neither was the rent. Sure, it was quite a climb up those stairs, and it had been a bitch hauling his thrift store furniture up here when he'd first moved in, but other than that the place was perfect for Jason.

Wasting no time on pleasantries, Jason led the man straight to the bedroom. He'd left a lamp burning there, and it beckoned to them. The closet door stood open, waiting.

Jason turned and suddenly the man was on him, tongue questing into Jason's mouth, hand sliding up under his shirt to pinch his nipple. It was all Jason could do to push the man off him long enough to gasp, "Wait, slow down."

"Slow down? I believe you're the one who invited me back here to fuck."

"Yeah, I know, it's just that . . . well, there's something I want to show you."

"There's only one thing I'm interested in seeing," the man said, tugging at Jason's belt.

"No, wait, really. In the closet, I want you to see."

The man paused in his efforts to de-pants Jason, glancing back toward the closet. "What you got in there? Toys?"

"Yeah, toys. Lots and lots of 'em."

"You think what I got won't be enough?" the man asked, rubbing his own crotch. Jason could see the outline of the man's erection through his pants, and it was indeed formidable.

"Nothing like that," Jason stammered, forcing his eyes away from the man's groin. "I just think you'll like the stuff I got in there."

"So the little virgin's got a kinky side, huh? I like that. What kind of toys you got to show Daddy?"

"Take a look for yourself."

With a smile that was part quizzical, part indulgent, the man turned and walked over to the closet. Squinting into the darkness, he said, "Can't see shit in here."

"There's a light inside. Step in and pull the chain."

The man walked slowly into the closet, reaching out blindly for the nonexistent chain. When he was over the threshold, Jason rushed forward to close the door. The man apparently heard Jason's movement and turned, his smile replaced with a frown. He opened his mouth to say something as Jason slammed the door shut, leaning his body against it in case the man tried to get out.

Jason waited, expecting some kind of commotion, maybe a scream, but he heard nothing. At the very least, he expected the man to bang on the door, call to be let out, but there was only silence. Minutes ticked by on the wind-up clock next to Jason's bed. Five. Ten. Fifteen. Twenty minutes went by without so much as a sound.

Cautiously removing his weight from the door, steeling himself against the possibility of the man bursting out, Jason stepped back, unsure. Finally, half an hour after closing the man inside the closet, Jason gripped the doorknob in his hand, his sweaty palm almost sliding off the cold metal, and slowly opened the door. "Hello," he said lamely as he peered inside.

The closet appeared to be empty. Of course, it was so dark in there he couldn't be entirely sure. The man could have been standing in the back, behind the shirts, the shadows concealing him. Jason shuffled quickly to the switch and turned on the overhead light, enough brightness to illuminate the inside of the closet. The *empty* closet.

Jason stepped into the cramped space, unable to believe it. The man had disappeared like a magic trick. No trace of him left whatsoever. Of course, that was what Andros had told him would happen, but he'd expected *something*. A shred of clothing, a few hairs, or hangers knocked askew. But there was no evidence to suggest anything unusual happened here. It had been so quick and so quiet.

Jason stepped back into the bedroom, closing the closet door and leaving his fingers lingering on the wood for a few moments. He'd expected to feel guilt or shame for what he had done, but he was surprised to find he felt neither. It had been so *easy*. All he'd done was close the door behind the man. It was hard to feel guilty when he'd done so little. Still, the deed was done, and he was on his way to getting what he desired.

One down.

The second sacrifice wasn't quite so simple.

Jason returned to Liaisons the following evening and found it nearly deserted on a Sunday night. Apparently homosexuals, like God, rested on the seventh day. Besides himself and the bartender, there were only five other men in the bar, two of them together. Jason took a seat at the bar, the same stool he'd occupied last night, and waited for one of the other men in the club to approach him.

None of them did.

The two that were together left shortly after Jason arrived and two of the others hooked up soon after, groping each other on the deserted dance floor. That left one other man standing over by the pool tables. Several times Jason caught the man staring at him in a way that suggested he was interested, but for whatever reason he did not approach Jason.

Maybe he's waiting on me to make the first move, Jason thought after forty-five minutes of waiting.

The only problem was that Jason didn't know how to make the first move. Hell, he didn't know how to make *any* move. In the movies, men in singles bars always offered to buy young ladies a drink. Would that work with two men? Or were there different rules that governed gay society?

After the couple from the dance floor staggered out of the club together, Jason figured he had to make his move. He stood up and strolled as nonchalantly as possible to the pool tables. When he stepped up to the man, Jason had a sudden inspiration and said, indicating the nearest pool table, "Wanna shoot a game?"

The man smiled in a way that was remarkably reminiscent of the man last night. "You wouldn't be trying to get a look at my stick and balls, would you?"

"As a matter of fact . . . " Jason said with a sigh, relieved to be back on familiar ground. He figured the rest of the encounter would follow much the same script as the previous evening.

"I'm just teasing," the man said, reaching around for one of the pool cues. "I'd love a game."

Jason stood frozen for a moment. He'd only been looking for an opening; he didn't actually know how to play pool.

"You wanna set 'em up?" the man asked.

Jason decided his best course of action would be to use the line with which he'd already had proven success. "I'd rather just go back to my place and fuck."

"You certainly cut right to the chase, don't you?" the man said, which was similar to what the man last night had said, although this one used a completely different tone.

"I just know what I want," Jason replied, trying to appear confident.

"Yeah, me too." The man returned the cue to the rack. "Have a good night."

"What? You're leaving?"

The man just nodded and pushed past.

"Wait a minute," Jason said, reaching out and grabbing the man's arm. "Are you going to tell me you didn't come here looking for sex? I saw the way you were watching me."

"Yeah, I thought you were hot, and maybe I was even hoping I would get laid tonight, but that doesn't mean I don't want a little conversation first. At least an exchange of names. A guy that opens with 'Let's fuck' is too nasty for me. Who knows what kind of STDs you got floating around in your bloodstream?"

The man jerked his arm loose of Jason's hold and left the club. Jason was too stunned to follow. He had assumed that one approach would work with most guys, but obviously he'd been wrong. And as he was the only one remaining in the club, that left him with no one to take back to Andros tonight.

As he headed for the exit, Jason reminded himself that he had a month to get twelve more men. It wasn't like he had to get one every single night. This would give him time to strategize, mull over tonight's failure and figure out how not to repeat it in the future. He would just have to—

"Hey, wait a minute sexy."

Jason stopped and turned toward the bar. He had thought himself alone in the place, but of course that wasn't true; there was the bartender. The man looked to be in his mid-thirties, a tight T-shirt showing off his muscular chest and arms, blonde hair a mess of curls atop his head. He was deeply tanned, which made the brightness of his smile stand out.

"I'm sorry, are you talking to me?" Jason asked, thinking he sounded like a sad imitation of Robert De Niro in that *Taxi Driver* movie.

The bartender leaned across the bar, beckoning Jason closer. "I wasn't exactly eavesdropping or anything, but I couldn't help but overhear your conversation. I just wanted to tell you that guy is a fool. If a hot little thing like you had asked me to fuck, I'd have been all over it in about two seconds."

Jason was suddenly excited. Not in a sexual way . . . well, not *only* in a sexual way. Maybe his luck wasn't out tonight, after all. "Would *you* like to go back to my place with me?"

"I'd love to, but I really have to close up the bar. I'm the only one working tonight."

"I can wait. Really, I don't mind."

"Why wait?" the bartender said and came out from behind the bar. He passed Jason and went to the door, turning the lock and flipping a switch which Jason assumed turned off the neon-sign outside. He returned to Jason and kissed him roughly, practically raping Jason's mouth with his insistent tongue.

"Wouldn't you be more comfortable if we went to my place?" Jason asked weakly, even as the bartender undid his pants.

The bartender put a finger to Jason's lips. "Shhh, don't say another word."

And Jason didn't. Not even when the bartender bent him over one of the pool tables.

Jason got no sleep that night. He sat up in the bed remembering what he'd allowed to be done to him at the club earlier, tears streaking his cheeks. The acts that had been perpetrated on his body had been vile, disgusting, sinful . . . and he'd *liked* it. All those nasty things the bartender had done to him, they'd felt so good. Jason had ended up urging his violator on: faster, harder, deeper, rougher. By the time the bartender was done with him, Jason had been sore all over, but the aches were pleasurable in a way he was certain was damning.

He now knew this sickness went deeper than he had dreamed, had sunk roots into his very soul. It was more imperative than ever that he rid himself of this affliction. He had to get twelve more men for Andros. Then the demon would grant Jason's wish.

Twelve more men. No matter what.

Since he figured that *Liaisons* would be as deserted on a Monday night as it had been on Sunday, Jason decided to change his tactics. It was for the best, he figured. It's probably not a good idea to collect all twelve men from the same place. But that left the question, where to go? There were no other gay clubs in town and he doubted that if he went to another city he could convince anyone to come all the way back to his place. So what options did that leave?

Barnes & Noble.

Jason had never been much of a reader, but he had heard rumors that the B&N was quite a pick up joint for the gay crowd. Apparently there had even been a glory hole in between the two men's room stalls before they had replaced the plaster wall with a metal one.

He went that night around nine, an hour before closing, figuring anyone left would be getting desperate and he wouldn't have to work as hard. Even at that hour, the place was full of people sipping flavored coffees in the café, lounging in the deep chairs, and flipping through newspapers they had no intention of buying.

There were several single men about, but Jason found himself at a loss. At the bar, at least he knew most everyone there was gay and looking for the same thing. Here, how was he to differentiate between gay men on the prowl and straight men looking for caffeine and reading material? It wasn't like anyone here wore a T-shirt with the logo LOOKING 4 COCK!

Jason perused the magazine rack until he found a stash of gay publications. *Advocate*, *Out*, *XY*. He picked up an *Advocate* and flipped through it without really paying any attention to the articles. He positioned his body so that the cover was facing out toward the store, hoping it would act as a beacon to draw someone in.

After only a few minutes, his approach seemed to have done its job. Jason became aware of a middle-aged man watching him at the other end of the magazine rack, short and stocky with a mischievous glint in his eye. Jason couldn't be certain the man was gay, but the way he stared so intently at Jason without looking away certainly seemed telling. Deciding to take a risk, Jason reached down and squeezed his package, making it seem like he was scratching his balls. That was all it took. The stocky man abandoned whatever magazine he'd been reading and headed Jason's way.

"Hey there," the man said, his eyes not on Jason's face but below the belt.

"Hey yourself."

"Good magazine?"

"Not bad."

The man nodded, glanced briefly at Jason's eyes, let his own wander downward again. "Boring night, huh?"

"Yeah, I'm just looking for something fun to do."

"I hear that. I'm Eric, by the way."

"Ja . . . mie." He wasn't sure why he didn't give his real name since the guy wouldn't have the chance to share it with anyone. He just didn't want this man knowing.

"Nice to meet you, Jamie. So what are a couple of fellas like us to do for fun on a boring night like this?"

Jason reached down and cupped his balls again. "I've got a few ideas."

"You do, do you? I'm all ears."

They were lying on the bed, making out and rubbing one another through their clothes, while Jason tried to figure out how to get Eric into the closet. Although Eric was shorter than Jason, he had a good hundred pounds on him, mostly muscle. It didn't seem likely Jason would be able to physically overpower and force him into the closet. He could always try the ploy that had worked last time, saying there were sex toys in the closet, but so far he'd been gagged by Eric's tongue the entire time and had been unable to speak.

Luck being with Jason tonight, Eric suddenly pulled back—Jason denying the disappointment he felt when the man's tongue was removed from his mouth—and said, "Sorry, think I had too much coffee back at the bookstore. Can I use your bathroom before we go any further?"

Jason raised his hand to point toward the closed bathroom door but hesitated, instead moving his finger until it pointed directly at the closed closet door. The two doors were nearly indistinguishable, no reason Eric should suspect Jason was lying to him.

Jason propped himself up on his elbows and watched the man cross the room. He found he was still hard, as if the anticipation of what was to come was a major turn on. As Eric approached the door, Jason got to his feet and followed quietly.

Eric opened the door and stood there at the threshold for a moment, frowning into the dark closet. He started to turn, saying, "This isn't the bath—", then Jason shoved him roughly from behind, sending the man tripping into the closet. Without a pause, Jason slammed the door shut, backing away as if fearing it would explode back open.

It didn't. It remained closed, and there was only silence from inside. After a few moments had passed, Jason opened the door and found the closet empty, like last time. He remained there, staring in at the nothing there was to see and a smile slowly spread across his face.

He started to believe that he could really do this, deliver all thirteen men to Andros.

After all, it was easy.

Having built a certain momentum, Jason delivered the next four men all within a week. Numbers three and four—that's how Jason had come to think of them, as mere numbers—came from Liaisons, one in his fifties, the other barely in his twenties. They'd come back to his apartment willingly enough and had disappeared into his closet, almost as if they had ceased to exist altogether. Number five was another pick-up from the Barnes & Noble, a nervous married man who kept fiddling with his wedding band as if it were some magical talisman. Number six was actually the bartender from Liaisons that Jason had fucked after closing one night. During one of Jason's fishing trips to the club, they'd arranged a date. Instead of cooking the bartender dinner, though, Jason had shoved him into the closet, but only after repaying the earlier favor and drilling the bartender's ass for almost an hour.

Almost halfway to his goal, Jason discovered the Man Web, a gay exclusive website for personal ads. Answering an ad from a couple who were looking for a threesome, Jason was ecstatic to get numbers seven and eight in one go. He didn't get them in the closet right away, first he got on all fours and let one pound him from behind while the other filled his mouth. Number nine also came from the Man Web, an older man with far too much hair on his back. He had introduced Jason to the joys of being rimmed before Jason introduced him to the inside of his closet.

He'd gone back to Liaisons for number ten, a twenty-something so drunk he'd passed out seconds after getting to Jason's apartment. Jason actually fucked the man while he was unconscious before dragging him into the closet and closing him inside.

Number eleven was from the Man Web, a self-proclaimed virgin who looked no older than seventeen, eager for his first sexual experience. Jason, who was not without heart, fulfilled all the boy's fantasies before knocking him upside the head and tossing him into the closet.

Number twelve was a man named Robbie, who Jason knew from work, a flamboyant man who'd always made Jason uncomfortable with his openness. He invited Robbie over on the pretense of needing help moving an armoire and gave Robbie a thrill by letting him suck on Jason's cock for a while before pushing him into the closet.

Afterward, Jason reclined on his bed, smiling up at the ceiling. Only one more to deliver and he still had three days before the next full moon. He should be able to get that last one with no trouble then he'd have what he wanted. Heterosexuality. A normal life. No more giving in to these wicked urges that caused him to partake in the vile, nasty, decadent acts he'd indulged in since he'd first met Andros. He tried not to think of those things right now, as it was getting him hard again.

Hell, if he was about to get the cure, Jason figured he might as well enjoy the sickness while it lasted. He had just slipped his hand into his underwear when the closet door creaked open and Andros stepped out, a playful smile curling his lips.

"What?" Jason exclaimed, jumping up from the bed and pulling his hand back out of his underwear.

"Not happy to see me, mortal?"

"What are you doing here? I haven't delivered all thirteen souls to you yet."

"Ah, but you have." Andros paused, closed his eyes and inhaled deeply, a soft moan issuing from deep in his throat. "I can just smell the sex in this room. All that man sweat, testosterone, drying semen. Why would anyone want to give this up?"

"What do you mean? I *have* delivered all thirteen souls? I know how to count and I've only delivered twelve men to you."

"Yes, twelve . . . plus you."

Jason felt his skin go cold and his erection deflated like a punctured balloon. "What are you talking about?"

Andros stepped close to him, reaching out and running his fingers down his cheek. "You were always to be the thirteenth soul."

Jason batted the demon's hand away and sidestepped him, inching his way to the door. "I'm not part of the bargain. The deal was that I provide you with the souls of thirteen homosexual men and you grant me my wish to be straight. That's the deal, we shook on it."

"Silly mortal," Andros said with a laugh. "You think demons know anything of honor or fairness? You think that handshake sealed a promise of some kind? You should know better than to take a demon at his word. We are liars by our very nature."

Jason had almost reached the door when Andros made his move. The demon was so fast that he registered only as a blur. Andros was there by Jason's side, seizing his arm in a vise-like grip and jerking him toward the closet.

"This can't be," Jason whined, trying to resist but being dragged along nonetheless. "What about the reformed lesbian that sold me the copy of *Transformations*? You healed her."

"She isn't reformed; she's still a pussy-licker extraordinaire. No, she's merely one of my faithful servants, offering her services to help me perform my sacred duty."

"What duty?"

Andros grabbed Jason roughly by the hair and brought his face close. Jason could smell sulfur on the demon's breath. "To punish pansy-ass homosexuals like yourself who don't have the balls to accept who they are."

"Where are you taking me?" Jason said, renewing his efforts to pull loose of Andros's grasp, all to no avail.

"I'm taking you to hell, of course. But don't worry, there's no fire, no brimstone, no souls crying out in agony. Hell is a more *personal* affair."

Jason screamed then, hoping one of his neighbors would hear and come to his rescue. But Andros yanked him into the closet and the door swung shut behind them.

Only they weren't in the closet. Gone were the clothes, the hangers, the rod, even the walls. Instead there was only a black void that seemed both limitless and claustrophobic at the same time. As Jason's eyes began to adjust to the gloom he made out a writhing mass in the distance. The sounds came next—moans and grunts and squeals and gasps. The scene came into sharper focus, as if without moving Jason had somehow gotten closer. It was the twelve men Jason had delivered to Andros, all of them naked and covered in sheens of sweat, seeming to be joined into one being as their flesh melded in a raw, animalistic orgy. Hard cocks plunged into tight asses, rigid members suckled by hot, hungry mouths, juice spurting into every available orifice, faces bathed in the transcendent light of orgasm. Jason was so hard it was almost painful, his erection straining to join the festivities. He tried to step forward but found himself bound in place by heavy, rusty chains.

"Quite a sight, isn't it?" Andros said, stepping up next to the immobilized Jason. The demon was completely naked, his chest sprinkled with a fine dusting of dark hairs. A ten inch cock with large mushroom head pointed straight up from a tight nest of pubic hair, balls slicked with sweat hanging low like ripe fruit. "They certainly are having fun, aren't they? And they never tire. They never go soft."

Jason made a mewling sound that spoke of hunger and desire. He strained against his chains, but they were sturdy and seemed to get tighter the more he struggled.

"This is your hell," Andros said intimately into his ear. "For eternity you get to watch the orgy, but you never get to join in, never even get to touch yourself."

Without another word, Andros walked over to the pile of flesh and rammed his large dick into Robbie's ass, causing the man to cry out with ecstasy and pain.

TRANSFORMATIONS

From his own private hell, Jason watched a heaven of which he would never be part.

THE BONADVENTURE

"CANE, ARE YOU sure this is a good idea?" Kinsley asked, gripping the flashlight to her chest so that the light hit the underside of her chin and spread around her face.

Cane knelt by a large angel monument, unpacking equipment from his duffle bag and lining it up on the ground next to him. "It's a great idea. This investigation is going to put S.C.A.D.P.I.T. on the map."

"Dude, are you still going with that name?" Topher asked, stepping onto the monument's base and scrutinizing the angel up close.

"The Savannah College of Art and Design Paranormal Investigation Team. What's wrong with that name?"

"Well, other than the fact that Scad Pit sounds like a condition you'd need penicillin for, the acronym is almost as long as the name itself."

"I'm the founder of this group, so I get to name it."

Topher hopped down from the monument. "I still vote for the Artistic Spirit Squad."

"A.S.S.?" Kinsley said with a giggle. "You're joking, right?"

"I think it has a certain appeal to it."

"You would think that," Cane said under his breath.

"What's that? It wasn't a homophobic slur from our fearless leader, was it?"

Cane rose to his feet. Topher was at least three inches shorter, slighter of build, but he seemed not a bit intimidated by Cane, which actually irritated Cane more than he wanted to admit. "Look, I don't care who you have sex with. You can screw chipmunks in your spare time for all I care, but I would appreciate it if you two would stop being so loud. We are trying to fly under the radar here."

"Gotcha," Topher said in a stage whisper, reaching up to run his fingers across his lips as if zipping them shut.

Cane rolled his eyes then reached down to pick up the EMF reader. He held it out to Topher. "Here, you're going to measure the electromagnetic fields tonight."

"No way, I always do the EVPs."

"Not this time. Kinsley's going to have the voice recorder and ask the questions tonight."

"How come?"

"How about because last month at 432 Abercorn you asked the ghost of the little girl if she'd ever seen *Dreamgirls*?"

Topher laughed and stroked his goatee. "Yeah, that was a good one."

"See, you don't take this seriously at all."

"Come on, dude. You think the dead don't have a sense of humor just because you don't?"

Cane said nothing, just stared at Topher until the other young man relented and took the device. Next he handed the voice recorder to Kinsley.

"I still don't know if we should be doing this. We had permission to be in all the other places we investigated. You know no one's supposed to be in the cemetery after 5 p.m. unless they're part of an official tour."

Topher sidled up next to Kinsley and threw an arm around her shoulders. "If I didn't go where I wasn't supposed to go, I'd miss out on an awful lot of fun."

"This isn't exactly the same as sneaking into some underground club," Cane said. "We're doing an exhaustive and in-depth paranormal investigation of one of the most famous cemeteries in America. This is going to—"

"—put us on the map," Topher and Kinsley finished in unison.

"Mock all you want, but I think it's a shame that Savannah has the reputation as the most haunted city in the country and yet S.C.A.D. doesn't have a single sanctioned paranormal organization. And they won't approve any new groups or clubs without a minimum of five members. Look around and do the math; you'll see we're short."

"And you really think this will help?" Kinsley asked.

"Hell yes. Once word gets out that we did an all-night investigation of Bonaventure Cemetery, people are going to be lining up, begging to get in."

"Just like some underground club," Topher said with a snarky grin.

Ignoring him, Cane selected the digital video recorder with infrared night-vision. "When we get sanctioned by the school and start collecting membership fees, we can finally get some decent equipment like the professional outfits use."

"Maybe we can even get Chip Coffey to pay us a visit," Topher said. Cane shot him a heated glare, and Topher pulled the corners of his lips down in a severe, exaggerated frown. "Sorry, forgot I was supposed to be Mr. Serious."

"Enough fooling around. Let's start over at little Gracie's grave."

The trio headed to one of the many roads that cut through the expansive graveyard. Topher remained silent for about ten seconds, which was pretty much his limit, then said, "So I think I've come up with a name for this little excursion." Cane didn't respond, but he knew that wouldn't stop Topher. "The Bonadventure. What do you think?"

"I think that sounds ridiculous."

"It's fun and whimsical, like me."

"I want this organization to be taken seriously, not seen as some colossal joke."

"Yes, God forbid anyone laugh at the Scad Pit."

"Look Topher, I know you think you should be in charge of this group, just because you lead those little walking ghost tours around the downtown area, but you're not."

"Hey, my ghost tours are the most popular in the city, and one hundred percent historically accurate, so don't go shooting your fat mouth off."

"I'll say whatever—"

"Guys," Kinsley said, stepping between the two. "Whatever happened to keeping our voices down? I suggest you save the pissing contest for later so we can get the job done."

Cane and Topher stared at one another for a few seconds, then turned without a word and continued down the road.

So far S.C.A.D.P.I.T. had done three investigations, Bonaventure being the fourth. Already Cane was sick to death of Topher and his unprofessional demeanor. Other than their interest in the paranormal they had absolutely nothing in common. Their personalities clashed like a cold and warm front colliding to create a massive thunderstorm. More than once he'd considered kicking the jokester off the team, but seeing as he already hurt for members, he couldn't really afford to give anyone the boot. Besides, much as it pained Cane to admit it, the guy's tours were immensely popular and could potentially draw in new members.

As they approached the grave of six year old Gracie Watson, Cane started up the recorder, looking at the display screen to check the picture quality. The night-vision rendered everything a glowing green, but the picture was clear and focused. "Anything registering on the EMF?" he asked without glancing at Topher.

"Everything's in normal range, Cap'n."

They stopped before the grave, enclosed by a tall wrought-iron fence. Inside, the life-sized marble statue of the girl shone ghostly in the moonlight, startlingly lifelike in its detail. Foliage exploded around it. Cane positioned the camera through the bars and trained it on the statue. "Still nothing?" he asked Topher.

"No unusual spikes in the electromagnetic field. Maybe she's sleeping?"

Cane pointed the camera at the collection of dolls and trinkets that had been left just outside the fence. Little Gracie's grave was purported to be one of the most haunted sites at Bonaventure Cemetery. People claimed they could sometimes hear Gracie, who had died of pneumonia in 1889, laughing or singing, sometimes even crying. Supposedly, the statue even wept blood at times. Cane highly doubted the latter, but there may be truth to the other tales. He hoped to find out tonight.

"Okay, Kinsley, you're up."

She seemed distracted, staring off at something to the left of them. Cane called her name again before she turned on the recorder. "Okay, um, here we go. Is the spirit of Grace Watson with us?"

Kinsley paused, and they all remained silent, even Topher. The night seemed to be totally devoid of sound. Even the insects held their breath. All Cane could hear was the rustling of leaves. But with electronic voice phenomena, the answers could often not be registered by the human ear. Only when the recordings were played back could the voices of the dead be heard.

"Are you lonely?" Kinsley asked. "Do you want someone to play with you?"

Cane zoomed in on the toys, hoping that maybe one of them would move, but nothing.

"Do you miss your parents? Are you looking for them?"

"Have you tried a Google search?" Topher said in a quiet voice.

Cane instantly turned on him and growled, "Will you knock that shit off? You're not helping."

"What is your problem? Why do you think ghosts are more likely to manifest to sour-faced stick-in-the-muds? Maybe the dead could use a little levity. Ever think about that?"

"I really don't get you, man. I mean, I've taken one of your tours and you don't act like this."

"Well, I get paid for the tours."

"Oh, I see, so it's all about the paycheck for you. Since you're not making anything from this trip, why don't you just go home?"

"Hey, you can't kick me out of here?"

"I founded this organization so I assure you I most certainly can."

"Fine, maybe I will leave. And the first cop I find, I'll just report to him that I know of two individuals who are in the cemetery after hours."

"You little bastard, I ought to—"

"Enough!" Kinsley hissed. "I'm sick of dealing with your bickering. If I didn't know any better, I'd swear you were an old married couple. Maybe we should just pack up our stuff and get out of here, call the investigation off."

"No way," Cane said. "This is too important."

"I'm not leaving either," Topher said. "Whatever our fearless leader may think of my personality, I am very devoted to paranormal studies. I'm just as interested in finding hard evidence about the afterlife as you are, even if we approach things differently."

Cane felt a sharp retort bubbling up like vomit, but he swallowed it down and took a moment to calm himself. He pulled his wallet from his back pocket and took out a crumpled twenty, slapping it into Topher's palm. "There, you're getting paid now. If you're going to stay, I expect some professionalism."

Topher just stared down at the bill in his hand for a while, before he stuffed it into his back pocket. "You got it, boss."

With a sigh, Cane said, "We're getting nothing from Gracie right now. I say we move on, come back later and try again."

Topher nodded, but Kinsley just walked past him, heading to the left. She stopped before a large plant. The thing was almost as tall as her, with large palm frond-like leaves, and cupped in the center of the fronds were some kind of round spores as big as basketballs. It looked tropical. "What exactly is this?" she asked.

Cane walked over, scrutinizing the plant. "I think it's a Sago Palm."

"You're just an expert on everything, aren't you?" Topher said, stepping up next to him.

"Of the three of us, I'm the only one actually from Savannah, and these are fairly common."

"I don't recall seeing anything quite like it before," Kinsley said. "But they're all over the cemetery. What are these big spores?"

"I think it's the plant's fruit, or seed, or whatever."

Kinsley shone her flashlight on one of the spores. "They look almost woven from vines, creating some kind of mesh. And I think—" With a startled yelp, she jumped back.

"What's wrong?" Topher asked.

"I swear there was something moving in there, inside the spore."

Cane laughed. "You're just spooked."

"I'm telling you, I saw something moving."

She shone the flashlight on the spore again. Cane and Topher leaned forward to get a better view. Nothing.

Kinsley looked at the two men, the blush in her cheeks evident even in the scant light. "Stop looking at me like I'm crazy. I know what I saw."

"It could be a haunted plant," Topher said. "That would be a first, huh?"

Kinsley slapped his arm. "Knock it off."

"I think we've all wasted enough time," Cane said. "Let's do a tour of the cemetery to see if we get EMF spikes in any particular location. If so, we'll concentrate there for a while."

Cane and Topher started off. Kinsley remained, staring at the strange plant, before she followed.

They'd been at it for hours and they had absolutely zilch to show for it. There wasn't anything on the camera and no unusual EMF readings. Cane could only hope they'd caught an EVP or two, otherwise this night was proving to be a total bust.

They were taking a break near the Wilmington River, while Kinsley changed out the batteries in the digital voice recorder. When she first announced the batteries were dying, Cane got excited. Inexplicable draining of batteries was often a sign of spirits trying to manifest. But then Topher admitted he'd forgotten to charge the batteries before they left.

"Do we really have to keep this up 'til dawn?" Kinsley asked.

"That's what we all signed on for."

"Yeah, but it's dead out here."

"Pardon the pun," Topher added. He stood on the base of a large monument, taking a closer look at a life-sized statue of Jesus that was partially covered in moss. The statue had one hand stretched out, and which Topher grabbed it as if they were shaking. "Hey, someone get my picture. Topher Bridges and the Son of God, having a meeting of the minds."

Kinsley laughed, but Cane just sighed. He sat on the ground with his back propped against a tombstone. He was tired. No, beyond that. Exhausted. He had such high hopes for this investigation, truly believing it would be the one to put S.C.A.D.P.I.T. on the map. How could Bonaventure have yielded nothing? The prior three investigations had all resulted in *some* findings. Nothing definitive or earth-shattering, but a few orbs and EMF spikes, and outside the Mercer House they'd captured some garbled static on the voice recorder that sounded like someone (Jim Williams?) hissing, "I was poisoned."

But here, at a site purported to be one of the most haunted places on the planet, they were coming up empty-handed. It didn't seem possible. Worse, he'd bragged to several people about this investigation (although he'd sworn Topher and Kinsley to absolute secrecy). How would he face them later to admit he had nothing to show from spending the entire night in the cemetery?

With another weary sigh, Cane said, "Let's just call it a night."

Topher, who had gone on to pretend the Jesus statue was strangling him, straightened up so suddenly that he almost toppled off the monument. "Are you serious, dude?"

"Yes, I'm serious. Let's just pack everything in and go home."

Hope and doubt seemed to be warring in Kinsley's eyes. "Even though we haven't found anything yet?"

"That's precisely *why* we're calling it quits." Cane stood up. "If anything was going to happen, it would have happened by now."

Topher jumped down and walked over. "It's not like you to give up. You feeling okay?"

"I just don't see the point of continuing a fruitless investigation. Having zero findings isn't going to earn us any recognition or get the group any closer to being sanctioned by the school."

"Yeah, but we'll try again, right?"

Cane looked from Topher to Kinsley, making an effort to rekindle his passion for the hunt, but he just felt drained. Maybe his father was right. Maybe this whole paranormal investigation thing was a childish waste of time. "Why don't we—"

He was interrupted by a loud noise that startled them all. It sounded like cables snapping. Lots of them. Coming from all around.

"What the hell is that?" Kinsley said, sidling up behind Cane to grip his elbow.

Cane took a moment to thrill at her touch—when he'd first met her at school he had harbored a major crush, but once she joined the group he had put such thoughts out of his mind.

The sound of cables snapping intensified . . .

. . . then stopped altogether.

A silence, so profound it felt like going deaf, replaced the noise. The trio stood perfectly still. Cane, intending to break the silence, was cut off when a new noise arose. This softer sound was somehow more ominous. Scrambling and scratching, like something clawing its way along the ground and pavement. Several somethings, actually. Perhaps dozens. It came from everywhere, surrounding them.

"I think we should go," Kinsley said, an unmistakable tremor in her voice.

Topher, his usual prankster persona discarded like an old sock, nodded mutely.

"Are you guys insane?" Cane asked. "This is what we came here for. Finally something is happening. Get your equipment ready and let's investigate."

Kinsley gripped his elbow tighter. "This isn't like the others. This isn't ghost lights or creaking floorboards. Listen to that . . . something is out there."

"Yeah, and I'm going to find out what." Cane raised the camera and scanned the cemetery around him. He didn't focus on any one area since the sound was everywhere. He stared intensely at the display screen, his surroundings becoming a green and black otherworld. At first he saw nothing, but then an object zipped across the screen, low to the ground like an animal. It moved so quickly any real details were indiscernible.

"There," he said, pointing. "Something darted between the grave markers about twenty yards that way."

Topher started to speak, but his voice cracked. He cleared his throat and tried again. "What kind of something?"

"I'm not sure, maybe an—oh shit! There went another one! And another!"

"What are they?" Kinsley asked. The tremor of her voice replaced with an edge of hysteria.

"I can't say for sure. Topher, are you getting anything on the EMF?"

When Topher didn't respond, Cane tore his gaze away from the camera's display to look at the other man. Topher's face resembled little Gracie's statue, pale contrasting against the darkness. The EMF reader hung at his side, forgotten as the chaos escalated. Cane repeated his question louder, making Topher jump into action. "Um, no, there's nothing. Nothing at all."

"Are you sure that thing's batteries aren't also dead?"

"I'm sure. Look, maybe we should get out of here. Whatever this is, it doesn't sound supernatural."

"It's certainly not natural," Cane said softly, turning back to the camera. The things seemed to swarm around them, surrounding them. From what he could see on the display they looked similar to scorpions, complete with stinger-tipped tail raised above them. They were far too big to be scorpions, though. About the size of a full-grown bulldog.

"Let's just go," Kinsley said, grabbing Topher's elbow. "Cane can stay if he wants."

"Dude, come with us," Topher said. "Sounds like whatever it is, is getting closer."

Cane heard them but didn't respond. He slowly turned full circle, watching the night through the camera display. Yes, Topher was right. Those things swarmed around them in a constricting circle that tightened like a noose. Still, he couldn't force himself to leave.

Topher took Kinsley by the hand. "Suit yourself. We're out of here."

The two started off, back in the general direction of the main gate, where they'd have to scale the fence to get to the car—parked two blocks away behind an abandoned gas station. They had the flashlights, whereas Cane had the night-vision camera.

"Fuck, look at that," Kinsley exclaimed behind him. This grabbed Cane's attention. He hurried over to the other two to investigate the discovery.

They stood in front of another Sago Palm. Cane was about to turn away when he noticed what caused Kinsley to shout out. Kinsley trained her light on the spores again, which were ruined, shredded. The woven vines had broken open, lying in tangled heaps.

"I told you I saw something move in the spores," Kinsley said. "Whatever it was, I don't know, *hatched* out of them."

"That's ludicrous," Cane said with no real conviction. This seemed the most logical explanation under the circumstances.

Topher said, "This shit is too fucked up for me. I signed on for a ghost hunt, not a creature feature." He took off toward the main gate, not pausing to see if anyone or anything followed.

Kaitlin turned to Cane. "Please, don't be such a mule. Let's get out of here."

Cane studied the ruined spores again and decided she was right. He was about to say so when the palm before shook furiously, as if caught in a high wind. Only there was no wind. They both started to back away, but not fast enough.

Something leapt out of the fronds and onto Kinsley's chest, knocking her to the ground. She screamed, crab walked as she tried to shake it off, but before she could free herself from its grip the thing's tale whipped around and the stinger punctured her left eyeball. She screamed again, this time more of a high-pitched shriek.

Cane was frozen in place. He knew he should go to Kinsley, try to help her, but the monstrosity before him rendered him incapable of moving. It did indeed resemble a large scorpion, only without the claws and with more than eight legs. Encapsulated in a blue-gray shell, shining like metal in the moonlight, the *thing's* multi-jointed legs ended in sharp points that stabbed into Kinsley's flesh as it crawled up her torso. Her left eye socket was a bloody crater. Somewhere along the line, her screaming stopped, replaced with a wheezing rattle. Her limbs jerked, the flashlight still gripped tightly in one hand. At least, until she brought it down on the ground so hard it shattered. The night was bright enough, however, that Cane could still see her one good eye roll toward him, pleading silently.

Then the creature leapt onto her face, and from the crunching sounds, Cane assumed it had some kind of mouth on its underbelly. Sharp teeth made quick work of cartilage and bone. Much to his horror, Cane realized he was filming all of this on the digital camera.

When three more creatures emerged from the shadows, scuttling quickly toward Kinsley's body, Cane finally overcame his paralysis and took off running in the direction Topher had gone a few moments ago.

Only a few moments ago, when Kinsley still breathed.

The sound of the creatures moving through the cemetery overpowered Cane's senses, filling his ears like apocalyptic thunder. In his mind, however, he could still hear Kinsley's high-pitched shriek. He had to alter direction more than once when the creatures scrambled into his path. He leapt over one, barely avoiding its whipping tale. Soon, though, he'd become disoriented.

Then, he saw little Gracie sitting in her wrought-iron cage. A landmark, something to help him get his bearings straight. With renewed vigor, Cane picked up speed. He still carried the camera, evidence of the night's fatality. When he got out of here—and he would not allow himself to even entertain the idea that he wouldn't—he would need it as evidence so the authorities wouldn't think him insane.

When he heard Topher calling his name, he did not stop. He did slow, eyes darting around for some sign of the man. Then he realized the voice was coming from above, and he glanced up to see Topher straddling a branch about twenty feet up in a live oak.

"What the hell are you doing up there?" Cane hissed, standing directly beneath him.

"Hiding from those things. You need to get your ass up here, too."

Cane actually made a move toward the lowest hanging branch, but then stopped. He kept visualizing the creatures' legs, the way they ended in those lethal points. Seemed to him, the damn things wouldn't have any trouble climbing.

"Get out of there," Cane said. "It's not safe."

"It's a lot safer than being down there with those . . . whatever the hell they are. The cemetery is crawling with them. Where's Kinsley?"

Cane tried to answer but his voice was locked away and he could only shake his head.

"Damn man, that a—"

He never got to finish his thought, because one of the creatures suddenly dropped from a higher branch, landing directly on Topher's back. He screamed as he flailed. Then another dropped onto his back. Topher leaned too far to one side and toppled off the branch.

Cane backed up quickly. Topher hit the ground with an audible *crack*. A dozen creatures attacked at once, covering him completely.

Cane turned and ran. He wasn't used to this much physical exertion and a painful stitch stabbed in his side. Still, he pumped his legs harder. Morbid as it was, he hoped that Topher would keep the creatures occupied long enough for Cane to make his escape.

As if an answer from Heaven itself, the main gate came into view. He was almost home free. Relief flooded his system, which perhaps made him drop his guard. Cane didn't see the creature until it was almost upon him. He side-stepped it, stumbled, nearly fell but managed to keep his balance. For a moment, he thought he'd avoided disaster.

That is, until he felt the pain in his left ankle. Looking down, he saw the stinger retracting. He kicked out, his foot connecting squarely with the creature's side. It felt like kicking a boulder. He made for the gate once more.

His left leg tingled, but the tingling gave way to total numbness, and his leg gave out. He collapsed onto the pavement, banging an elbow and skinning his palms. Cane gritted his teeth against the pain and crawled forward. The gate was so close. So close. He could almost touch it.

The numbness spread throughout his lower torso. Pretty soon everything below the waist was dead weight. Still, he used his fingertips like claws to drag himself forward, inch by excruciating inch. The moon dipped behind a cloud, bringing total darkness over the cemetery. Cane felt the numbness spreading up his body. He knew he wouldn't be able to move at all, sooner rather than later. Maybe he wouldn't even be able to breathe.

Then he heard that sound, the scrambling and scratching as the creatures closed in on him. It sounded like an army of creatures were approaching him from behind. Not rushing. As though they were savoring every agonizing moment Cane spent incapacitated. He glanced back, peering into the shadows. With trembling, numbing, hands, he brought the camera up to his face. Cane aimed it back to the cemetery, staring at the display screen.

He would have screamed if he had any strength left, but all that came was an asthmatic gasp.

He'd thought it sounded like an army, and it was. Hundreds by the look of it: glowing green on the display, advancing slowly but steadily.

He let his head drop to the pavement, closed his eyes against his approaching death. He only prayed he'd lose consciousness fast.

Cane's last coherent thought was that someone was going to find the camera, review the footage, and then he would have gotten his wish.

This would put S.C.A.D.P.I.T. on the map.

A HELPING HAND

THE BABY WAS crying again. Erica heard her through the baby monitor sitting on the nightstand. She pushed aside the James Patterson novel she was reading, got up, and started toward the nursery, down the hall. Halfway there, she heard Brett coming down the stairs.

"I've got it," Erica called over her shoulder and stepped into baby Patricia's room. As she lifted the baby into her arms, Erica felt the diaper's dampness. "Does Pat need to be changed? Yes she does, oh yes she does," she cooed.

"I'll do it," Brett said, reaching for Patricia.

"You're supposed to be working."

"I know, but I heard the baby crying."

"That's what I'm here for," Erica said, carrying Patricia to the changing table. "The whole purpose of me moving in here was so that I could take care of the baby, allowing you to get back to writing."

"I know, I know, but when I hear her crying, I have to come. It's instinctive. Pavlovian, I guess."

Brett gently elbowed Erica aside and started to remove his daughter's diaper. Patricia giggled and squirmed, repeating "Da-da, Da-da" over and over, obviously delighted to see her father. Erica stood off to the side, feeling useless. "So, have you got much work done on the new novel?"

"Some," Brett said evasively, taking the moist wipes from the box and cleaning the baby.

"You know the deadline for the publisher is just around the corner."

"What are you now, my agent?"

While Brett dusted baby powder onto Patricia's bottom to prevent diaper rash, he made silly, cartoonish faces at her, causing the baby to laugh even harder as she pumped her fists in the air.

"I'm just saying, Cassie always told me how important your writing was to you, and you really haven't done much since . . . well, since Pat was born."

Brett said nothing as he diapered Patricia, picked her back up and bounced her as she tried to snatch the glasses off his face. "It's been a rough adjustment," he conceded. "Learning to be a single father has taken up a lot of my time."

"It's been a year." Erica smiled compassionately, placing a hand on Brett's forearm. "I know losing Cassie in childbirth was painful. She was my daughter, and I miss her, too. I also know raising Pat by yourself took a lot of your time and focus away from your work. But I offered to move in to shoulder the burden. Yet, in the three months that I've been here, your writing continues to suffer, because you can't let me take care of my own granddaughter."

Brett placed Patricia into her crib, handing the child her favorite stuffed animal—a yellow rabbit with one ear straight up and the other flopped over. "Hoppy," Patricia exclaimed.

"That's the thing," Brett said. "You said 'shoulder the burden,' but I don't view Pat as a burden at all."

"You know that's not what I meant."

"Yes, I know, but the truth is I *want* to take care of her, I like it. I don't feel right pawning her off on you."

"I don't mind, Brett. Grandmothers love to dote on their grandchildren. It's what we live for."

"I know you don't mind, and I'm glad you're here to spend time with Pat and help out when I need you, but I don't intend to leave all the work to you. Like I said, I want to do it."

"What about your writing?"

"What Cassie told you was right, my writing was one of the most important things in my life, but my priorities shifted since Patricia came along. There's nothing more important to me than Pat. *Nothing.*"

"Aren't you worried about your career?"

"Not really. Having sold the film rights to my first two novels—for a hell of a lot more money than I got for the books themselves—I don't *need* to work for a very long time. I might even take some time off from writing. I can go back to it when Pat's older."

"What about your fans? They're clamoring for more."

Brett looked down into the crib, flicking a finger under Patricia's chin and making her smile. "What Pat needs is a lot more important to me than what my fans want."

Erica looked at her son-in-law with misty eyes. She smiled, wiped her eyes, and said, "Well, it's almost time for Pat's feeding so—"

"I got it. You can relax."

"Are you sure? It's no trouble for me to feed her."

"I'm sure," Brett said, taking Pat back into his arms, kissing her on her soft head with the peach-fuzz of hair growing in. Red, like her mother's had been. "I think Pat here needs a little Daddy bonding time."

"Da-da, Da-da, Da-da, Da-da."

With one final glance at the family tableau presented by father and daughter, Erica left the nursery. Back in her own room, she looked at the Patterson novel she'd left on the nightstand. With a disgusted flick of her wrist, she knocked the book off the table and into the wastebasket. What a waste of dead trees.

She went to her closet and opened the door. On the top, small shelf, she had lined up all seven novels Brett had written. *Crutches, The Unexamined Life, Washed in the Blood, Fancy Junk, The Last Resort, All the More Reason,* and *Climbing the Mountain.* The last was completed a few short months before Patricia had killed Cassie when she ripped her way into the world, leaving Erica's daughter nothing but an empty shell.

It was bad enough Patricia had killed her mother, but she'd also killed her father's writing career. No one wrote like Brett. His novels were full of such rich emotion, such layered themes, such complex characters. They moved Erica, made her laugh and cry and fear and rejoice. No other books satisfied her like these. She wasn't merely Brett's mother-in-law; she was his biggest fan. She practically salivated over the prospect of something new, being lucky enough to read most of his novels in manuscript form long before they were available to the general public.

Only there were no more novels, no more manuscripts, and the way Brett talked there wouldn't be for quite some time. Erica had thought moving in would free him up to go back to what he did best; she would tend to her murderous grandchild and Brett could produce more extraordinary novels. Obviously, things weren't going according to plan. It was as though Patricia had cast some spell over her father, keeping him from his important work, which left Erica with no new novels to look forward to.

Sitting on the edge of her bed, Erica reached over, took one of her pillows and hugged it to her, squeezing tight. Tonight, after both father and daughter were asleep . . . tonight she'd employ Plan B.

Tonight she'd remove the one thing keeping Brett from his work.

THE POSSESSION

OKAY, LET'S GET one thing straight. I did not murder Dirk Vandercock. I mean, I know how it looks, but what you see ain't always what you get. That thing I killed, it may have looked like Dirk and it may have sounded like Dirk, hell his own mama would probably have thought it was him, but it wasn't him. It was some *thing*, a hell-beast taking residence in his body, like a squatter.

I guess, in a way, you could say I *did* murder Dirk, because what happened to him—the possession and all—was my fault. I didn't mean for it to happen, didn't even believe in demons and shit like that, but I'm responsible all the same.

You see, what you got to understand is that I have a reputation in the gay porn industry for being a writer/director with real vision and ambition. My productions ain't just a bunch of mindless fuck flicks. Shit no. They got plotlines, character development, the whole shebang.

I'm not the winner of five Golden Cock Awards for nothing.

Hey, a little patience, please. All this is relevant, trust me. Now with each film I really tried to push myself, to come up with something more mind-blowing than the last. Take *Black Holes* for instance. It's not just an interracial orgy set on a space station. I mean, it is that but there's more to it. It also explores issues of race and stereotyping, as well as the results of prolonged isolation. Real deep shit, you better believe it. And *Backdoor Justice*, with its storyline of an Average Joe who gets revenge on the guys who gang-raped his daughter by tracking them down one by one and ass-raping them? That film takes a long, hard look at vigilantism in this country. No pun intended.

So I'm sure you can see it was important to keep coming up with something bigger and better, to constantly top myself. So when I hit on the idea for *The Devil's Pitchfork*, I knew I had a real winner on my hands. The subject matter would be controversial which was sure to get the film lots of attention, and I figured it would be a perfect vehicle for Dirk.

Well, I guess at this point I should back up and tell you about me and Dirk.

He was the star of my films for the last three years, true, but he was also my lover. I met him when he was eighteen, new to the city and working as a waiter for a catering company while trying to make something happen with his acting. He'd only been at it for a couple of months, but he seemed depressed that all he'd gotten so far was a two-line part on some soap. Like the perfect cliché, he'd stepped off the bus expecting to find someone standing there ready to hand him bug bushels full of fortune and fame.

He'd moved into my building, down the hall from me. A real fleabag of a place. I noticed him right away. That dark hair and strong jawline, the slender body and bubble butt. He had a twinkle in his eye that a wordsmith, such as myself, can only describe as devilish. Dirk made my mouth water, I can tell you that. I introduced myself, offered to show him around the city, told him I was in the film business without getting into specifics. Just enough to get him interested.

We started spending a lot of time together, and I admit I was laying it on thick. I mean, in my line of work I got plenty of action, tasty young boys willing to do almost anything for a screen test or audition. But I hungered for Dirk in a way that I hadn't experienced in a while. Him playing hard to get made me want him all the more.

When I finally admitted that I made gay porn for a living, there was disgust, but excitement at the same time. He asked me lots of questions, so I offered to show him one of my films so he could see firsthand what I did. Dirk was reluctant, or at least acted like he was, but agreed nonetheless. We had a little private screening in my apartment. Needless to say, it had the desired effect. Got him all hot and bothered, which is how I finally got him into bed.

Where I was shocked to find out Dirk was a virgin. A guy as hot as all that and still untouched . . . It was like rooting around in shit and finding a gold nugget. I showed him the ropes, though. You can take that to the bank.

Dirk was awkward and shy about things in the beginning, but before long he was sucking like a pro. And that ass . . . that sweet, tight ass! If there's a heaven, it ain't in the clouds but buried deep in Dirk Vandercock's ass.

First time I brought up the idea of him starring in one of my films, he refused. After all, he had plans of being a serious actor. The next Vin Diesel. I shit you not, he actually said that. I figured I could bide my time, and after only three more months of not booking a single gig, not even a dog food commercial, he caved. That's when I gave him his name, Dirk Vandercock. Got a real ring to it, wouldn't you say? His real name was just so bland and forgettable. I'm not sure I even remember what it was anymore.

First film we did together was called *The Fuck-It List*, about a young man who discovers he has a terminal illness and decides to go out fucking up a storm. Dirk had a touching death scene at the end while a gang of strapping young men did a circle jerk over his body. It was a huge hit. Dirk became an instant gay porn sensation.

About that same time, Dirk and I moved in together, getting a nicer apartment in a better part of town. Financially it made sense, but I also wanted to keep him all to myself.

He was mine, I found him and I wasn't planning to share him.

I know what you're thinking. Wasn't I jealous with him fucking all those hot guys in the films? Hell no, *that* was business, nothing personal. Besides, I got to hand-pick all his co-stars, remember? If he seemed to enjoy himself a little too much with a certain actor, I made sure they didn't work together anymore. When the cameras were off, though, he belonged to me and me alone. He seemed okay with that.

After all, I had taken him under my wing when he was new to the city and painfully naïve, I taught him the art of fucking, and I gave him not only a job but a career. Dirk showed his gratitude in a variety of pleasurable and increasingly inventive ways.

Things went on like that for about three years, give or take. We made one hit movie after another. In our personal life, Dirk was completely devoted to me. I ain't exaggerating when I say it was damn near perfect.

Then came *The Devil's Pitchfork*.

I curse the day I ever came up with the idea for that film.

I'd recently watched *The Exorcist* on late-night cable, and I got to thinking how cool it would be to incorporate Satanism and the occult and animalistic fucking all into one story. It would piss off the Christian types more than gay porn normally did. Over the years I'd learned that pissing off Christians was a sure-fire way to make some money.

While writing the script, I did a lot of online research into satanic rites and rituals, and found this one ritual for supposedly inviting a demon into someone's body. I instantly knew I wanted to use it in the film, because from a cinematic point of view, the scene would be breathtaking with all the candles, the pentagram, and the chanting. Plus, having Dirk chained down to an altar would be the perfect segue into a hardcore bondage scene.

So we started shooting, and everything was peachy up until the ritual sequence. We shot the scene and things seemed to go perfectly, but afterward Dirk complained that he didn't feel well. He did look a bit pale, and he was throwing up. I'm not a tyrant or anything, so I let him have a whole day off before we finished up the movie. It was released, and as predicted there was quite an uproar over it. *The Devil's Pitchfork* quickly became our most downloaded production to date.

But something still wasn't right with Dirk. It wasn't anything obvious, not at first. He simply seemed . . . *different*. At home, there was coldness and distance. There were times when I caught him looking at me, not with the adoration I was used to, but with what I thought might be contempt. I shook it off, figuring it was my imagination.

And then we stopped fucking. Or more to the point, Dirk stopped. All of a sudden he was always tired or had a stomach ache or some other lame excuse. Finally I put my foot down and told him he owed it to me after all I'd done for him. That worked. He let me fuck him. Dirk just didn't participate. He just laid there like a blow-up doll or something, his expression almost bored. He didn't even get hard.

After that, he began to go out without me, staying out late, coming home smelling like strange cologne and cigarettes. When I confronted him, he'd get angry, tell me I didn't own him and he didn't have to account for his whereabouts every second of the day.

These kinds of arguments became commonplace and soon escalated. He told me I was smothering him, that he needed some space, a life apart from me and the movies we made. Said he wanted to start auditioning for *legitimate* films again. As if the work we'd been doing was shit, you know? He was slipping away from me, becoming a stranger, and it seemed like it happened overnight.

Then I went out of town to receive my fifth Golden Cock for *The Devil's Pitchfork,* ironically enough. Dirk said he had an important audition and couldn't go with me. I was supposed to be gone three days, but after two days of not getting any calls from Dirk, I cut the trip short and went back to the city.

I walked into the apartment to find Dirk having a threesome on the living room sofa.

Not even with two guys, one guy and a chick. Dirk was fucking her while he sucked the other guy off. It was disgusting.

I went ballistic, sent those two hetero freaks packing without even giving them time to put on all their clothes. Dirk just sat on the sofa, bare-ass naked, looking not the least put out. He smiled up at me. Not even a smile, more a smirk. I yelled. The longer he stayed silent and detached, the louder I yelled.

Finally I wore myself out and collapsed on the other end of the sofa. Dirk looked at me for a minute then spoke for the first time since I'd gotten home. He told me he was leaving.

I told him he couldn't leave me. I'd created him for Christ's sake. Everything he had, *I* had given to him. If not for me, Dirk Vandercock wouldn't even exist. He was mine.

Dirk said he belonged to no man and that he didn't know why he'd allowed me to keep him prisoner for so many years. That's what he said, that I'd 'kept him a prisoner'. He told me he was finally breaking free, and he didn't give two fucks if I liked it or not.

He left me there in the living room to pack. At that point, I was too stunned to really react. I mean, this wasn't the Dirk I had known and loved all these years, this wasn't him at all.

Then I realized it wasn't Dirk.

Insane as it seemed even to me, I suddenly knew what had happened, why Dirk had changed so drastically in such a short period of time. He wasn't himself anymore, he was something else entirely. Something dark and evil.

The ritual in the film had been real, and it had worked. I had allowed a demon to take possession of Dirk's soul when we were filming *The Devil's Pitchfork*. What else could it be? It would explain why he'd become so cruel and vicious and ungrateful. I had opened a doorway to Hell. The sweet, devoted man I'd molded into a star was no more, He'd been replaced by a wicked imposter.

Maybe, though, it wasn't too late to get Dirk back.

I didn't have an iota of doubt, which is how I knew it was the right course of action. Conviction is always a sure sign of righteousness. I went into the bedroom where Dirk was at the closet, pulling out the expensive clothes I'd bought him and tossing them into the suitcase I'd also bought. I picked up one of the four—soon to be joined by a fifth—golden phallic statues sitting on a table by the doorway, and used it to bash Dirk in the back of the head. He was down but not out. I had to hit him two more times before he lost consciousness.

I dragged him across the room, tied him to the bed and stuffed a pair of red silk boxer shorts in his mouth, putting duct tape over that. Then I got online and did a little research on exorcisms.

Turns out, there's a hell of a lot of conflicting information on the subject. There seems to be no one accepted method of casting a demon out of someone, so I decided I'd try them all. Holy water, which isn't as easy to come by as *Buffy* would have you believe, didn't work. Neither did bleeding, burning, or the ever-popular gospel recitation. Nothing seemed to work. Dirk thrashed around on the bed like . . . well, like he was possessed. When I took his gag out, I endured the foul curses he spit my way. Exactly like Linda Blair, only minus the projectile vomiting and head spin. Luckily my neighbors were used to hearing shouting and obscenities from our apartment.

Finally, not knowing what else to do, I decided I'd try to starve the demon out of him. I left him tied and gagged for nearly a week without food, occasionally removing the gag to let him suck water through a straw. The thrashing gradually became weaker until it practically stopped altogether. His body, which had once inspired such desire in me, seemed to be shriveling up. His skin took on an ashen look. His eyes glazed over like smudged glass.

The last time I took his gag out, he told me in a hoarse croak that he hated me and he would make me suffer if it was the last thing he ever did. And that's when I knew. Dirk was gone for good. There was no getting him back.

That left me with only one option.

The butcher knife left a clean cut across his throat.

It was easier than I'd thought it would be, because I knew I was probably setting his soul free with this one selfless act.

And that's what happened. Honest to God, hand me a Bible and I'll swear on it. I ain't making excuses or nothing. I'm telling it like it is. If you want to hold it against me then so be it, but I know I did what had to be done.

What killed Dirk was possession, plain and simple.

THE LOCKED TOWER

ALEC STEVENSON PULLED into a space in the school's small visitor's parking lot and cut the Cadillac's engine. He sat there, staring out the window at the campus. Several years had passed since he'd been to his alma mater, Limestone College, but he marveled at how few superficial changes had occurred. There were, of course, little differences—the old wrought-iron sign at the main entrance was replaced by one that looked like a tall brick wall, the driveway had been repaved, a few of the buildings renovated—but for the most part it looked like it had fifteen years ago, when Alec had been a student.

Making sure he had his cell phone with him so he could take a few digital photos, Alec stepped out of the car. The clear sky promised a bright afternoon. The activity on-campus was minimal, which was the reason he'd chosen to come so late on a Friday afternoon.

He started across the quad, past the library and the auditorium, making a direct line for Winnie Davis Hall.

In Alec's day, Winnie Davis had been in sorry shape, closed off to students. Alec, however, had been inside once. On a dare during his sophomore year, he'd broken through one of the ground level windows and crawled through, taking a tour of the first two floors. He didn't risk going any higher because the floorboards bowed dangerously under his weight. Each step felt like it could send him plummeting to the basement. The whole place smelled of mildew and rot. When he stood in the rotunda, staring straight up to the tower, he'd seen the skeletal framework of a skylight that would normally have separated the tower from the rest of the building, only there was no glass.

Of course, those days were in the past. Alec recently read on the Limestone website that a massive restoration project for Winnie Davis, costing millions of dollars and lasting many years, had been completed. Apparently the building now boasted such state-of-the-art amenities as an elevator, a flat-screen television mounted to the walls of each classroom, and even automated shades that would lower themselves over the windows at the push of a button. From the outside, Winnie Davis still looked the same, gothic and a bit like a miniature cathedral, but from what he'd read the inside was new and modern.

This was why Alec returned to Limestone after so long.

Winnie Davis Hall had lingered in the back of his mind ever since that dare all those years ago, but reading about its recent renovation brought the memories to the foreground. Inspiration seized him by the balls. As always he had no choice but to follow where it led.

Alec stood before Winnie Davis for a moment, on the newly paved courtyard, appreciating her refurbished beauty. The buildings at Limestone were truly magnificent, both architecturally and historically. Many of them dated back to the early 1900s, some even earlier. That was why so many were on the National Registry of Historical Places. But Alec had eyes for only Winnie Davis Hall.

He climbed the stone steps that led to the double doors, feeling weird about entering this way. He still identified the place as off limits. Once he stepped inside the entryway, he knew this wasn't the Winnie Davis of his past. Fresh paint, hardwood floors buffed to a shine, marble busts of historical figures housed in alcoves behind Plexiglas—the building had gotten a serious facelift. To either side of him staircases twisted their way to the top floor. Alec stepped to the circular railing of the rotunda. Since the main doors of the building opened onto the second floor, he could look down to the ground level below. Nothing to see but a wooden table with a vase of flowers centered on it. He craned his neck and looked straight up, into the tower. Only he could no longer see all the way into the tower. The skylight had been fitted with opaque glass, and a stunning chandelier hung down for at least two stories. Quite an impressive sight. Alec held up his cell phone and took a picture of it.

He was interested to see what else Winnie Davis had to offer, but the grand tour would have to wait. He'd come here specifically to see the tower and he wanted to get up there right away.

He started up the stairs, his footsteps echoing throughout the quiet building. He paused on the fourth floor, the last one before the tower. The skylight overhead reminded him of a scene from *Titanic*, although he doubted water would break through the glass and sink the building. He would file away that surreal image for later, along with the rest of the random sights and sounds, snatches of dialogue and dream fragments. All tools of his trade.

Off the fourth floor rotunda was a narrow staircase, blocked off with a velvet rope. He assumed it led to the tower. Without giving it much thought, he unclipped one end of the rope and headed up the stairs. Halfway up, Alec noticed a trap door, which opened onto the tower, bolted with a massive padlock.

Alec stopped and stared at the padlock, frowning at the sight. Why would the school lock up the tower? Was it being used for storage? Regardless, Alec knew he had to get up there. He would have to find the right person to—

"Excuse me, do you need some help?"

Alec started at the sound of the voice, nearly losing his balance. Putting a hand against the wall to steady himself, he looked down at an older gentleman with glasses standing in the doorway of an office. Alec recognized the face immediately.

"Dr. Rob," he said, making his way down the stairs.

The older man frowned quizzically. "I'm sorry, do I know you?"

"And here I thought I was unforgettable. You're messing with my self-image."

"Well, you do look vaguely familiar. Were you a student of mine?"

"About a million years ago. Alec, Alec Steven—"

"Alec Stevenson!" Dr. Rob finished, stepping farther out of his office. "I'll be damned, I haven't seen you in . . . how long has it been?"

"Well, I graduated in '95."

"No. Can't be."

"Afraid so."

"Well, how've you been?"

Alec shook Dr. Rob's proffered hand. "Can't complain, you?"

"Not bad. So what brings you back to Limestone?"

"Just visiting some ghosts of the past. Checking out the new and improved Winnie Davis."

"She's something, isn't she? A real beauty. Want to see my new office?"

"Sure," Alec said, following his former professor inside. The large office was almost as impressive as the skylight, with an entire wall dedicated to bookshelves. "Wow, you have a lot of space here."

"Tell me about it," Dr. Rob said, wearing a youthful grin. "And I have closets on either side that are almost as big as the office itself. It's almost like having three offices, more than enough space to keep my hundreds of books."

"Yeah, I remember the office you had when I was a student, it was kind of a . . . "

"Book cave?"

"I was going to say a 'shithole' but book cave works, too."

Dr. Rob dropped into the chair behind his desk. "I'm pretty happy with it. If it only had a window, it would be perfect."

"You're moving up in the world, and it only took you, what? Three decades?"

"Closer to four, I've been at Limestone since '73."

"Man, that was the year before I was born."

Dr. Rob peered at Alec over his glasses. "It's not nice to insult a fan."

"A fan, huh?"

"Oh yes, I have all three of your novels."

"Really?" Alec said, turning to peruse the shelves.

"Not here, I keep those at home."

"I see. I couldn't help but notice you said you *have* all three of my novels, not that you've actually *read* them."

"I've read the first two, but I have to admit I haven't gotten to the latest one yet."

"Well, if you listen to the critics, you're not missing much."

"I particularly liked your second book, the one about the shape-shifters. Really creepy stuff."

"That surprises me," Alec said, taking a seat across from Dr. Rob. "I never pegged you for a horror fan."

"Love the stuff. Stephen King, Dean Koontz, Greg Nigel, and of course Alec Stevenson."

"If you think I'll respond to flattery, then I'd say you know me pretty well."

"Last I heard you were living in New York."

"For about ten years now."

"You're a long way from home. Visiting friends?"

"No, actually I came here specifically to see Winnie Davis Hall."

"What for?"

"Research."

This seemed to snag Dr. Rob's attention. The man leaned forward with his elbows on his desk. "Planning to write a book about this building?"

"I have the beginnings of an idea," Alec answered.

"Care to tell me a little something about it?"

"Well, it's nothing solid yet, not like I even have an

outline or anything. I'm thinking maybe something—some spirit or as-of-yet unidentified entity—will be awakened by the reopening of Winnie Davis Hall after so many years. I'm even toying with having a character in there loosely based on you."

"Ooh, I get to be in the book?"

"Well, not *you*, a character with a few of your traits and qualities."

"Do I get to do something really nasty?" Dr. Rob asked with a strange gleefulness.

Alec held out his arms in a *'who knows?'* gesture. "Like I said, it's nothing solid. May not even be anything that gets written. I mean, not every idea I have gets turned into a novel. I am, however, intrigued enough by this idea that I want to spend some time on it, do some research, see if I can develop it into something worthwhile."

"That's exciting. Maybe it could be the beginning of a whole series set at Limestone."

"Turn the college into my very own Castle Rock?" Alec asked, smiling.

Dr. Rob returned the *'who knows?'* gesture. "Anything you need, feel free to ask. No one knows the history of this building like I do."

"Since you're offering. You wouldn't happen to have a key to the tower, would you?"

The professor's flinched at the unanticipated question. "The tower? They keep that locked."

"Yeah, I know, that's sort of why I need a key."

"There's no public access allowed. It's dangerous up there."

"How so?"

"Well, the walkways are very narrow. If one were

to slip, you'd crash right through the skylight, and you know how college kids can be. A bunch of daredevils is what they are. No, it's better to keep the place sealed up tight."

"Okay, I understand that, but people are allowed up there sometimes. Haven't you been up there?"

Dr. Rob shook his head. "Nope, and I don't have a key either."

"I really want to get a look. I'm thinking that whatever the reawakened something is in my story, it'll reside mainly in the tower. There's something kind of medieval about that idea, which appeals to me. So if you can't help me out, who can I talk to about getting access to the tower?"

"I don't know, maybe Public Safety."

"Of course, those guys have a key to everything."
***

"What do you mean, you don't have a key?"

The overweight security guard stared at Alec and slowly repeated, "I. Don't. Have. A. Key. I'm not sure how to make that any plainer."

"But you're security. Don't you have a key to everything?"

"I got keys to what I need keys. Guess they don't think I need a key to that tower."

Alec and the guard stood outside the Public Safety office, between the Curtis Administration Building and Ebert dorm. The guard saw Alec's presence as an annoyance, like a fly he couldn't quite shoo away.

"Someone has to have a key for that lock," Alec said.

The guard shrugged. "Try the maintenance crew."

Alec sighed and rubbed at his temples. "It's like I'm

on some weird scavenger hunt. All I want to do is go up in the tower, I can't figure out why that's so difficult."

"They probably stashed them heads up there."

"I'm sorry, did you say *heads*?"

"Yeah, you know, all them white heads of dead famous people."

"Oh, you mean the busts. They have those out on display."

"Uh-uh, not all of them. They got some real old ones, all chipped up. They didn't wanna put them out, so they stashed them away somewhere. Maybe locked them in the tower where no one could get at them."

"Right. Old busts with broken noses, I'm sure that's some precious treasure that needs protection."

The guard shrugged. "I don't really give a damn."

With that, the guard turned and went back into the office. Alec barked a surprised laugh then looked back, across campus, toward Winnie Davis's tower.

He would figure out who was in charge of maintenance. Then, by God, someone was going to let him in that tower.

"They won't let me in the tower."

Alec sat up in the hotel bed with his cell phone in hand. Dr. Rob's home number had been listed in the phone book. Alec hadn't thought twice about calling, despite the late hour. He had stewed all evening and Dr. Rob was the only person he knew that might be able to help him.

"You're talking about Public Safety?" Dr. Rob asked.

"No, they didn't even have a key to the tower, but some geriatric guard told me maintenance might be able to get me in. So I located the head of the maintenance crew, Dale something or other."

"Trilling. I know Dale; he's a good guy."

"Good guy or not, he wasn't a damn bit of help."

"He didn't have a key, either?"

"Oh no, he had a key, but he still wouldn't let me in the tower. Said there was absolutely no access to anyone, except the maintenance crew."

There was a pause on the line, before Dr. Rob said, "Well, I guess that's that then."

"That's crazy. If they want to keep it secured, fine, but come on, the idea that *no one* can go up there doesn't make any sense. I tried to explain about the book and all, but he wasn't hearing it. I even told him someone from his crew or security could accompany me, make sure I didn't try to leap from the windows or swipe whatever secret cache they're squirreling away up there. He told me the subject was closed. And let me tell you, he wasn't too polite about it."

Another pause, and when Dr. Rob spoke, Alec could clearly hear the irritation in the man's voice. "Alec, I'm not exactly sure what you want me to do about this."

"Surely you've got some pull with the administration. Hell, you've been there since God was a boy."

"If Public Safety and maintenance can't get you in, there's not going to be much more I can do."

"Come on, Dr. Rob, you said if I needed any help with this book—"

"I meant it. If you want to know anything about the

history of Winnie Davis, I'm your man, but I can't help you gain access to the tower."

Alec felt like tossing his cell phone across the room, but resisted the urge. He tried to keep the growing frustration out of his voice. "Dr. Rob, all I want is to take a look up there. Five minutes, that's all I ask. I want to walk around, snap a few pictures, get a feel for the geography of the place. If I'm going to write about it, I need to *see it*, for Christ's sake."

The longest pause yet, and if Alec hadn't been able to hear Dr. Rob breathing over the phone, he'd have thought he'd lost the connection. Finally Dr. Rob said, "Alumni/Development."

"What?"

"Try Alumni/Development. You are a graduate of Limestone, after all, and considering your reputation, I'm sure they'll view you as one hell of a potential donor. Play it up that way. I bet Alumni/Development will get you whatever you want, including access to the tower."

"Hey now, that's a great idea, Dr. Rob."

"I do have my moments of brilliance. Few and far between, but I have them."

"I'll give them a call first thing in the morning."

"Offices are closed over the weekend. You'll have to wait until Monday."

"Damn. Well, first thing Monday morning then. Thanks a million, Dr. Rob. Alumni/Development. I never would have thought of it, but I'm sure that's the answer."

"The answer is no."

Flabbergasted. That was the only word Alec could think of to describe how he felt. Why was it so difficult to get in that damn tower? When researching his third novel, he'd requested access to the F.B.I. headquarters in New York and been granted it within hours. It was ridiculous that this should prove the more arduous task. He'd come to the Alumni/Development office in McMillian Hall to personally meet with Mr. Brackett, head of the department, fully expecting all doors to be opened to him. Instead he faced more locks.

"I'm sorry," Mr. Brackett said, leaning on the corner of his desk. "I simply can't help you on this matter."

"I'm not asking you to give me access to one of the girl's dorms after midnight with nothing on me but a switchblade and a hard-on. All I want is to get up in the tower for one quick little tour."

"Again, no," Mr. Brackett said firmly.

Alec started laughing at the absurdity of it all. "How much?"

Mr. Brackett blinked at him. "Excuse me?"

"Just tell me how big the check needs to be to get me access and I'll write it."

Mr. Brackett smiled at him then, and it was a smile Alec recognized instantly. It was the smile you gave your buddy at the bar when he'd had a few too many and was making a colossal ass of himself. The kind of smile you gave an unattractive woman who kept throwing herself at you even after you'd made it clear she wasn't in your league. Basically it was a smile that said you were deeply embarrassed for someone.

"Mr. Stevenson, we of course always welcome

donations, and would appreciate any gift you are willing to give, but you can't bribe your way into the tower. It is off limits due to safety concerns."

"It can't be that dangerous. I'll sign a waiver, stating that if I get injured I won't hold the college liable. That should cover all your bases."

"Sorry sir, but we simply cannot allow it."

"Jesus, what do you guys have up there? Dead bodies? Bars of gold?"

Mr. Brackett pointedly checked his watch. "Thank you for coming by, Mr. Stevenson."

"Wait a minute," Alec said, refusing to be dismissed this way. "Don't you know what I'm trying to do here? I want to write a book set here at Limestone. It could really put the school on the map."

"We're doing just fine," Mr. Brackett answered with a tight smile.

"But you could be doing even better. I'll donate half the profits from the book to the school. *Half.* All you've got to do is get me up in that tower for five minutes."

Mr. Brackett didn't respond right away. Alec watched a war raging in his eyes. He was resisting, but he wanted that money, Alec could practically smell the want in the air. "Why is the tower so important?" he finally asked.

"It will be the focal point of the story."

"Why not choose some other location to be the focal point instead? Why not the basement of Winnie Davis? We'll be more than happy to let you roam around down there all you want."

"No, it has to be the tower."

But did it, really? If Alec examined the situation objectively, the idea he entertained didn't absolutely hinge on the tower. He could move the lair of the entity to the basement without changing anything integral to the story. Yet, the more access was denied to him, the more he felt it *did* have to be the tower. He hadn't taken many psych courses as a student, but he knew that depriving someone of something often left that person more desperate than ever to get it.

"I have an idea," Mr. Brackett said. "Why don't I describe the tower to you?"

"What?"

"I could tell you what it looks like up there, and you could use my description for the story."

Alec considered this. It could work. Accuracy wasn't necessary in fiction.

But damn it, he wanted to *see it!*

"Okay, now I have a counteroffer," he said. "If I'm not allowed up there, what if you went and took some pictures for me?"

Mr. Brackett visibly stiffened. "That isn't possible."

"Why not?"

"Mr. Stevenson, I really don't have time to continue this repetitive conversation with you. I have a lot of work to do, so I suggest you go."

Alec stood, anger bubbling inside him like the carbonation of a shaken soda. "This isn't the end of it. I'll get in that tower one way or the other."

He began to make his way out of the office, but paused when Mr. Brackett called his name. Alec looked over his shoulder. "Yes?"

"Don't do anything crazy."

"This is crazy," Alec mumbled to himself.

He felt like a spy in some espionage movie, or more accurately, in some parody of an espionage movie. Night had settled when he slipped into Winnie Davis through the back door. The guards would soon lock up the building for the night, so he needed to be quick, but also cautious.

Despite the warm weather, Alec wore a jacket to conceal the bolt cutters he'd tucked under an arm. He hated to admit that he wasn't doing a terribly good job. The blades poked out at his waist, but chances were he wouldn't run into anyone. The building should be mostly deserted. He hoped.

Alec thought it wise to avoid the stairs, so he took the elevator to the third floor. He crept through the building, pausing each time his shoes squeaked on the floor, listening for any sound that would indicate that he wasn't alone. All was quiet, but he didn't let his guard down.

Jesus, this really is crazy, he thought. He couldn't understand why he felt like a criminal. It wasn't as if he was breaking into a bank. After getting nowhere with Alumni/Development, Alec had called the office of the president of the college. Dr. Grey, he had been president since the late 80s and had always seemed to like Alec. In fact, he had sent a letter after the release of Alec's second novel asking if he would be interested in teaching a creative writing seminar at the school. Alec had responded by thanking Dr. Grey for the offer but taking a pass due to other commitments. But at this point, Alec was willing to reconsider if it would mean getting up in the tower.

Unfortunately, Dr. Grey wouldn't even talk to him.

He sent a message through his secretary, saying he needed to take a pass on meeting with Alec, due to other commitments. The other commitments could be anything, but Alec had heard Dr. Grey's twenty-six year old daughter had gone missing a few months ago.

When Alec's options ran out, he decided to break into the tower. It was a desperate, stupid act, but he felt fairly desperate and stupid. He didn't even know if the bolt cutters would work. Still, he had to try.

When he reached the stairs, he stood on the landing, straining to hear if anyone descended from above. When nothing sounded, he started up the stairs, praying Dr. Rob wasn't in his office this late.

There were two faculty offices on the fourth floor, and both doors were shut. Without pausing, he hurried to remove the velvet rope that cordoned off the staircase. He pulled out the bolt cutters as he approached the trapdoor. The lock looked bigger and more daunting today than last Friday. He felt foolish, breaking into a restricted area, like a character in a bad novel he'd be ashamed to write. He should turn around right now and get out of here, but he continued forward, stopping only when he could go no farther. He opened the blades of the bolt cutter and fitted them on either side of the U-ring of the padlock. It would be like trying to cut through a tree trunk with a butter knife.

As the saying goes: Nothing ventured, nothing gained.

Alec heard someone below clear his throat.

He froze.

He wanted to move, to at least glance back and see who it was, but it felt as if the air had solidified like cement, encasing him in place. He tried not to panic. It might be a student, if so he could talk his way out of this. Taking a deep breath and slowly lowering the bolt cutters, he turned his neck, hearing it creak like rusty hinges. He looked down and saw not a student, but several familiar faces.

The old security guard, Dale Trilling, Mr. Brackett and Dr. Grey all stood at the bottom of the stairs, looking up at him. "I told you he was going to try something like this," Mr. Brackett said, addressing the president.

Dr. Grey shook his head, like a disappointed parent. "Alec, what are you doing, son?"

He wasn't sure how to respond to that. He couldn't exactly deny his attempted breaking and entering. In the end, Alec only said, "I tried to call you today."

Dr. Grey sighed wearily. "What are we going to do with you?"

The group of men suddenly seemed more menacing. Alec found himself gripping the bolt cutters tighter. The guard noticed this and stepped forward, his right hand resting lightly but meaningfully on the butt of the gun in his holster. "I think you need to put those down and come with us."

"Listen to Chief Simms," Dr. Grey said. "It's in your best interest to do what he says."

Alec hesitated for a moment then sat the bolt cutters on one of the steps, resting the handles against the wall. He slowly made his way back down.

He'd really done it now, let an obsession impede his better judgment, and he had a feeling he'd be talking to the cops very soon.

✻ ✻

"We're not going to call the cops," Mr. Brackett said.

Together in the security office, Alec was being fenced in by the other men. Alec threw up his hands. "What then? Do you want me to say that I'm sorry and I'll never do it again?"

"What we want is for you to go," Chief Simms said, his bulldog jowls quivering as he stared down at the writer as if he'd like nothing more than to pistol-whip him. "Get off campus and don't come back. If we see you around here again, we will call the police."

Alec looked at each man in turn, a smile curling the corner of his lips upwards. "Is that so? I don't think you'll call the cops at all."

"Alec, please," Dr. Grey said.

"I'm right, aren't I? If you were going to call the cops on me, you'd have done it by now. No. I don't think you want the cops out here, because maybe they'd start asking questions about what's up there, and I don't think any of you want that."

Now it was Dale Trilling who threw up his hands. "Why won't you let this go?"

"I'm tenacious. I am not going to drop this matter until I find out what you are hiding up there."

"We're not hiding anything," Mr. Brackett said. "I swear there's nothing in the tower. Nothing."

"Then what are you protecting? And don't feed me anymore of that 'it's dangerous' bullshit."

"But it *is* dangerous," Dr. Grey said, his voice imploring. "You have no idea how dangerous, but maybe it's time you did."

Chief Simms reached out and put a hand on the president's shoulder. "Sir, I really don't think you should."

"Perhaps if we tell him, if we make him understand, he'll leave it alone."

"Make me understand what?" Alec said. "This whole cryptic vibe you're giving off is getting old. Now either you tell me what's in the tower or *I* go to the police."

Chief Simms snorted a laugh. "And tell them what? We ain't breaking any laws here."

"Well, maybe I think you are. Maybe I think you have young girls trapped up in the top of Winnie Davis."

"That's ridiculous," Trilling said.

"Be that as it may, I bet I could convince the police to at least check it out."

"You little piss-ant," Chief Simms said, advancing on Alec. "I ought to tear your spine out and beat you with it."

"Enough!" Dr. Grey said in a loud, sharp voice. Chief Simms backed off, but he didn't seem happy about it. Dr. Grey pulled up a chair and sat across from Alec. Meeting the writer's gaze, he said, "We can't let you go up in the tower because . . . because you may not come back."

"What?"

Dr. Grey took a deep breath before he continued. "Sometimes people go up in the tower and they don't come back."

Alec squinted at the older man, waiting for the punch line. "Uh-huh. Where exactly do they go?"

"No one knows. They simply . . . vanish."

A thick, suffocating silence filled the security office. Finally Alec cut through the smoke with a wild laugh. "You can't seriously expect me to believe that."

"It's the truth," Dr. Grey said. "Doesn't happen every time, there were plenty of people through the tower during the renovation that came back down fine, but every so often, someone goes up there and simply disappears."

Alec was in shock. What was Dr. Grey playing at here? Did he really think such a preposterous story was going to keep him away from the tower? Or had grief over the loss of his daughter driven the man insane? That would mean the rest of them were crazy, too. None of the others confirmed Dr. Grey's story, but none of them denied it either.

"Okay," Alec said, deciding to play along for the moment, "exactly who is supposed to have disappeared in the tower?"

Mr. Trilling was the one to answer. "The first was the foreman of the construction crew doing the renovations, Lester Todd. There were a lot of men in the tower at the time, installing the panes of the skylight. At the end of the day, no one could locate Lester, and the last time anyone remembered seeing him was in the tower. It was assumed at the time that he had left without being noticed by anyone, although his truck was still parked behind the building and no one knew why he would walk out on a job. Weeks, then months, went by and no one heard from him, not even his family. The missing person's case is still open."

"One of my guards was next," Chief Simms said. "The building had already been renovated, but wasn't open for classes. Pete was on his routine rounds; a kid really, couldn't have been no older than twenty-five. Had a girlfriend and a kid on the way. Anyway, I get this call from him over the two-way, saying there was something strange going down in the Winnie Davis tower. I asked him what the problem was, but there was so much static on the radio, I couldn't tell for sure what he'd said. Thought it was something to do with snow, but that didn't make no kind of sense. Then the line went dead. So me and one of my other guards went over to Winnie Davis and straight up to the tower. The trapdoor was propped open but when we went up there, no sign of Pete anywhere. We searched the entire grounds but he was gone. His girlfriend thinks he freaked about the baby and took off."

"Maybe he did," Alec said. "I mean, what do you guys really know? Both men were in the tower at some point shortly before their disappearances, but that's flimsy reasoning to support the theory that the tower is eating them up or whatever."

Dr. Grey nodded, his eyes cast to the floor. "That, of course, wasn't the first conclusion we drew from the disappearances. At least, not until the third person went missing."

"And who was that?"

Dr. Grey took a shuddering breath and the expression on his face suggested it hurt him, as if he were inhaling thorns. "Have you heard about my daughter, Melanie?"

"Yeah, I read that—wait a minute, are you trying to tell me she vanished in the tower, too?"

Dr. Grey started to speak, but then he grimaced and choked back a sob. He stood and walked to the corner of the room. Mr. Brackett took the chair vacated by the president and answered for him.

"We were getting ready for the building dedication ceremony to commemorate the reopening of Winnie Davis. Melanie was here helping out. She wanted to see the view from the tower."

"I said I'd take her up myself," Dr. Grey said, still facing the wall. "But when we got to the fourth floor, Dr. Robinson was there setting up his new office and asked to speak with me for a moment. I sent Melanie ahead, told her I'd be there as soon as I was done. I didn't even go in Dr. Robinson's office. We stood right out in the rotunda the whole time. When we finished our conversation, I went up the stairs to the tower, but Melanie wasn't there. I checked both levels, but she simply wasn't there."

"There's only the one way in and out of the tower," Mr. Trilling said. "She couldn't have come back down without passing her father. A few of us met, discussed the situation, and decided to lock up the tower and not let anyone in there."

"And no one has been in the tower since?"

Mr. Brackett shook his head. "No, although we have done experiments."

"What kind of experiments?"

"Every so often we'll open up the trapdoor and set an object just inside the tower. Books, music boxes, clothing. We'll come back later to see if the objects are still there. Sometimes they are . . . sometimes they aren't."

Alec stared around him at this group of older men. A realization hit him with the force of a sledgehammer. "You all really believe this, don't you? You actually think people are going up in the tower and vanishing into thin air."

"It's the truth," Dr. Grey said in a raw, scratchy voice. "You have to trust us on this."

"I don't think so. I may write about spooks and supernatural happenings, but I don't actually believe in that nonsense. I can't believe a group of intelligent men would believe in it either."

"Then where is my Melanie?" Dr. Grey shouted suddenly, turning and advancing on Alec. "What do you think happened to her?"

"I don't know," Alec's voice softened with sympathy. "I really am sorry for your loss, but I don't believe there's some kind of black hole or whatever in the Winnie Davis tower."

"You don't got to believe it," Chief Simms said. "What you believe or don't believe don't change what we know."

"Look, the bottom line is that you let me up in the tower or I'm going to go to the police and let them decide how to proceed from here."

"Let him go," Dr. Grey said in a whisper.

Mr. Trilling, Mr. Brackett, and Chief Simms all exclaimed "What?" at the exact same moment with such perfect synchronicity that it would have been comical under other circumstances.

"We can't let law enforcement get involved in this," Dr. Grey said, regaining his composure and authority. "And it has become painfully obvious that Mr. Stevenson won't drop this matter until his curiosity has been satisfied. So let him go. He knows the risks."

"Thank you," Alec said.

The president walked over to Alec and stared into

his eyes. "But before you go, I want you to ask yourself one question, are you sure you want to do this?"

Alec wasn't sure he wanted to do this.

Not that he was afraid he'd step up into the tower and melt away into nothing, but these men seemed more than a little unstable. What if he got up in the tower and they locked him in?

He had his cell phone on him, should anything happen.

Mr. Trilling climbed the stairs to the tower's trapdoor and used a key to remove the padlock, sitting in on the top step. Then he made his way back down the stairs and stepped aside. "Have at it."

"No one coming with me?" Alec asked with a small, somewhat sadistic smile. None of the other men would meet his gaze.

Alec hurried up the steps, feeling oddly excited now that he was finally going to get into the tower after such a protracted quest. He pushed open the trapdoor, hesitated to lend the moment a bit more drama, then stepped up into the tower.

There wasn't much to see, really. After all the effort he'd expended trying to gain access, it was rather disappointing. The tower was split into two levels. The first level consisted of a platform circling the skylight. A narrow staircase led up to an identical second level. The walls were painted plain white.

Alec started toward the stairs to the upper level, pulling out his cell phone to take a few photos. He was finally getting what he needed for his story idea.

Although his desire to get into the tower had ceased to have anything to do with the potential book and more to do with getting what was denied him. A childish motivation, perhaps, but despite finding nothing of particular interest up here, it still felt good to have reached his goal.

As he climbed to the upper level, he paused by one of the tall windows and looked out across campus. The view was quite stunning. He could see all the way to Lake Limestone, down by the dining hall, and he was struck anew by the college's picturesque grounds.

Something caught in his eyelashes, a piece of dust perhaps, and he blinked it away. He felt several cold spots on his arms and looked down to see droplets of water. Was the roof leaking? He glanced toward the ceiling and gasped at the snowflakes fluttering down from above. Big, fat white flakes drifting down at first but then began to really pour.

Which was insane.

It didn't snow this time of year, certainly not indoors. Still, the snow rained down so hard he couldn't even make out the ceiling. He glanced back toward the stairs, ready to call out to the men gathered down on the fourth floor, but he couldn't even make out the walkway. There seemed to be inches worth of snow and ice already built up. It didn't make any sense. Alec moved forward slowly, feeling along for the stairs he knew had to be close.

There was no end in sight.

Large drifts of snow, as tall him, rose up on either side to create a valley through which he walked. The frigid air made his breath come out in thick plumes. Dressed in only jeans and a light shirt, Alec wrapped his arms around himself for warmth, shivering violently. The exposed skin of his arms and face already felt numb.

In the distance Alec thought he detected a flickering orange glow, a beacon in the oppressive darkness. He started toward it, stumbling several times along the way. Alec felt like he'd already walked for at least an hour, but he wasn't sure. His joints were stiff, and he found moving a chore, but he trudged on.

Alec arrived at what looked to be an ice wall, with a fissure at the base opening into a cave. He ducked through the entrance and found himself in a narrow tunnel sloping down into an open cavern. In the very center of the space was a fire, the smoke drifting up, into an opening high above. A young woman sat by the fire, bundled up in layers of clothes. Thin and pale, her curly brown hair fell over her shoulders. Meat had been jammed onto a stick, roasting over the fire. She was surrounded by a few books and an ornate silver music box that sat on top of a rock.

"Hello," she said, quietly. "Come get warm before you freeze to death."

Alec shuffled forward, dropping to his knees in front of the fire. He was so cold he wanted to dive headfirst into the flames, but he settled for getting as close as he could without actually burning himself. He allowed the heat to bake into him and thaw his flesh.

"What is your name?" the woman asked.

"Alec Stevenson. Are you Melanie Grey?"

She seemed a bit stunned. "I am. Did you come through the tower?"

"Yes, I did. Your father is very worried about you."

"My father," she whispered, tears glistening in her eyes. "How long have I been gone?"

"Three or four months, I think."

"It's hard to tell, there is no day or night here."

Alec still clutched his cell phone. Unclenching his fingers was painful, but he did it anyway.

"Your phone won't work here," Melanie said matter-of-factly. Alec tried it nonetheless, but couldn't even get the phone to turn on. "I'm sorry you got stuck here, too," Melanie said, wearing a sad smile, "but I must admit, I'm glad to have someone to talk to again."

"There were two others here before," Alec said, not quite a question.

"Yes, Lester and Pete. Pete died shortly after I arrived. He got very sick, was coughing up blood. Lester and I weren't sure what was wrong with him, but after a few days of screaming and crying, he went to sleep and didn't wake up."

"Is that what happened to Lester?"

"No, Lester gave up hope. While I was sleeping a few days ago—or maybe longer, like I said it's hard to keep track of time here—he slit his wrists with a pocketknife he had with him."

Alec didn't know what to say to that, so he stared into the flames for several minutes. Finally he said, "How did you start the fire?"

"Pete had a cigarette lighter with him, and this cave is full of sticks and twigs. Of course, the lighter is almost out of fluid. I'm not sure what I'll do when it runs out entirely."

Reaching into his pocket, Alec pulled out a half-used book of matches. "Isn't much, but it's something."

Melanie smiled. "You wouldn't happen to have a steak and baked potato in your pocket as well, would you?"

"Afraid not." Eyeing the meat roasting over the fire, Alec went on, "Speaking of which, what are you surviving on?"

Melanie looked uncomfortable and stared off toward the cave's only entrance. "I . . . I've had to make do."

Alec didn't pursue the topic any further. He scooted a bit closer to the fire. Ice had collected in his hair and was now melting and running down his face like tears. "Do you think there's a way out of here?"

"There has to be," Melanie said with conviction. "If there's a way in, there has to be a way back. Periodically I go out searching for it, but I can only go so far. If I lose sight of the fire, I may never be able to find my way back here."

Alec nodded. The aroma of the cooking meat caused his stomach to grumble loud as thunder.

"Want some?" Melanie asked, waving the stick his way. "There's plenty to share."

Alec shook his head vigorously, thinking about Lester and Pete and wondering where their bodies were.

"You say that now," Melanie said. "You'll change your tune when the hunger pangs start. I hope there's some left when the time comes."

A black despair settled over Alec. It was like he'd stepped into one of his own horror novels. Maybe that was how he needed to think of this situation; if he thought of this as a plotline, perhaps he could come up with a solution, a way out, a happy ending.

When Melanie dug into her meal, Alec looked away, wondering if he'd ever get home again.

"I wonder if they'll ever get home again," Chief Simms said as he snapped the padlock back into place.

EXPECTANT

MARCH

RHONDA LITTLE CHECKED her reflection one final time before answering the door. She hadn't been on a date since she and Steven broke up last year. She felt horribly out of practice, anxious, too.

Putting on her most brilliant smile to mask her jitters, she opened the door and said, "Hi there."

"Hello," Darren said, looking exceedingly dapper in his orange turtleneck and dark khaki pants. He was a copy editor at Unrequited Press, the company that published Rhonda's series of historical romance novels. He'd begun flirting with her three months ago, and while Rhonda had enjoyed the attention, she'd never expected it to go further.

"Do you want to come in?" Rhonda asked, hoping it wouldn't be misconstrued as an invitation of a more illicit sort. It had been so long, she wasn't sure what the rules were for dating these days.

"Actually I have tickets for the symphony. We should be going if we're going to get there on time."

"The symphony, I'm impressed. Let me grab my wrap."

"Oh, and you might want to find a vase."

"A vase? For what?"

"For these," Darren said, pulling a bouquet of daffodils from behind his back.

"Darren, they're lovely."

"Just a token."

Rhonda took the flowers and held them close to her face, breathing in their sweet perfume. Her nose twitched as she inadvertently inhaled spores or pollen. She sneezed three times in rapid succession, demurely into the palm of her hand.

Darren frowned. "Dear, I hope that's not a bad omen."

"Not at all," Rhonda said, smiling. "Excuse me, I'll be right back."

After depositing the daffodils into a crystal vase on the coffee table and grabbing her best black wrap with the pearl clasp, she linked her arm through Darren's and allowed him to escort her to his car.

MAY

Rhonda sat on the edge of the bed with her best friend, Anna, staring at the plastic stick in her hand.

"Are we happy or sad?" Anna asked, placing a comforting hand on Rhonda's shoulder.

Rhonda smiled weakly and said, "Mostly we're dazed, but with a side of happy, I guess."

"Are you going to try to get in touch with Darren?"

"He never even bothered to call me after our one date. If he didn't want anything to do with me, I don't know why I should think he'd want anything to do with a baby."

"Screw him," Anna said. "You make a good living,

and you've got Auntie Anna here to help out. This kid's going to have a great life. She's damned lucky to have you for a mother."

"She?" Rhonda asked with a raised eyebrow. "You've already determined the sex, have you?"

"It's a feeling. Call it a sixth sense or whatever you want, but I have a hunch you're going to have a little girl."

Rhonda smiled and hugged her friend, though she knew Anna was wrong. She didn't know how she knew, but she had no doubt that the child she carried was a boy.

Rhonda didn't tell Anna this, however. Like she didn't tell Anna she hadn't had sex with Darren. Oh, she'd wanted to, she'd made advances on their date, but he had rebuffed all her attempts at seduction.

Rhonda hadn't had sex with anyone in the past year and a half.

SEPTEMBER

"Could I have some more rolls, please?" Rhonda asked the waiter as he passed.

"Slow down, girl," Anna said from across the table, nibbling on her Caesar salad. "You're not going into hibernation, no need to stuff yourself to last all winter."

Rhonda blushed. "I am eating for two, you know."

"Not that anyone could tell. You're still as thin as ever. No one would guess that you were six months pregnant."

"Some girls are lucky that way."

Anna's lips tightened and she squinted, a look that

Rhonda knew meant her friend was about to get serious. "Rhonda, are you sure everything's okay? What does your doctor say?"

Rhonda put her fork down and favored her friend with a harried smile. "I'm fine, I promise you. We've been over this a hundred times already. Dr. Matthews says the baby is perfectly healthy. He says not every woman gains a ton of weight, and as long as I'm eating right and taking care of myself, the baby will be perfectly fine."

Rhonda hated lying to her best friend, but she didn't know how to explain to Anna that she hadn't been to see a doctor since finding out she was pregnant. Dr. Matthews was an invention of her imagination. Anna would worry and insist Rhonda see a doctor right away, but Rhonda's baby had advised her against it.

Rhonda knew it would sound crazy if she told anyone, but her unborn son talked to her. Not out loud, not with words, but on the inside. His thoughts surfaced in her own. He told her that he was a special child and that she had been chosen to be the vessel through which he would enter this world.

"What is that perfume you're wearing?" Anna asked. "It smells heavenly."

"What? Perfume? I'm not wearing perfume today."

"Oh, well, someone must have put out some fresh flowers," Anna said, looking around the restaurant. "I could swear I smell daffodils."

MAY

"Rhonda, are you sure you don't want me to come up there?"

Rhonda closed her eyes and sighed into the phone. "Anna, really, you don't have to worry about me. I'm enjoying the peace and quiet, and I'm working on a new novel."

"I don't like the idea of you being all alone. What if something happened?"

"It's not like I'm in the middle of the desert." Rhonda laughed. "I'm at my lake house in Maine."

"When are you coming back home?"

"I don't know. I need some more time on my own, away from my life there in New York, away from all the memories."

"Rhonda, honey, I love you, but you need to get on with your life. It has been six months since the miscarriage. You need to come back and face things, dismantle the nursery, reclaim your life."

"In time. I'll call you before the weekend, I promise."

"You better."

Rhonda hung up the phone and placed a hand over her extended stomach, feeling the movements of the child inside her. It had been the baby's idea to tell everyone she'd had a miscarriage then seclude herself away at the lake house. No one would understand the protracted gestation period. She'd been pregnant for fourteen months now and she still hadn't come to term.

"I can be patient," she whispered to her son. "I

know you'll come when you are ready. I look forward to meeting you."

OCTOBER

Rhonda lay back on the bed, sweat glistening on her forehead. She knew she was in labor, but she felt no pain. She looked down at her body and knew she should've been repulsed by what she saw, but she wasn't.

From her waist down, Rhonda's body was covered by a hard, yellow shell—a cocoon of some sort. Large veins ran below the surface. A thick layer of mucus covered the entire thing. The cocoon pulsed, inflating and deflating with contractions that would soon bring her son into the world.

Rhonda bit her lip and breathed deeply, listening to her child whisper assurances inside her head. A sharp pain, almost orgasmic in its intensity, ripped through her as she felt the cocoon split open. She arched her back and moaned softly as a pungent white liquid poured from a rift in the cocoon, soaking the sheets and carpet. Her son crawled out into the world, unfolding himself and standing on slightly shaky legs.

He was full grown, at least six feet, with a thick head of dark hair and piercing gray eyes. Rhonda realized he looked exactly like Darren. He glanced down at her and smiled, mouthing the words, "Thank you, Mother," though Rhonda could hear no sound.

The world blurred around the edges, growing gray, and Rhonda knew she was leaving this life as her son entered it. She could not survive now that he was no longer a part of her; she felt too hollow inside.

EXPECTANT

As Rhonda slipped away, her son leaned over and kissed her on the forehead.

He smelled like daffodils.

THE LAST MEN ON EARTH

BOBBY AND I have been together for a year now. Not 'together' as in a couple, although if you ask me that's what we are. I mean, we spend almost all our time together, we sleep together. Hell, we're practically married. Still, Bobby balks at the use of the word 'couple'. He claims to be straight, after all, and said until he met me he'd never 'messed around with'—his words, not mine—another guy before. He says what we have is not romance, merely desperation and convenience.

You see, Bobby and I are the last two people on Earth. Or at least, as far as we know. It's been a year. We've been traveling all across the U.S. on motorcycles and we haven't seen another living soul. According to Bobby, what we have is what happens in prisons, necessity.

Six months after we started traveling together he let me go down on him for the first time. He never returns the favor or kisses me or holds me afterward. He does make love to me—though he'd cringe if he heard me call it that—but always from behind so he doesn't have to see my face. Still, I hold out hope that eventually he will grow to see me as more than the scratching of an itch; I hope that one day he will love me.

The way that I love him.

The world ended by some kind of plague—a sickness, sort of like in that Stephen King book. Only faster. People got sick and were dead within hours. It was no more than a week before the entire planet was wiped out.

Except for me and Bobby.

For some unknown reason we are immune.

I met Bobby about two weeks after everyone in my hometown died. I was wandering around in some kind of numbed dazed; I actually think I was on the edge of losing my mind. Then Bobby drove into town on a Harley. He came from the next state over. Bobby said I was the first living person he'd seen. I was instantly taken with him, and I readily accepted the offer to join him.

We've been traveling ever since, scavenging grocery stores for nonperishable foods and water. There are bodies everywhere, and the smell has become quite rancid. We've taken to staying away from places that were heavily populated. Recently I've been lobbying for us to settle down, somewhere away from the remains of civilization and the stench of decay. Bobby wants to keep going, keep searching for other survivors. Although after a year of looking, I think he is giving up hope, accepting that it's just him and me. That's one step closer to us becoming a real couple. An Adam and Eve of the new world, only minus one Eve and plus a second Adam.

I met Andrea on a Tuesday. I think.

At first I made a point of keeping track of the days, marking them off on a calendar I carried with me, but I had grown lax, letting several days pass before going back to X them out. The day of the week is unimportant. What's important is that I was alone.

We were in the North Carolina Mountains, and we'd spent the last couple of days at a cabin in a wooded area, miles from the nearest town. Whoever once lived here had apparently not been home when the plague hit. I actually thought I was getting close to convincing Bobby to make this place our home, to stop our fruitless search of a dead world.

As midday approached on our second day at the cabin, Bobby told me he was going to hike to the nearest town and see what there was to salvage. I offered to go with him, but he said no, he needed to be alone. Hurt, I did not press the matter. I suspected he wanted some time to consider the issue of settling down or moving on. If I gave him his space, I knew there was a chance I might get what I wanted. As if in confirmation, before he left, he gave me a quick, tentative kiss. Our first.

After he was gone, I began gathering up firewood. It was early September, not yet cold, but it was beginning to get chilly at night. I figured I'd get a fire roaring, making the cabin as cozy and homey as possible for when Bobby returned. He'd been gone two hours and I was deep in the woods gathering branches and sticks when I heard movement in the brush behind me. I turned with a smile, expecting to see Bobby. Instead, I was shocked to find a young woman standing there.

She looked to be in her early twenties, thin with pale skin, red hair that fell about her shoulders in tangled curls. She wore jeans and a stained T-shirt. She stood completely still, staring at me with wide eyes and an expressionless face. She seemed almost afraid of me.

"Are you real?" she asked after several moments of silence. "Or are you only in my mind?"

I tried to speak but at first couldn't seem to make a sound. I took a few deep breaths, tried to calm myself, and then said, "Where did you come from?"

"I've been staying at a place a half a mile down the mountain, but I ran out of food so I came looking for other cabins. And I found you. God, I'm scared to believe you're real."

"I'm as real as you. What's your name?"

"Andrea," she said and started to cry. Huge, racking sobs shook through her body. "I thought I was the last one, all alone on this planet. I never thought I'd see another living person. I'm so glad you're here."

With arms full of firewood, I stared at this intruder, this interloper into my future bliss with Bobby. Even though she looked slightly malnourished and was covered in filth, it was clear that Andrea was beautiful, and hungry for human contact. I could imagine how quickly she and Bobby would hit it off. The many dreams I had for my life with Bobby began to crumble, and it was all Andrea's fault.

"Are you alone?" she asked, taking a step closer. "Is it only you?"

"No, there are many of us," I said without thinking, acting on instinct. "Two dozen, we're living in a sort of commune here."

This reeled Andrea in like a trout on the line. "Really? Two dozen people. I want to meet them all. I've been so horribly lonely."

"You're welcome to join us," I said. "There's plenty of room. It's up this path."

Andrea didn't hesitate. She rushed past me, heading up the path toward the cabin, babbling the whole time. Obviously it had been a long time since she'd had anyone with which to converse. I waited until she passed me, then dropped all but the largest branch and swung it with every ounce of strength. When I connected with the back of Andrea's head, I heard a *crack* and the limb broke in two. Andrea went down hard, crumpling to the ground. I continued to bash her head until it was nothing but mush and bits of shattered skull. Just to be sure.

I felt nothing. Not guilt, not horror at my actions, but no particular pleasure either. Moving in this emotionally numbed state, I hurried back to the cabin and found a shovel in a storage shed around back. I returned, dug a shallow grave, and buried Andrea deep in the woods where I hoped Bobby would never find her.

When he finally returned from his trip into town, darkness had already settled outside. I'd started a fire and prepared a meal of potted meat, crackers, and bottled water. Bobby had brought back boxes of food and water, as well as candles and matches. We sat in front of the fire and ate in silence. Only after we had finished the meal did Bobby speak.

"It's a nightmare down there. Bodies everywhere and the smells are overpowering. I had to tie a bandanna around my mouth and nose. The world is dead, I really am starting to think there's no one left but us."

I said nothing.

"I know you want to stay here," he said, looking at me with an intensity that both scared and thrilled me. The fire cast dancing light on his face, licking his features. "I think you're right, I think it's time to stop traveling and make a home for ourselves here."

I felt ready to burst with joy. Tears sprang to my eyes, caused by the happiness bubbling within.

That night, we made love by the fire, and Bobby finally looked me in the face while we did it.

SIMILAR INTERESTS

IT **WAS INDEED** a dark and stormy night. Starting like every round-the-campfire horror story that ever terrified Neil Ferwin as a child. Not that the weather was a crucial factor in Ferwin's plans. Although Ferwin had to admit the rain falling in sheets, hitting the pavement with a deafening roar, and the intermittent strobe-flash of lightning, created a suitably ominous atmosphere. Ferwin smiled as he drove his Cadillac down the highway, pleased with this ambiance. He felt as if he was playing the role of the villain in one of those horror tales from his childhood.

Ferwin had no illusions about himself. He didn't try to rationalize his actions or sugarcoat them with lofty motives. He was a killer, plain and simple. He liked to pick up hitchhikers, take them off to a secluded area and brutally murder them. It was a hobby. He delighted in finding new and innovative ways of ending another person's life.

Earlier in the evening, while watching television at home, that familiar itch revealed itself again. So, despite the bad weather and poor road conditions, Ferwin had grabbed his car keys and headed for the highway. Visibility was minimal. The road, almost completely deserted, belonged to him. He'd driven for an hour and had yet to see a single hitchhiker. Not surprising, really, in this downpour.

Perhaps it was for the best. Ferwin had indulged his hobby far too often lately.

He was a tall man, towering over most people he met, his bulky body shaped into hard muscle by a meticulous regimen of exercise. He'd yet to meet the man he couldn't overpower. Despite his intimidating build, though, he had a friendly face. His slightly chubby cheeks lent him the appearance of everyone's favorite uncle. His disarming smile never failed to win the trust of others. It was easy for him, but if he didn't cut back on his late night highway excursions, he was bound to slip up sooner or later.

Ferwin looked for a turnabout, resigning himself to the fact that tonight had been a bust, when up ahead he saw a figure by the side of the road. In the glare of the headlights and through the slanting rain, the figure quivered like a mirage. As Ferwin drew closer, he clearly saw the figure extend its arm and stick out its thumb.

Colin Hagan stood on the shoulder of the highway, drenched by the relentless rain. His clothes were soaked through, clinging to his flesh like a second skin. His round wire-frame glasses were spotted and streaked, making it hard for him to see. Hagan didn't mind the inconvenience of the weather. It was worth it, after all, for his art.

Hagan considered himself quite the artist, albeit a novice, but he didn't paint or sculpt or even compose.

Hagan's area of expertise was murder. Twenty years old, he had been practicing that particular craft for the past five years. He had a natural affinity for it, a sort of inborn aptitude. He'd started simply but gradually became more creative and imaginative, always striving for perfection, hoping for a masterpiece that would confirm his genius.

Usually Hagan picked up his victims at gay bars, confused lonely souls who were all too eager to go back to Hagan's place. He was classically handsome, blonde hair and blue eyes, with a lithe body that looked good in tight black clothing.

Though Hagan was a slight man, short and thin, he was quick and agile, and he never had any trouble with his victims.

Hagan had tired of the bars and the poor saps that haunted them nightly, though. They were so pathetic, most of them, that they practically welcomed death. Hagan needed something more challenging, more satisfying. That was what had brought him here to this lonely stretch of highway on this godforsaken night.

Over the rise, he saw two headlights appear, spearing through the gloom and the rain. Hagan stuck out his thumb, eager to get started on his next creation. The long yellow Cadillac rolled to a stop next to Hagan and a smiling middle-aged man leaned across the front seat and opened the passenger's side door.

"How ya doing?" Ferwin asked as the hitchhiker climbed into the car and closed the door on the wind and the rain.

"Wet and cold," the hitchhiker said, forcing a smile. "Thanks for stopping," he added.

"No problem." Ferwin pulled back onto the highway, the tires slushing on the wet pavement. He cut a discreet sideways glance at the hitchhiker. Young, dressed in a black T-shirt and jeans with only a light jacket to protect him from the harsh elements outside. His hair, so doused that Ferwin couldn't even guess at its true color, was plastered to the top of his head like a swimming cap. A black backpack hung from the hitchhiker's left shoulder.

"You can put that in the back," Ferwin said, flashing his most charming smile.

The hitchhiker placed the pack on the floorboard between his feet. "No thanks, I'd rather keep it close."

Ferwin nodded. "I understand. I'm a stranger, and you don't trust me. That's cool. So how far ya headed?"

"As far as you are," was the hitchhiker's response. He never once glanced at Ferwin. He seemed immune to Ferwin's usually irresistible magnetic personality. This was going to be a tough one, Ferwin thought, but he was up for that. He was confident he would win this game in the end, like he always did.

The driver of the Cadillac made Hagan nervous, which was practically unheard of. Hagan had nerves of steel and prided himself on his unshakable confidence. However, something about the driver's cheerful persona seemed forced, a façade of some kind. Hagan tried to dismiss this feeling as paranoia, but the driver kept giving him quick furtive glances. The driver was muscular, but aging. His gut evinced the first signs of flab, forewarning a potbelly sometime in the not-too-distant future. His hair receded from his forehead like a shoreline steadily eaten away by erosion. Hagan had nothing to worry about should this man decide to put up a fight, but he couldn't quite squelch the unease gnawing at him.

The car passed a large green sign, the headlights temporarily spotlighting it. Hagan had an idea.

"There's a rest stop at the next exit. At this time of night and in this storm, it's likely to be deserted."

"Yeah?" the driver asked noncommittally.

"I was thinking we could stop there," Hagan said, placing a hand high up on the driver's inner thigh. "We could have some fun."

The driver said nothing for several seconds. Hagan worried he'd taken the wrong course of action, but then the driver smiled. Hagan considered it to be the man's first genuine smile of the night. Without a word, the driver turned the car onto the ramp leading to the rest stop.

🦋 🦋

Ferwin could not believe his luck. At first he had been revolted by the hitchhiker's obscene offer and the feel of the young man's questing hand, but then Ferwin realized how perfect the situation was. The hitchhiker was inviting his own doom, and Ferwin would be more than happy to oblige him.

"You know, I've never done anything like this before," Ferwin said, infusing his voice with a mixture of insistent lust and harmless naiveté.

"Don't you worry. I'll show you the ropes."

Hagan's excitement built, but so too did his cautiousness. The driver was a fool, driving himself to his own funeral. However, Hagan still could not shake the nagging feeling that something was wrong. He needed to be careful with this one.

The Cadillac crested a small rise and they found themselves in the parking lot outside the rest stop. There were bathrooms quaintly labeled GUYS and GALS, vending machines filled with drinks and snacks, and a row of payphones all housed underneath a slanting overhang. As Hagan suspected, the Cadillac was the only car in the lot.

"Here we are," Hagan said. "Shall we get started?"

"No, not in the car," Ferwin said. "Let's do it in the restroom."

The hitchhiker shrugged, grabbed his pack and opened the door. The rain was letting up, but the wind grew stronger.

The hitchhiker hunched his shoulders against the gusting air and started toward the bathroom.

Ferwin followed suit, stepping out into the drizzle. He never handled his victims in the car. It was too risky and too messy. Ferwin could be a bit sloppy at times.

It wouldn't do to have blood all over the upholstery.

Hagan led the way, the driver trailing close behind. The restroom door creaked as it swung open on old, rusted hinges. Hagan was instantly assaulted by the stench of urine and mildew. He resisted the urge to gag. The filthy restroom, with puddles of stinking piss collected on the floor, disgusted Hagan. At the same time, though, the scene elated him. The stained green tiles of the floor and the utter corruption of the restroom seemed an appropriate burial ground for the middle-aged man, whose life Hagan imagined was as empty and squalid as this restroom.

The door swung shut, cutting off the light from the lamps in the parking lot, leaving the restroom in darkness. Hagan reached out to the wall, found the light switch and flipped it. Nothing happened. In the impenetrable blackness, Hagan smiled.

At first Ferwin couldn't even make out his own nose in the darkness that enfolded him, but gradually his eyes adjusted to the gloom. The hitchhiker stood a few feet away, shrugging off his backpack.

In the dark, the hitchhiker's eyes seemed to burn with some inner fire. Ferwin couldn't wait to snuff out that flame.

"Want a beer?" the hitchhiker asked, reaching into his bag.

"Sure." Ferwin stepped farther into the restroom, glancing at his surroundings, what little of it he could see. The restroom was narrow and ran straight back, one wall equipped with a long metal trough-like sink. The other wall held six urinals and six toilet stalls, only two of which had doors. Ferwin hated this place, hated the stench of human excrement.

He could hear the clinking of glass against glass behind him and the sound of the young man's footsteps on the tile as he approached. Yes, Ferwin could definitely use a beer, even if it was lukewarm from being in the hitchhiker's pack for a while.

Ferwin started to turn when something hard smashed against the side of his head, and he went sprawling to the floor. In the last few seconds before he lost consciousness, he could make out the hitchhiker standing over him, staring down and laughing.

The driver lay on the floor, blood seeping from the wound in his right temple to pool beneath his head. He was motionless except for the steady rise and fall of his chest—evidence that he was merely unconscious and not yet dead. That was good. Hagan wanted to get inventive with this one.

Hagan pulled a bundle of sturdy rope from his pack and tied the catatonic driver's wrists securely together. Dragging the man to the nearest stall, Hagan propped him up on the toilet. He returned to his backpack and unloaded some of his goodies; the tools of his trade. He had knives of every variety, pliers, a hammer and nails, a small blowtorch, a battery-operated electric drill, and his personal favorite, a corkscrew. Hagan never used guns, considering them too crude and unimaginative. He laid these items out on the floor and mulled them over, deciding which he would start with.

When Ferwin came to, his vision blurred and his mind was groggy. Gradually he became aware that his wrists were bound. He wiggled his hands, trying to free them, but the rope was too tight. He could hear the hitchhiker breathing somewhere beyond the stall. Ferwin knew he had to act quickly and had only once chance—the switchblade he kept tucked inside his sock.

He bent over and snagged the blade with his fingers, flicking it open with the ease of someone who had performed this act countless times. Ferwin began cutting through the rope, aware of a soft murmuring coming from somewhere outside the stall. It sounded like the hitchhiker was naming off items from a list.

Ferwin managed to cut through the thick rope in a matter of minutes. When he tried to stand, the world went gray around the edges. Ferwin slumped back against the toilet. His head pounded. Eventually the dizziness passed and he stood, a little uncertainly, but this time he maintained his balance. Crouching so that his head wouldn't show over the top of the stall, he clutched the switchblade in his right hand, and waited for the hitchhiker.

For starters, Hagan settled on the blowtorch. It may have been compact, but it was capable of generating intense heat—an unavailable prototype, obtained through one of Hagan's illegal suppliers. Hagan got his hands on any weapon he wanted, illegal or not, with only a few simple phone calls and an exchange of cash.

Although he trembled with anticipation, an inner calm had descended over him. Working on his art was the only time Hagan felt truly at peace. Everything shifted into perspective, and life was full of purpose and meaning.

Hagan walked slowly toward the stall where he'd left the driver. As much as he loved his art, he dreaded that moment when his victim took his last breath. It always left Hagan feeling empty. Therefore, he liked to make the kill last as long as possible, like a lover trying to hold off orgasm to receive the fullest possible pleasure.

As he reached the first stall, a well-honed intuition told him something had gone wrong. He'd learned over the years to trust that intuition, so he stopped short of the stall and stood very still. He held his breath for a moment, his ears straining to hear the slightest noise. He heard nothing, only the even rasping of the driver's breath. Steeling himself and lighting the torch, Hagan stepped in front of the doorless stall.

Ferwin listened as the hitchhiker walked toward the stall, ready to pounce as soon as the young man was in view. Before the hitchhiker reached the opening though, he stopped. The hitchhiker's breathing also stopped, momentarily.

He's on to me, Ferwin thought.

He quickly sat down on the toilet, holding his

hands together between his knees as if they were still bound. He closed his eyes and opened his ears, biding his time to make a move.

Hagan stepped in front of the stall, torch held out in front of him, expecting to find the driver poised to strike. Instead, the middle-aged man was as Hagan had left him.

You're getting paranoid, Hagan told himself.

He turned off the torch, not quite ready to use it, and leaned over the driver.

"Wakey, wakey," he called out softly. "C'mon now, I want you awake for this. It wouldn't be as much fun if you weren't."

Ferwin sensed the closeness of the hitchhiker, felt the heat of his breath as he lowered forward. When Ferwin's instincts told him the time was right, he raised the blade and thrust it toward the hitchhiker, sending all his weight flying forward. The blade sank into the hitchhiker's left shoulder, up to its polished-wood hilt. The force of Ferwin's assault caught the hitchhiker by surprise, and the two men went sprawling onto the floor.

When Hagan collided with the floor, his glasses flew from his face, transforming the world into an indecipherable collage of blurred images. Miraculously, he managed to maintain his grip on the blowtorch.

The driver was on top of him, trying to pull the blade from Hagan's shoulder. Hagan knew he had to act before that could happen. If the driver got the blade free, he would no doubt find a deadlier location in which to plunge it.

Hagan fumbled for the torch's switch, his sweaty fingers almost losing their purchase, but then the flame ignited with a soft hiss. Hagan brought the blowtorch up without hesitation, flaying away several layers of skin from the driver's cheek.

Ferwin screamed.

The pain in his cheek was worse than anything he'd ever known. It felt as if his eye would explode. Relinquishing his hold on the blade, still buried in the hitchhiker's shoulder, he rolled off the young man. Scrambling backwards, Ferwin tried to put as much distance as possible between himself and that blowtorch.

The hitchhiker rose slowly, dusting off his clothes, wincing at the pain in his shoulder. He glanced at the hilt of the switchblade then shifted his gaze to Ferwin. Ferwin imagined the stare to be something he'd given his own victims, and he found he didn't like being on the receiving end.

Ferwin managed to get to his feet, expecting a charge at any moment. Instead, the young man remained in place, grabbed a hold of the blade and pulled it out of his flesh. It made a wet sucking sound like shoes in sticky mud. The hitchhiker tossed the blade casually over his shoulder.

It landed with a *plop* in one of the urinals.

Ferwin backed up, never taking his eyes off the hitchhiker. He made his way to the door, so that his back was covered. Ferwin got the impression the hitchhiker was merely toying with him, making a sport of it all, as Ferwin himself had done many times in the past. Was this some kind of poetic justice, Ferwin wondered? Karma, perhaps?

Ferwin's foot landed on an object that rolled away beneath him. For a terrifying moment he thought he was going to fall. He regained his balance though. Risking a brief glance down, he discovered the object at his feet was a screwdriver. There were other tools laid out on the floor—a hammer, a drill, an object it took several seconds to recognize as a corkscrew.

He plucked the hammer from the floor, grateful to have a weapon, and continued backing toward the door.

Hagan watched the driver pick up the hammer with amusement. This was turning out far better than he'd ever imagined it would. Never before had any of his victims put up this much of a fight. Hagan had hoped for a challenge, and he'd gotten one.

He advanced on the driver, holding the torch down and out.

The driver raised the hammer and said, "Stay where you are."

Hagan was impressed to hear not the slightest tremor in that voice. It was a voice of authority, a voice of someone who had power and knew how to use it.

The driver was shaping up to be a worthy adversary, and Hagan was going to find it gratifying to take him down.

"Stay where you are," Ferwin said again. He hadn't bargained for this. The question was: would he come out on top this time?

The hitchhiker continued forward at a leisurely pace, making it obvious that he had experience at this sort of thing. While holding the hammer in one hand, Ferwin reached out behind him with the other, searching for the door. His fingers brushed only the cool, clammy tiles of the wall. Ferwin's fear combined with this darkness disoriented him. He wasn't sure if the door was to the right or left. The hitchhiker advanced. Ferwin needed to make a decision. He chose at random and moved left, trailing his fingers over the wall.

Ferwin had gone only a few steps when there was a creaking to his left. The bathroom door swung open. He pushed himself back against the wall to avoid being smashed in the nose, concealing him from the elderly gentleman who stepped inside.

Caught off guard by the sudden interruption, Hagan lost view of the driver. Someone else entered the restroom. Without his glasses, Hagan couldn't make out any specifics. He could, however, hear his labored, halted movements and identified the newcomer as an older person.

The old man took two steps into the restroom before spotting Hagan. He stopped short, his eyes sliding down to the torch in Hagan's hand.

"Um, excuse me," he said as the door swung shut behind him. "I didn't mean to interrupt. I'll just be a minute."

Hagan grinned and raised the torch, starting forward again.

Two for the price of one.

The old man reached for the door behind him and said, "Please, me and my wife are on our way to see our newest grandbaby. Please, please don't."

When the old man started for the door, Ferwin acted on impulse, his ingrained desire for violence winning out. He lifted the hammer and brought it down hard, embedding it in the top of the old man's head.

The crunch resounded before the old man fell to his knees and toppled over.

Only after the initial thrill of murder had subsided did Ferwin realize his mistake. The hitchhiker was still waiting for him, and Ferwin had relinquished his only weapon. He could bend over and yank the hammer from the old man's skull, but could he do it before the hitchhiker could close the remaining distance between them? Ferwin didn't think so.

Hagan was shocked. He had respected the driver's will to survive, his cool-headedness in the face of danger, but now Hagan saw there was more to the driver than even he suspected. The killing of the old man, such an unprovoked and heartless act, shocked him. The driver's apparent lack of remorse made it obvious to Hagan that this wasn't the first time the driver had killed. There was an efficiency about the man, a professionalism, that told Hagan the driver was a seasoned pro.

Hagan started forward again, and the driver reached out for the door handle. "I'm not going to hurt you," Hagan said.

"The fuck you're not," the driver said, running his fingers over the burned flesh of his cheek.

Hagan turned off the torch and tossed it away, holding up his hands to show he was unarmed. He stepped over the dead man's body as if it were nothing more than a fallen branch. Along with Hagan's realization that the driver was also an experienced murderer came a feeling of kinship, of brotherhood. They were cut from the same cloth, Hagan and the driver. United by the spilling of blood.

✖ ✖

Ferwin didn't know what to make of this turn of events. The hitchhiker had thrown away his weapon. Did he intend to battle Ferwin in a fistfight, man to man? Thoughts of escape left Ferwin's mind and he stood his ground. Ferwin had no doubt that he could beat the hitchhiker in simple hand-to-hand combat.

But the hitchhiker didn't seem to have combat in mind. He stopped in front of Ferwin, a grin spreading across his face, and said, "I had no idea. Will you accept my apology?"

"What are you talking about?"

Instead of answering, the hitchhiker asked another question. "How many have you killed?"

The question caught Ferwin by surprise. He fumbled a moment before saying, "I'm not sure, probably somewhere in the double digits. I don't keep count."

✖ ✖

"Oh, I do," Hagan said, grateful to have someone with which to discuss his art. He'd kept it bottled up so long that he now found himself rambling. "I've killed exactly thirty-seven people to date, twenty-six male and eleven female, thirty-two over the age of eighteen and five under the age of eighteen. After I read a book about Dahmer, I tried eating one of my victims. Christ, it was disgusting. I don't see how anyone could be sick enough to enjoy something like that."

✖ ✖

Ferwin was mesmerized. Here was someone who had killed as many people as Ferwin—more in all likelihood—and the hitchhiker talked about it in such a nonchalant manner. It excited Ferwin, meeting someone who shared his dark desire.

"Pardon me," Ferwin said after a few moments, "I hate to interrupt, but the old man on the floor said something about his wife being with him. She's probably out in the car right now, wondering what's keeping her hubby."

"Of course, you're right. May I take her? It's only fair. After all, you got to do the old man."

Ferwin smiled and said, "Be my guest."

Hagan knelt on the floor and felt around until he found his glasses, thankfully still in one piece. He went back to his assortment of tools and picked out the corkscrew, hiding it in the pocket of his jacket. While the driver washed up at the sink, Hagan eased out of the restroom and stalked into the parking lot. The rain had stopped completely. Even the wind was letting up. There were two cars in the lot now—the driver's Cadillac and, a few parking spaces over, an ancient gray Pinto. In the passenger's seat was an equally ancient woman with fluffy white hair. She stared at Hagan, and he saw her push down the door lock. Hagan plastered on his most authentic smile and made his way to the Pinto.

The woman was visibly panicked. Hagan knelt by the car and rapped on the window. "Ma'am," he said, his voice all innocent charm, "I'm so glad you and your husband happened by. I'm in a bit of a pinch."

The woman looked toward the restrooms. "Where's Raymond?"

"Your husband's still in the bathroom, ma'am. I talked to him in there. See, my car's battery is dead and I'm stranded. Your husband—Raymond—said he'd give me a jump."

"We don't have any jumper cables," the old woman said, clutching her purse in her lap.

"Oh, I have the cables. If you'd open up—"

"Where's Raymond?" the woman asked again.

"I told you, he's still in the bathroom. He's, um, he's doing a number two."

The old woman blushed and looked away. "I'll wait for Raymond."

"I understand," Hagan said, and smashed his elbow into the window. Shards of glass rained down on the old woman. She scrambled across the seat, reaching for the driver's door, but Hagan had the passenger's door open and was hauling her out before she could even get hold of the handle. In the process, the old woman's blouse was torn open, revealing a raggedy bra with one strap held up by a safety pin.

Hagan rolled her over onto her back and held her down by the throat. He applied enough pressure to make it hard for her to breathe without completely cutting off her supply of oxygen. She thrashed and struggled, but her frail limbs were useless against him.

"Please, don't rape me," she whispered, trying to cover herself with her ripped blouse.

Hagan laughed. "Don't be silly, Grandma. I'm not going to rape you, just kill you." He pulled the corkscrew from his jacket and showed it to the old woman. She began to struggle again, but Hagan banged her head sharply against the concrete, knocking her semi-unconscious. With a hungry grin, the aches and pains of his body forgotten at that moment, Hagan lowered the corkscrew toward the old woman's left eye.

Ferwin came out of the restroom as the hitchhiker pulled the old woman from the Pinto. He watched with interest from afar, admiring the hitchhiker's technique, his zealousness. It reminded Ferwin of himself. How refreshing it was to see a young person so dedicated, with so much real passion and ambition.

When the hitchhiker finished his work, he stood, blood coating his hands. He tucked the corkscrew back into his jacket, looking down at the body with obvious pride. He stood that way for several moments, entranced, then collected himself and walked over to Ferwin.

"You do nice work," Ferwin said.

"That's not all that much. It was too sloppy, but I was in a hurry."

"Well, if that's how you work when pressed for time, I'd love to see you at your best." Ferwin tried to smile, but the pain in his cheek turned the effort into a grimace.

"Man, I'm sorry about that. I didn't realize . . . "

"That's quite all right. Hazard of the job. It seems I did a bit of damage myself."

Hagan looked down at the wound in his left shoulder as if noticing it for the first time. Blood soaked through the upper left part of his T-shirt.

"I've had worse," he said, shrugging his right shoulder. "I know a few doctors who'll fix me right up, no questions asked. Of course, they don't actually have a license to practice medicine, but killers can't be choosers."

They shared a chuckle then stood in silence. Hagan was surprised to discover he actually respected this man, and that was something he'd never been able to say about anyone else he'd met. As a gesture of his esteem, Hagan held out his blood-streaked hand. The driver took it without hesitation.

When the handshake was over, Ferwin didn't bother to wipe the blood from his hand. He liked its texture, the thick slickness. "Can I drop you somewhere?" he asked.

"Won't be necessary. I find long walks invigorating, helps me think."

"Well, I should be going. It's late, and I have to take care of my cheek."

"It was a genuine pleasure meeting you," the hitchhiker said.

"Same here. Maybe our paths will cross again sometime."

"Hope so. In the meantime, keep up the good work."

"I will," Ferwin said with a laugh. On the way to the Cadillac, he glanced approvingly at the old woman's body and all the new holes the hitchhiker had added to her head. As he drove back to the highway, Ferwin raised his hand in a wave to the hitchhiker.

Driving toward town, Ferwin whistled a tune to himself. The hitchhiker had certainly been dynamic and interesting. Ferwin felt better about the future of America knowing there were young people like that out there.

Hagan watched the Cadillac disappear down the ramp before going back inside the restroom. Raymond's body lay inside the door. Hagan dragged the corpse halfway out, propped it up against the open door so that the dingy light from the parking lot would filter into the restroom. Hagan set about collecting his tools and stuffing them into his pack. Before leaving, he went over to the urinals and looked into them one at a time. In the third one he found the switchblade, floating in the yellowish water. Hagan reached in and put the blade in his pack with the rest of his things.

Back outside, he inhaled the clean air deeply. The rain seemed to have purified everything, a freshness descending on the world. He closed his eyes and imagined he was the only person on the planet. That he had the whole Earth to himself, that he had ridded the world of every other living soul.

Except for the driver. He would let him live. Together they would reign.

Hagan's pleasant reverie was interrupted by the sound of an approaching motor. He opened his eyes and took off across the lot, rushing into the surrounding woodland. When he felt he'd put enough distance between himself and the rest stop, he made his way back to the highway. It was a five mile trek back to his home, but he didn't mind.

Walking along the highway like this, backpack hanging heavy on his back, Hagan felt a little like that character from the old *Incredible Hulk* television show. This amused him and he said aloud to the night, "Don't make me angry. You wouldn't like me when I'm angry."

A few cars passed him, but he didn't bother to raise his thumb. He'd had enough for one night. He wanted to get home and get some rest.

He'd probably sleep though the day then wake refreshed and ready for another night of pursuing his art.

WALKING TALKING JESUS

I WAS KNEELING at the altar of the old church when a voice said, "Excuse me."

This startled me, because I'd been sure I was alone in the sanctuary. I quickly scanned the pews for a new arrival, perhaps someone else waiting to say a prayer, but the place was still empty.

"I'm up here."

The voice was no less startling the second time around, although I did pinpoint its location. I raised my head and blinked rapidly, sure I was seeing things. The large wooden Jesus hanging on the cross at the back of the pulpit stared down at me with his head cocked. His lips creaked up into a slight smile. "Could I trouble you for some help?"

At first I couldn't speak. Ironic, I thought. Here was a thing that shouldn't be able to speak, speaking, whereas I am supposed to speak and couldn't. The Jesus waited with a patient expression on his splintery face.

When I finally regained my voice, I said, "Are you talking to me?" Perhaps not the most intelligent question in the world, but my wits seemed to have fled.

The Jesus turned his head one way and then the other, making a show of looking around the sanctuary. "I don't see anyone else here."

I stammered a bit, cleared my throat, swallowed as if I had a large wad of bread stuck in my throat, and said, "What kind of help do you need?"

"I was hoping you could help me down from here."

"Off . . . you mean off the cross?"

"Well, yes. You see, I've been up here for centuries and it is more than a bit uncomfortable."

"But, um, you can't get down."

"I could if you would offer me a little assistance."

"But . . . you're Jesus."

"Yes, I know."

"We need you on the cross. It's what saves us from ourselves."

"I know, and I don't want to be down forever. I just need to stretch my legs a bit, work out some of the stiffness."

"I guess that would be okay."

"Sure it will. You can trust me, after all. Help me down, let me get a taste of the world, and I'll hop right back up here in a week's time. Two, tops."

I pondered this for a moment. It didn't seem an entirely unreasonable request. I knew how bad my neck hurt if I slept funny, so I could only imagine the discomfort of being in his position for as long as he'd been. Besides, it would only be for a little while. He'd promised, and surely Jesus wouldn't lie to me.

So I stood up, went over to the corner where I knew there was a supply closet. I located the ladder and returned to carefully help Jesus down from the cross, getting a few splinters in my fingers for my trouble. He was unsteady on his feet and I let him lean against me.

"Thank you, child," he said. "What is your name?"

"Paul."

"Oh, I used to know a Paul. I hate to do this, you've been so kind already, but I have yet one more favor to ask."

"What?"

"Do you have a place I can crash?"

I took the sofa and let Jesus have my bed—it seemed the Christian thing to do.

He was a polite and thoughtful guest.

I awoke the next morning to the smell of sizzling bacon. Entering my tiny cubbyhole of a kitchen, I found that he had prepared breakfast fit for a king, with pancakes and eggs, bacon and sausage, homemade biscuits with rich gravy, even some fried ham.

I stared at the feast with wide eyes. "Did you go to the store?" I asked.

Jesus shook his head. "I used what you had around."

"I didn't think I had this much food in the fridge."

"I make due." Jesus shrugged.

The food was delicious, and I only had to pick out a few stray slivers of wood, which I then used as toothpicks. Jesus seemed to delight in his meal as well, scarfing down three full helpings.

"You'll have to forgive me," he said, "I haven't eaten in so very long."

I frowned. "But how can you eat anything? Aren't you, you know, *solid*?"

Jesus considered this then shrugged again. "I guess it's a miracle."

"That makes sense, I suppose."

When we finished breakfast, we both did the dishes. I washed, Jesus dried. Once that was done, I said, "I have to go to work. Will you be alright here on your own for a while?"

"Sure, maybe I'll watch some TV."

Two days later Jesus asked if he could borrow some clothes. He'd worn nothing but a loincloth for so long, he thought it might be nice to dress like everyone else for a change. I lent him an old Pearl Jam T-shirt, some cargo shorts, and a pair of sandals. He found a slightly beat up fedora on the top shelf of my bedroom closet and asked to wear that as well. It looked rather silly with the outfit, but you don't exactly say no to Jesus.

I took him out to the park near my apartment. He sat on a bench for a long time, watching the children climb all over the playground equipment, smiling and laughing. Jesus, after all, loves the little children. We then strolled along the bike path for a bit, feeling the sunshine on our faces. It was a nice afternoon.

That evening Jesus insisted we go up to the roof of the apartment building and watch the sun set. I'd never actually taken the time to watch a sunset before. It was indeed magnificent. A celestial light show like none I'd ever seen. We stayed out there long after night fell, not saying much. Jesus seemed entranced by the stars. For someone whose Father created the universe, everything seemed new to him.

When we went back down to the apartment, Jesus surprised me by grabbing me and planting a kiss on my lips. "Sorry," he said. "I've never kissed anyone before, and I wanted to experience it."

"And how was it?" I asked, feeling a bit flabbergasted.

Jesus shrugged. "Nice, but I think I'd need to do it some more to really know what I think of it."

This time I put my arms around him, leaning in for the kiss. This one was longer, deeper. His lips were hard and his tongue tasted vaguely of sawdust, but the experience still sent a tingle up my spine like an electrical current.

When the kiss broke, I was panting as if I'd just sprinted a hundred yard dash. Jesus took my hand and told me I didn't have to sleep on the sofa that night.

We spent all day Saturday in our pajamas watching television. He seemed enamored with cable, all the many different options. He watched a little of everything for five to ten minutes then flipped to something else. The only thing he seemed to have a real distaste for was the news.

"Everything is war and murder and scandal and famine," he said, grimacing. "Is it always like this?"

I considered the question then shrugged. "There has always been bad stuff in the world, but it seems to have gotten worse, more hopeless, in the past week. Ever since . . . Well, you know."

Jesus changed the channel and the subject along with it.

The next day I asked if he wanted to go to church with me.

"I don't think so," he said, rummaging through my closet, looking for an outfit. "I've spent so much time there, you understand. I was thinking we could go somewhere different today, somewhere fun."

"What did you have in mind?"

He smiled at me.

We went to Wacky World, a local amusement park. We rode all the rides—some twice. We ate tons of junk food, petted the animals at the petting zoo, and zip-lined over the lake, something I'd never had the nerve to do before. The day was unforgettable. I had an absolute blast. Although I don't think I was enjoying myself nearly as much as Jesus. He whooped and hollered and laughed like a kid.

I couldn't help but notice, however, that those around us did not seem to be having as good a time as us. The people seemed morose and unenthusiastic, even the children. I noticed it, but decided not to dwell.

After all, it had been such a glorious day.

It was the middle of the next week when I came home from work to find Jesus making love to the mail lady in my bed, what I had come to think of as *our* bed.

She had the decency to seem embarrassed, quickly dressed, gathered up her mailbag, and rushed out the door. Jesus, on the other hand, seemed not the least bit ashamed.

"I'm trying to experience everything I can," he said. "The world has so much to offer."

"But what about me?"

"What about you?"

"I . . . I thought you loved me."

"I do. I love everyone in the world."

Over the course of the next week, I started seeing less and less of Jesus. He stayed out late, apparently making new friends who took him to nightclubs. He got a tattoo, a Chinese water symbol carved right into his wooden forearm. He also had people over to the house at all hours, playing loud music, smoking and drinking.

A few times when I actually managed to catch him alone I tried to broach the subject of him going back on the cross where he belonged, but he was always too busy to discuss it.

I tried going to church the following Sunday, but no one was there. Not even the preacher. I guess with the cross empty, no one saw the point.

The news became more disheartening every day. The world wasn't becoming more violent or more dangerous, simply more apathetic. People had stopped caring—about each other, about their jobs, about their homes.

It was as though the collective lives of mankind had lost all meaning.

Jesus had been in my home for nearly two months when he came to me excitedly one day and said, "I got a job."

"What? Where?"

"I'm bagging groceries down at the Food Emporium."

"You're going to work at a grocery store?"

Jesus looked offended. "Hey, it's decent money and within walking distance. I can save up to get a car and eventually my own place."

The whole conversation was causing me to feel a little dizzy so I sat down heavily on the sofa. I couldn't say I was entirely surprised; part of me had known this was coming. "Your own place?"

"Yeah, I can't keep living with you forever."

"But you've got to get back up on that cross."

He folded his arms and shook his head. "I don't think so."

"But you have to. It's your . . . I don't know, your duty."

"I think I performed that duty long enough," he said, walking around behind me. "It's time I got to have a life."

"But don't you see what's going on in the world? Mankind needs a Savior."

"I know," Jesus said, and I heard real mourning in his voice. "I'm sorry."

I turned to look at him in time to see the bat swinging toward me.

✖ ✖

When I came to, I didn't know where I was. After my initial disorientation passed, I looked at the church's sanctuary. Looking *down* at the sanctuary. The pews were full again, some people with their heads bowed in prayer, others with faces and hands upraised. There was singing and laughing and shouts of "Amen."

The preacher stood directly beneath me, his face beaming with joy. "We knew you would not forsake us, Lord. We praise you and thank you for returning to us."

I did not speak, didn't know what I would say even if I could. I could feel the nails through my wrists and feet, the thorns digging into my forehead, the spear gouging my side, oddly, there was little pain. Discomfort, yes, but no real pain.

I looked across the sea of worshippers.

In the very back, near the exit, I spotted Jesus wearing my best suit. He smiled sadly at me then walked out the door.

SURVIVAL OF THE FITTEST

DRU WAS HER NAME. She wasn't exactly sure of her age. Such abstract concepts as years, months, and days meant little to her. The last birthday Dru remembered was her sixteenth, and that had been shortly before her mother had fallen victim to the Plague. That could've been five years ago or fifteen; she wasn't sure and figured it didn't really matter.

She rode through the streets on a motorcycle, a big bitch of a Harley she had lovingly restored herself. The city seemed deserted, the silence of the night shattered only by the rumbling of the Harley's engine. The raw power of the machine vibrated up Dru's crotch to radiate throughout her body. She reveled in the feeling, leaning forward into the wind as she edged the machine's speed up a few more notches, rocketing down the street, winding her way effortlessly through the burned-out husks of long abandoned automobiles as if through a labyrinth.

The dark buildings of the city loomed over her in their dilapidated splendor. Glass and debris littered the cracked sidewalks. From certain darkened doorways, curious, clandestine eyes peered out and tracked her passage, betraying her feeling of isolation.

She brought her Harley to a stop in the middle of an intersection, the extinguished traffic light hanging overhead. Dru was running low on fuel, both for the Harley and her own stomach. It wouldn't be difficult to scrounge up some food, but gasoline was another matter altogether. Luckily, a friend had given her the name of a man who had a stockpile of fuel and sold it to those able to pay what he charged. It wasn't money the man was after; in this drastically altered world, money no longer had any real value. But the man had an insatiable craving for tobacco, which unfortunately was almost as hard to come by as gasoline. It just so happened that Dru had several cartons of cigarettes in the duffel bag strapped to the back of her cycle. Tit for tat, it would be a fair trade.

As Dru checked over the directions one last time, a figure shambled out of the blackness of a nearby alley. He wore a ripped trench coat, and his scraggly hair obscured his eyes. He staggered toward the intersection, but one piercing glare from Dru and the derelict quickly changed course and disappeared into a shadowy storefront.

Dru was a menacing figure, standing at six feet four inches tall, her body lean and as well-muscled as that of any man. She wore her shockingly red hair close to the scalp in a military-style buzz cut. Her face was full of sharp angles with thin lips and emerald-green eyes that were lethal in their intensity. She dressed almost exclusively in black, favoring jeans, tank-tops, and heavy work boots. Her expression was always one of extreme seriousness and cruelty, and only the foolhardy ever attempted to mess with her.

She refolded the directions and stuffed them in her

pocket, glancing to her right where she'd last seen the derelict. No sign of him now, but something did catch her eye. On the side of a four-story brick building a message was scrawled in neon-pink spray paint. The sign was faded but still legible. Dru's face evinced no emotion as she read the message, a desperate plea:

PLEASE FIND A CURE!

Four little words, but they spoke volumes. There were similar messages all around, memorials to a dead world.

Dru turned the Harley onto the intersecting street and shot off toward the city limits. Up ahead, she could see the glow from a fire burning in an old trash barrel, and voices drifted to her over the cacophony of the cycle's engine. As Dru rode by, she saw two men screeching and laughing as they mercilessly kicked a third man lying crumpled on the ground. Dru considered riding on—it wasn't any of her business— but she knew that her conscience would never stop needling her if she didn't try to help. Making a quick U-turn, she drove back to the men. The two halted their assault as Dru pulled up and cut the engine on her motorcycle.

"Well, lookee what we got here," one of the assailants, a short man with the face of a particularly ugly sewer rat, said. Dru smelled the liquor on his breath even from a few feet away. "I thoughts it was a man at first."

Dru said nothing as she dismounted the bike.

"Nope, that ain't no man," the other man said. He was about the same height as his friend but at least a couple of hundred pounds heavier, his doughy flesh jiggled when he moved. "This is one of them butch chicks, pro'ly *wishes* she was a man."

Rat Face giggled. "Well, what can we's do for ya, Butch?"

"I was wondering what crime this man committed to deserve such a vicious beating," Dru said evenly, her voice surprisingly feminine and melodic.

"Oh, the crime of weakness," Dough Boy, who seemed to be the leader, said. He grinned, revealing a few blackened teeth that protruded from his gums like tombstones. He grabbed the beaten man by the hair and pulled him to his knees. "This here boy's a queer."

Dru eyed the battered man, kneeling in a pool of his own blood. Tall, pitifully scrawny, with long black hair falling into his face and down his back in matted clumps, Dru noticed. His facial features were distorted by countless bruises and abrasions, his left eye swollen shut. His hands were tied behind his back, and his clothes hung from his emaciated frame in tattered shreds. He made mewling sounds deep in his throat, like a frightened animal. Dough Boy pushed him to the ground.

"That's a crime punishable by death?" Dru asked.

"You know it," Rat Face said, striding over to deliver a swift kick to the captive's ribs. Rat Face then sat on a crate by the fire and laughed as he watched the captive's obvious agony.

Dru said nothing.

"Few days ago we caught this 'un and some other guy sleepin' together in a warehouse," Dough Boy said. "They didn't even have the decency to deny they was doing the dirty deed. It was like they wasn't 'shamed of it."

"Where's the other man?" Dru asked.

Rat Face spat into the fire. "He up and died on us. Guess he wasn't as strong as his butt-buddy here."

"Say, you's kind of pretty," Dough Boy said. "I's don't usually go for you butch types, but I'm just drunk enough. I bet you's a real wildcat in the sack, huh?"

Dru smiled tightly. "Why don't you come find out?"

"Alrighty, this my lucky day."

When Dough Boy was within range, Dru spun around and kicked out with her right leg. The heel of her boot smashed into Dough Boy's face, crushing his nose and sending hot blood gushing from his nostrils. Dru punched him squarely in the gut. He *woofed* out all the breath in his lungs and fell to the ground.

Rat Face was still immobile on the crate, too stunned to react. Dru turned and started toward him, but then Rat Face's paralysis broke. He jumped up, grabbed Dru by the neck, and slammed her against a nearby telephone pole, slivers of the splintering wood digging deep into her back.

"You's gonna die now, bitch!" Rat Face spat, pulling a serrated hunting knife from his belt and pressing it against Dru's throat. The tip dimpled the soft flesh on her neck and sent a thin line of blood trickling down into the collar of her shirt. "I'm gonna kill you slow; make you hurt."

In one quick, fluid motion, Dru grabbed Rat Face's wrist and gave it a violent twist, efficiently snapping the bones in two. Rat Face cried out and dropped the knife. Dru took this opportunity to ram her knee into his crotch. Whimpering, he crumpled to the ground at her feet.

Dru saw that Dough Boy had managed to struggle

to his knees, clutching his still-gushing nose and screaming bubbly curses at her. Dru hurried over and planted a strong kick under Dough Boy's jawbone, snapping his head back and sending him sprawling onto his back. She retrieved Rat Face's knife and hacked through the ropes that bound the captive's wrists together.

"Thank you," the captive croaked as Dru helped him to his feet.

"No time for thanks. We've got to get the hell out of here. Come on."

After situating herself on the bike, she helped the scrawny man onto the back and urged him to hold on tight. She peeled away. They were long gone by the time Dough Boy and Rat Face regained their strength.

Miles away, in a barn on the outskirts of the city, Dru tended to the wounded man's injuries. He told her his name was Lowell. Outside, an elderly black man in faded overalls and a straw hat gassed up the Harley while happily puffing away on two unfiltered cigarettes at once.

"I'm sorry about your friend," Dru said in a neutral voice.

Lowell grimaced. "Yeah, me too."

Dru cleaned the gashes on Lowell's back. Dough Boy and Rat Face had used a whip on him. The wounds were deep and Dru hoped they wouldn't get infected.

"What was his name?" she asked to distract Lowell from the pain.

"Rick."

"Again, I'm sorry."

"If only I'd had the strength to fight back, to make those bastards pay for what they did. If you hadn't stopped, I'd be dead, too."

"Well, I did," Dru said, applying makeshift bandages. "And you're going to be okay."

"I want to get out of the city," Lowell said softly. "Rick and I were planning to head down to the coast soon, maybe spend the summer there."

"Really? That's where I'm headed myself."

Lowell perked up and said, "Take me with you. I won't be much trouble, I promise."

"I don't know about that, trouble seems to follow me."

"Please," Lowell said, taking Dru's hand. "I need to get out of here, away from the memories. I don't have anything to pay you, but I'll do anything you ask. It's not even that far, really."

Dru stared at him for a moment. "Okay, but once we get to the coast you're on your own."

"That's fine," Lowell said, smiling. Dru hadn't seen the man's smile before, and she was surprised by its beauty. His teeth were even, if a bit yellowed, and the grin lit up his entire countenance. "Maybe you can even teach me some of your moves. You know, so I'll be prepared the next time a couple of Neanderthals try to beat me to death."

Dru smiled crookedly. "I think that would take more time than we're going to have together. Lie back and get some rest. You're going to need some time to recuperate."

Lowell didn't argue. He closed his eyes and reclined in the hay. Within moments, his breathing evened out and he snored quietly. Dru watched him for a while, listening as he called out for Rick in his sleep, then she walked out into the night. The stars shone in the sky and the crickets sang in the grass as if all were still right with the world. Dru knew better.

The old black man limped over, a gap-toothed grin on his wrinkled face. "The tank's topped off, and I'm giving you an extra can of gas for the road. You and your companion are welcome to stay the night if you want."

"Thanks, I think we will," Dru said with a nod.

The old man tipped his comical hat and went inside the barn. Dru lingered outside, feeling the need to spend some time alone. She sat on the ground, head tilted back. A shooting star streaked across the sky, leaving a trail of vapor in its wake. Dru felt the sudden need to cry.

But she didn't.

LAND OF PLENTY

BENJAMIN FULLER WAS executed this morning.

The execution wasn't a public affair—those were discontinued when I was still a little girl—nor was there an announcement in the paper. Everyone in the village knew about it though. We'd known it was going to happen for the past nine months, but the birth of Fredda Jones's baby boy last night had solidified it into an inevitability.

While I was working this morning in the garden behind the house, my callused fingers lovingly kneading the fragrant, fertile soil of the tomato patch, I heard the clock from the town square chime eleven times to signify the hour. I paused in my work, closing my eyes and letting a shuddering breath escape my lungs, allowing it to pass through my clenched teeth with a faint *hiss*. Each chime struck me like a physical blow, and if I hadn't been kneeling in the dirt already, I might have collapsed to the ground.

Ben Fuller's death at the age of eighty-one meant that my grandfather, with whom I've lived since my parents' death ten years ago, was now the eldest living citizen of Pleasant Hills.

I tried to ignore the chimes and their cheerfully

ominous music, but I could not block them out. I was painfully aware of each thunderous chime. The sound reverberated through my entire body, causing me to shiver as if in the grips of palsy.

"Isabella," my grandfather called out from behind me, his voice weak and quavering. "Isabella, love, have you fallen asleep amongst the tomatoes?"

I opened my eyes with a great effort and turned toward my grandfather's voice. He stood at the back door, inside the threshold, leaning his full weight against the doorjamb. He looked so frail to me in that moment—his back bent, his shoulders stooped, his thinning hair the color of dirty dishwater, his clothes hanging limply from his emaciated frame—his image quivered like a mirage as my eyes moistened.

"No, Pee-Paw," I said, using the childhood sobriquet that neither I nor my grandfather had ever outgrown. "I'm not asleep, just resting my eyes a bit."

Pee-Paw looked past me toward the village. He did not comment on the chimes. "The sun is merciless today."

I rose to my feet, my knees cracking like burning kindling. "Do you need something? Are you having another one of your spells?"

"No, no, dear," Pee-Paw quickly assured me. Recently, Pee-Paw had been suffering from debilitating bouts of dizziness and exhaustion. He would be reduced to lying in bed for weeks at a time, unable to muster the strength to rise. I would prop his head up with several pillows and feed him soup as if he were an infant.

"You should be resting," I said, hurrying across the heat-dried grass, the brittle blades crunching like hard-shelled insects beneath my feet. Placing the back of my hand against Pee-Paw's sweaty forehead, I added, "It's too hot for you out here. You'll tucker yourself out."

"I was going to make lunch for us." Pee-Paw grinned. Several of his teeth were missing, those remaining spelling out some Morse code message that I was incapable of deciphering.

"You shouldn't be making lunch," I chastised, clucking my tongue disapprovingly against the roof of my mouth. "I'll fix something."

He took my proffered arm and allowed me to lead him back into the shadowy coolness of the house. "It doesn't look as if anyone will be fixing anything. That's what I came out to tell you; it seems we are pitifully low on supplies."

"Oh yes, that's my fault. I've been meaning to go to the market all week. There's so much to do around here."

I instantly regretted my last comment. Although Pee-Paw didn't actually say anything, I could feel his body sagging against mine. I knew how he hated the frailty that came with old age, his inability to do even the simplest household chores like washing the dishes or picking vegetables. He told me once that it was as if his body had betrayed him, and I usually tried my best to make him feel useful. Sometimes, however, I made innocent statements that came out sounding like accusations.

"It is a beautiful day," Pee-Paw said as I helped him into his bed. His room was sparse, the drab gray walls bare of shelves or pictures, the splintering wood of the floor unadorned by rugs. The only furniture in the room was his sagging bed and near-empty wardrobe. He'd given his most valuable possessions—monetarily valuable, like his gold pocket watch, and sentimentally valuable, like photographs of my parents—to me over the years. Most of his clothes he'd given to various families in the village. I did not even like to think what significance this throwing off of worldly possessions might have.

"Would you like for me to sit with you awhile, Pee-Paw?" I asked, smoothing back his oily hair. Not for the first time, I felt more like his mother than his granddaughter. At times, I wanted to wrap him in my arms and never let go.

"That won't be necessary, my dear Isabella. Go on to the market. The walk will do you good. It is a beautiful day."

"You've said that already."

"Have I?" he asked, his bushy eyebrows coming together above his nose as if to shake hands. "Well, it is truly glorious. Not a cloud in the sky. Who would guess that on such a day as this . . . " Pee-Paw's words trailed off, and I was more than happy to let them go.

"Are you sure you'll be okay here by yourself?" I asked, reluctant to leave. In my mind, I kept hearing the chimes of the clock and seeing poor Ben Fuller's weatherworn face.

"I don't need you hovering over me like a nursemaid. I am perfectly capable of lying in bed without any assistance. Besides, if you don't go to the market, we'll both surely starve before long."

"I should only be a half an hour or so," I promised, and he waved at me, his arm dropping back to the coverlet as if weighted with lead.

LAND OF PLENTY

After twisting my shoulder-length black hair into a tidy bun, I placed a faded pink sunbonnet atop my head and tied the straps under my chin in an elaborate bow. Stopping in front of the water-spotted mirror in the bathroom, I inspected my reflection in the glass. What I saw saddened me greatly. Staring back was a plain woman with bland features and a sallow complexion. My ankle-length dress, the same faded pink as my bonnet, bulged slightly at the midsection. Sickly purple sacks hung under my eyes like rotten fruit, standing in stark contrast to the paleness of my skin. I found it hard to believe that the face in the mirror belonged to a girl of twenty.

I gave my head a resolute shake, trying to dispel all of these negative thoughts like a dog shaking off fleas. I grabbed a pristine white apron from the kitchen and tied it around my waist, efficiently covering my extended abdomen. After a momentary consideration, I changed into a more comfortable pair of shoes. It was only a ten minute walk into town, but the gravelly road could be murder on the feet.

Maroon-colored stepping stones led the way from the front door to the road. I remembered how as a child I had pretended that the lawn was a tumultuous ocean populated with child-hungry sharks. I would carefully cross the stones to keep from being gobbled up. A sudden wave of nostalgia hit me with such force that halfway to the road I swooned, in danger of toppling into the sea and falling victim to a shark attack. The spell passed after a few seconds and I continued on my way.

The road was made of packed dirt covered with loose pebbles. Hoof prints were embedded in the dirt, as well as the narrow ruts made by wagon wheels. I heard fanciful stories that men and women once rode in great metal machines that propelled themselves forward without the aid of horses. It was amusing science fiction, but I could not imagine such wild tales having any validity to them.

As I progressed toward the village, playfully kicking rocks into the weeds that bordered the road like sentinels, keeping an ear open for the jangling bells that would signal an approaching wagon, I studied the strange artifacts that littered the sides of the road. One object in particular caught my interest. It appeared to be a rusted rectangular box, partially buried in the ground with three busted glass circles covered with metal hoods set into the front. A length of black wire hung limply from the top like a dead snake. I could not comprehend what such a bizarre object could have been used for. This was merely another mysterious relic from a bygone age.

The oldest citizens of the village—those who still remained—sometimes told tales of a world gone mad, a world with too many people and not enough resources. There were stories of starvation, murder, and wars fought over land that was suddenly too scarce. These stories were both horrible and incomprehensible to me.

Pleasant Hills was a utopia by comparison. No one ever went without in Pleasant Hills; there was plenty for every citizen. Every family was guaranteed a warm home and good food on the table.

The houses I passed on my way to the market were a lot like the home I shared with Pee-Paw—small but sturdily built with four rooms and an outhouse, as well as a vegetable garden out back. I passed few houses, though. The entire population of Pleasant Hills was only seventy-five persons, and that number never varied. In order to maintain the plentiful lifestyle the citizens of the village had grown accustomed to, it was necessary that the population be kept low and steady. In a town meeting that was held a year and a half before I was born, it had been decided that seventy-five was all that the village's resources could adequately support.

I came out of my reverie to find myself in the town square, a cluster of shops and clerical offices with a small park at the center. I purposely averted my eyes from the clock tower on the west side of the square, shooting up several stories like an accusatory finger pointed at God.

Crossing a rickety wooden porch, the beams bowing under the weight of my feet, I pushed through the swinging doors into Nell's Market. Nell, a polite older gentleman with bright eyes and a ready smile, was in his usual spot behind the counter, playing cards laid out in front of him. As I entered, he flipped more cards over and placed them on top of others.

"Morning, Izzy," he said, rising from his stool like a proper gentleman. "Here for the usual?"

I nodded, taking a wicker basket from a pile by the doors. Nell continued to chat with me as I wandered about the store, placing various items into my basket— green apples, a sack of flour, a block of cheese, a few strips of cured bacon.

"That Ellis boy was in here askin' 'bout you the day 'fore yesterday," Nell said, causing me to turn quickly in his direction, nearly dropping a jug of fresh, frothy milk. "I was surprised to hear you two young'uns had split."

"Well, these things happen." I placed the basket on the wooden counter and deposited a few wrinkled bills into Nell's cupped palm. There were more items I'd intended to purchase, but I was suddenly eager to leave the market.

"Tell your grandpa I said hey," Nell called as I rushed out into the square. "Our prayers are with 'im."

As I began the trek back home, I started to feel foolish for the way I'd behaved, but the mere mention of Ellis's name never failed to upset me.

Ellis and I started dating when I was eighteen and he twenty. He was the only man who had ever told me I was beautiful, and being with him had made me *feel* beautiful. Everyone in Pleasant Hills had assumed the two of us would eventually marry, and I had assumed the same thing. Three months ago, however, I had abruptly broken off our relationship. Ellis had not taken it well; he demanded an explanation, but I didn't tell him the reason for my decision. I had not told anyone.

But I would not be able to hide it for much longer, and then it would be announced in the paper.

I suddenly paused in the middle of the road, my hand splayed across my belly and a few tears streaming down my cheeks, leaving shiny streaks like slug trails on my face. The wicker basket felt unaccountably heavy, as if filled with bricks. The air seemed to have substance, bearing down on me, threatening to crush me under its oppressive weight.

"Hey lady, move your ass!"

The voice startled me, and I realized that the

inelegant sound of bells filled the air. I turned to see a wagon pulled by two horses rapidly approaching. Gasping, I scurried to the side of the road, barely avoiding being run down. I actually felt the wind from the passing wagon buffet my body. Pebbles kicked up by the horses pelted my legs.

In my hasty retreat, the wicker basket tipped over a little too far, and the sack of flour fell out, hitting the ground with a dull *thump*. A snowstorm of fine powder circulated through the air, coating my shoes and ankles.

Badly shaken by this near-miss, I practically ran the rest of the way home, ignoring the painful stitch in my side. I stayed to the side of the road, mentally cursing myself for such foolishness. By the time I reached the house, I was so winded that I had to lean against the door for several moments, gulping air like water.

"Are you okay, Isabella?" Pee-Paw asked as I entered the kitchen. He sat at a butcher-block table, arranging a colorful bunch of flowers in a vase that had a noticeable crack up one side. "Your color is hectic."

I sat the basket on the table by the vase. "I'm fine. What are you doing out of bed, Pee-Paw? I thought we agreed you need your rest."

"Oh, pish-posh," he said, flipping his hand in the air. "I'm feeling much better. The weather is doing my old body some good."

Indeed, Pee-Paw did look better. There was some healthy color in his cheeks, and when he took the vase over to the window, he limped only slightly. Hating myself, I felt a pang of anger at Pee-Paw's improving health. It would be so much easier if I could believe he had only a little time left anyway.

"Isabella, dear, whatever is wrong?" Pee-Paw asked, and only then did I realize that I was crying. I collapsed forward onto the table, knocking the basket to the floor, the items inside scattering about like escapees, the jug of milk shattering.

Pee-Paw rushed to my side, being careful to skirt around the jagged glass, and cradled me in his arms like he did when I was a child, whispering encouragements that only seemed to intensify my agony. I felt that I didn't deserve his love or the comfort he wanted so desperately to give. I had betrayed him, and because of me he had only six months left.

He took my hands and kissed my forehead. "Honey, talk to me. What's the matter?"

"Pee-Paw," I said in a hoarse whisper, my head bowed. I couldn't bring myself to look him in the eye. "I think you'd better sit down. I have something to tell you."

WHAT SHE NEEDS

EXCUSE ME, LILY?"
Lily was on her way out of class, but she turned to find Keith standing behind her, his books held down in front of his crotch as if trying to hide something incriminating there. He didn't look directly at her, but instead gazed at her shoes. She and Keith only had this one class together, but she'd noticed him around before. With his muscular frame, shy of being what she thought of as a steroid build, his hulking figure was hard to miss. Yet the two had rarely spoken. In contrast to his appearance, Keith was shy and introverted and usually kept to himself.

When he didn't say anything for half a minute, Lily prompted, "What can I do for you, Keith?"

He shifted from foot to foot (the *pee dance*, Lily's father had always called it) and glanced up at her without raising his head. "Are you okay?"

"What?"

Keith gestured toward her face. "That's quite a shiner you have there."

"Oh," Lily said, raising a hand to her right eye. She'd used concealer on the purple-black bruising but apparently hadn't done a great job. Prodding the swollen flesh with her fingers, she inhaled air through her teeth. "Yes, it's just my usual klutziness. Got up in the middle of the night to use the bathroom, tripped over the shoes I'd left by the bed, and face-planted into the bedpost."

"Ouch," Keith said, wincing.

Lily nodded and waited for him to say more, but he merely stood there, staring at her shoes as if mesmerized by her footwear. The room had cleared out. Even Professor McNamara collected her things and left.

"Was that all you wanted?" Lily asked.

Keith closed his eyes as if saying a silent prayer, took a deep breath, then raised his head to meet her eyes. "I was wondering, um, you see they're showing the new Adam Sandler movie in the Student Center tonight. I thought maybe you'd want to go with me."

"I'm sorry Keith, but I don't think so."

"Not a Sandler fan? We could get coffee or something."

Lily tilted her head, wearing a pitying expression. Keith reminded her of her snot-nosed nephew, constantly asking his Auntie Lily to pick him up and hold him. She always told him no with the same look.

"Look, Keith, you're a nice guy and everything, but I'm not interested."

He nodded, returning his eyes to the floor. "I understand. A girl as pretty as you, I'm sure you have a boyfriend."

"It's not that. I mean, I am seeing Roy Vance but we're not exclusive or anything. You're just not my type."

"But you don't even know me," Keith said, a petulant whine threading through his voice.

"I know you enough to know you can't give me what I need."

That sounded cruel even to Lily's own ears, but she figured it was best to be totally blunt with him. It would save her the trouble of having to deflect his advances in more subtle ways over and over. *Cruel to be kind*, another of her father's pet sayings.

Keith didn't respond, but his entire body seemed to shake and she was suddenly afraid he was about to start crying. If there was one thing she couldn't stand it was the sight of a grown man crying. To save herself from the pathetic spectacle, she turned and left the classroom.

❧ ❧

The next time she talked to Keith was two weeks later, outside the Curtis Administration Building. She sat on one of the benches by the fountain, waiting for Roy. Keith walked up from the direction of Hamrick Hall and sat next to her.

"Hi, Lily. I noticed you hadn't been in class this week, now I see why."

She held up her left arm, showing off the cast. "Yup, more of my extreme klutziness. Don't worry the bone's not broken, just fractured."

"What did you do this—"

"Well, what in the hell do we have here?"

Lily and Keith both turned their eyes to the front of Curtis, where Roy swaggered down the steps toward them. He was not quite as tall as Keith, but definitely as muscular. His face was pinched so tight it seemed all the features were being drawn into the center.

"Hey baby," Lily said brightly, rising to her feet. "I was catching up with my good friend Keith here."

"Oh, is this another one you're fucking?" Roy spat, grabbing Lily's good arm and jerking her to him.

Keith got to his feet. "There's no need for that. We were just talking. We're in the same Intro to Psych—"

"I'm not talking to you, dickweed!" Roy shouted, jabbing a finger in Keith's direction while keeping a vice-like grip on Lily's arm with his other hand. "Right now I'm dealing with this little whore here, but when I'm done pounding some respect into her, then it'll be your turn."

"Stop being such an asshole," Lily hissed, trying to twist her arm out of Roy's grasp.

Roy whirled around and backhanded her hard across the cheek. She collapsed to the pavement, using her injured arm to break her fall, causing a red-hot explosion of pain. She cried out.

Raising her chin defiantly as Roy approached, she refused to scuttle away. Before he reached her though, with his fist held high like a wrecking ball about to knock down a skyscraper, Keith suddenly tackled him from behind. The two men went scrambling past Lily and into the grass.

Several people ran over, and a couple of them were helping Lily to her feet. She was so dazed by the sudden eruption of violence that she wasn't even sure if she knew them. Once she was steady on her feet, she turned toward the brawl, ready to yell for Roy to leave Keith alone . . .

. . . she was stunned by what she saw.

The reverse of what she expected to see. Roy lay flat on his back with Keith straddling his chest and punching him repeatedly in the face. Roy struggled feebly, his mouth and nose bloody. Keith made a high-pitched keening sound that sounded almost inhuman. His eyes were clouded over with rage, appearing to Lily as a force of nature.

Several men rushed over to the fighting duo (though Roy wasn't really putting up much of a fight), including one of the history professors and a security guard, and attempted to break them up. Keith lashed out at them, connected a few punches, but finally he allowed himself to be pulled off Roy. On the ground, Roy rolled onto his side and curled into a fetal position. One eye had already swollen shut and his nose was misshapen, obviously broken. He moaned and cried incoherently, something Lily had never seen him do. If asked before now, she would have said he was incapable of producing tears.

"Someone better call for an ambulance," the security guard said, looking at Roy, but then he turned his eyes to Lily. "Are you okay, lady?"

She couldn't make her brain work enough to actually speak, but finally she nodded dumbly.

"I'd have them check you out to be sure. In the meantime, I'll take this one down to the security office."

Though Keith still breathed heavily, he had calmed down considerably. In fact, the rage that Lily had witnessed in his eyes earlier had eclipsed to something like fear or shame. He docilely allowed himself to be lead down the hill by the security guard.

Keith sat across from her in the booth, staring down at his coffee as if it were a crystal ball. She'd ordered a salad and some pasta, but he wanted only the coffee that he seemed to have no interest in drinking.

"Is Roy okay?" he finally asked, his voice so soft it was nearly inaudible.

Lily chewed and swallowed before answering. "I don't know. I haven't seen or spoken to him since the fight last week."

"And you're okay?"

"I'm fine. I'm glad you didn't get kicked out of school over this."

"I'm on probation but a lot of people saw Roy hit you, so the administration was pretty lenient on me."

Lily smiled. "My knight in shining armor."

"I shouldn't have wailed on him like that," Keith said. He looked miserable and shaken, like someone who'd gone through a tax audit that didn't end favorably.

Reaching across the table, Lily placed her hand over his. "He was hurting me."

"I'm not sorry I stopped him, I had to keep him from hurting you, but I lost control. I could have subdued him, but instead I became an animal. I think a part of me wanted to kill him."

"You know, it almost looked like you were enjoying yourself."

Keith hunkered down closer to his coffee cup as if he wanted to dive headfirst into it. "Guess you could say I had a relapse."

"What?" Lily asked with a slight frown.

"I think I should come clean with you. I have a history of rage and violence."

"*You?* But you seem so . . . passive."

"Must mean I'm making progress," Keith said with a humorless laugh. "I don't know why, but I've always had a temper and very little ability to keep it under control. Ever since I was a little kid, I've gotten into nasty fights. Usually ones I started. Two years ago I was involved in a fender-bender, an older guy ran into the back of my car at a red light. It was a tap, didn't even really do any damage, but I certainly did some damage. I put the guy in the hospital. I don't know how I avoided jail, I guess because I was only sixteen. I did have to agree to go into therapy, anger management and all that. I've been trying so hard ever since, and that's one of the main reasons I self-isolate so much. I figure the less contact I have with people the less likely I'll lose control. Unfortunately, I lost control this time."

"Well, I know this will sound weird in light of what you told me, but I'm grateful to you. All I know is that you helped me."

Keith met her gaze and tried to smile but failed. "So I take it your black eye and the cracked bone was more than you being a klutz?"

Lily had a heap of pasta halfway to her mouth, but she paused and slowly lowered the fork back to the plate. "No use lying about it now. Yes, Roy beat me, often and quite viciously."

"Why'd you put up with it? Why didn't you leave him?"

Shrugging with one shoulder, Lily spoke softly. "My father was abusive. One of my earliest memories is of him beating me until I bled because I knocked over my milk at the table. I grew up thinking that type of behavior was natural. I'm ashamed to say it's a pattern that's became ingrained in me, and my relationship with Roy felt normal. Like what I deserved."

"You're wrong. You deserve to be treated right. You deserve to be with a nice guy."

Lily pushed her plate away from her, smiled at Keith and said, "I have an idea. Why don't you take me out to a movie tonight?"

Staring at her in slack-jawed silence, almost as if he hadn't understood what she'd said, Keith resembled a mentally handicapped person. Finally he blinked and shook his head as if to clear it of mental cobwebs. "Are you asking me out on a date?"

"No, silly, I'm asking you to ask me out on a date."

"Lily, I said you deserved a nice guy. I think I've proven that isn't me."

She reached over and squeezed his hand again. "How about you let me decide what I need."

They had been dating for two weeks when Lily showed up at the grocery store where Keith worked part-time as a bag boy to surprise him with hockey tickets. He took a break and walked outside with her.

"Lily, you know I love hockey, but these tickets are for Saturday night," he said.

"Yeah, so?"

"You know that's when I have my anger management classes."

Lily stuck her lower lip out in what her father had always called her *baby doll pout*. "So what? As long as we're together I'm supposed to spend all my Saturday nights alone?"

"With my school and work schedules, that's the only day I can fit it in. I suppose it wouldn't kill me if I skipped one Saturday though."

"Or why don't you skip *every* Saturday?" she said, putting her arms around him. "You told me you already fulfilled your court requirement for beating up the old guy that rear-ended you. You don't need those classes anymore."

"Are you forgetting what I did to Roy?"

"Those were special circumstances; the bastard had it coming. You are stronger than you realize. I'm telling you, you don't need the classes."

Keith looked into her eyes for a moment, biting his lower lip. "You really think I can do it on my own?" he finally asked.

"I'm sure of it. This will be the best thing for both of us, you'll see."

✲ ✲

By the end of the third month, they were living together. There had been no real discussion, but the decision was reached. The change happened gradually as Lily spent more and more of her time away from the dorm and at Keith's small apartment. Finally he told her she should move some of her things in.

He wasn't happy when he got home from work that Friday night, though. He stormed into the bedroom where Lily was placing her various creams, lotions and perfumes on the vanity. "What the hell is going on here?"

She looked up with a bright smile, all innocence and light. "What do you mean?"

"A bunch of my stuff is down by the street. My dresser, several of my lamps, my mattress and bedframe!"

Lily nodded, still smiling. "Yeah, I had the gay couple upstairs help me carry it all down."

Keith looked frantically around the room, as if searching for someone to help him understand his girlfriend's crazy behavior. "Why on earth would you do that?"

"You told me I could move some of my things in, didn't you?"

"Yes, but I didn't mean for you to throw *my* things out."

"Keith, I'm sorry, but there's not enough room in this cramped little place for both our things. Besides, your stuff was so old and beat up I thought you'd be glad to be rid of it."

Keith trembled all over and his face turned as red as a Valentine's heart. He looked like a cartoon character, and Lily almost expected steam to start shooting out of his ears. When it seemed his temper was reaching critical mass, an explosion inevitable, he closed his eyes and took several deep breaths. He didn't open his eyes again until the trembling subsided and his color mostly returned to normal. When he spoke, his words were slow and measured. "I'm sorry, you're right. You should feel at home in the apartment, which means having some of your stuff here. My bed and dresser were in bad shape and probably needed to go, but I did bring up the lamps. They belonged to my grandmother and I want to keep them."

"That's fine," Lily said. "We can put them in a closet or something. And maybe we can buy some new stuff soon that isn't yours or mine, but *ours*."

Keith smiled. "That would be nice."

"I also put some of my towels in the bathroom," she said, gesturing with her right hand, which drew attention to the bandage there.

"What happened?" he asked, his voice dripping with concern.

Lily touched her bandaged hand, a shiver working its way through her body. "Nothing. I burned myself on the stove earlier."

Keith crossed the room, taking her hand gently and delivering a soft kiss to the skin above the bandage. "I'm sorry, babe. You have to be more careful."

A week later, Keith came home unexpectedly right after his afternoon geometry class. Normally he went straight from school to work, but he stepped into the apartment saying, "Babe, I've lost my credit card somewhere. I need to find it before—"

He froze in the doorway. Lily stood in the center of the living room, looking at him sheepishly, like a child caught doing something naughty. But Keith's eyes weren't focused on her; they were zeroed in on the new furniture. Floral patterned sofa with a matching loveseat and recliner.

"Where did this stuff come from?" he asked.

"I bought it."

"With what money?"

With her hands behind her back, Lily twisted from to side, what her father had always called her *I'm so adorable you can't be too mad at me* posture. "Okay, thing is, you didn't lose your credit card. I sort of borrowed it."

"What? You *took* my credit card?"

"You agreed with me when I said we should get some new stuff."

"Yeah, I meant that we would go together and pick it out, make sure it was stuff we both liked and could afford. How much did this stuff cost?"

"Around three hundred," she said.

Keith stumbled over to the loveseat and sat heavily on the new cushion. "That's pretty much my entire credit limit."

"I know, I wanted to get more."

"Where's the old furniture?"

"The guys that delivered the new living room set hauled the old stuff away. It's part of the service the store provides."

Keith leaned over until his head hung between his knees, like he was afraid he was about to pass out or something. "I can barely pay the bills as it is, and now I'm going to have all this credit card debt to pay off."

"Yeah, I wanted to talk to you about that," Lily said, sitting next to him. "You need a better job."

His head whipped up and he fixed her with a poisonous glare. "What?"

"You don't make shit working part-time at the grocery store. If you had a better job, we could afford to move out of this dump to somewhere nicer."

"Well, sorry if this *dump* isn't good enough for you, princess, but my employment options are limited while I'm in school."

"So maybe you shouldn't be in school."

"What are you saying? You want me to drop out?"

"What are you going to do with an English degree anyway?" Lily asked with a derisive snort. "Teach? Bad pay and high stress. Might as well take one of the jobs down at the chemical plant.”

“What the fuck is wrong with you?” Keith screamed, his voice detonating in the apartment like an auditory bomb. “Where is all this coming from?”

“I’m trying to help you better yourself. Excuse me for thinking your life could stand a little improvement. I can see you have trouble showing gratitude.”

“God damn it!” Keith yelled, jumping to his feet and kicking over the end table by the sofa, sending Lily’s Tiffany lamp crashing to the floor where the glass shade shattered. “I need to get to work, I’m already late.”

Lily stood up, hands on her hips. “Are you just going to walk out in the middle of a discussion?”

“Trust me. You don’t want me here right now.”

He flung open the door, which banged so hard against the wall it knocked a framed photo of Keith and Lily off its peg. More shattered glass tinkled to the floor. Before Keith exited, he rammed his fist into the wall and punched a hole through the thin plaster.

Lily slowly lowered herself back the loveseat, her arms wrapped around herself as a shaky breath sighed past her lips. She reached down and idly scratched at her shin.

Even though she was wearing shorts today, Keith had failed to notice all the fresh cuts on her legs.

Lily waited an hour then drove directly to the grocery store. She spotted Keith as soon as she walked through the automatic doors, bagging groceries for a middle-aged woman with flaming red hair and a shirt cut too low for a woman of her age. Keith said something to the woman and she giggled.

"So that's why you ran off in such a hurry," Lily said loudly, stalking over to Keith. "Had to get to work so you could flirt with slutty cougars?"

"I beg your pardon," said the redhead.

"Why don't you keep your mouth and your legs closed for a change, honey?"

"Lily, have you lost your mind?" Keith asked. "What has gotten into you?"

"My eyes are suddenly open, that's all. You don't like my stuff. You get angry when I try to talk to you about ways to make our life better. It's so obvious. The thought of settling down terrifies you."

"This a friend of yours?" asked the lethargic checkout girl, popping gum as she watched the events unfolding before her with a look of ironic detachment.

Lily turned on her. "Why don't you mind your own fucking business?"

This seemed to shake the lethargy from the girl. "When it happens at my register, it *is* my business. And you should watch your mouth before someone punches you in it."

"Keith, are you going to let this skank talk to me like that?"

"Who are you calling a skank?"

"I don't mean to be rude," said the redhead, "but can you all save the soap opera for later so I can get my groceries bagged and get out of here?"

Lily reached into one of the bags, pulled out a nectarine and threw it at the woman. It hit her squarely in the shoulder. "I told you to keep your mouth shut."

Keith was frozen in shock, but the redhead started around the cart, her hands balled into fists.

"What is all this ruckus?" said a pimply faced teenager in a short-sleeve dress shirt and tie, approaching from an office in the far corner. He wore a nametag that identified him as 'Dave—Assistant Manager.'

"Nothing," Keith said quickly. "Just a little misunderstanding."

"Misunderstanding my ass," said the redhead. "This girl came bounding in here hurling insults, and then she assaulted me with my own fruit."

Dave turned to the cashier who blew a large bubble, sucked it back in, nodded and said, "She's a psycho."

"Do you know this person?" Dave asked, addressing Keith.

Keith ducked his head down, ashamed to admit to his association with Lily. "She's my girlfriend."

"I suggest you get her out of the store right this second."

"You can't tell me what to do," Lily said. "I mean, according to Keith you only got the assistant manager position because you sucked and swallowed the manager."

Keith recoiled as if he'd been slapped. "What? No, I never said any such—"

"Come on, you don't have to put up with any shit from this peckerhead. He's every bit the Nancy Boy you said he was. I bet I could even take him."

Dave looked simultaneously furious and hurt. His

voice was low and seething when he turned to Keith and said, "Take her out of here, and don't either of you come back."

"No man, seriously, I don't know what's gotten into her, but—"

"Go!" Dave roared.

"We don't have to go anywhere," Lily said, stepping forward and poking a finger pointedly in Dave's chest.

But then Keith started dragging her by the arm toward the exit. She yanked back, but his grip was like steel. Once outside, he grabbed both her arms, so hard she was certain there would be finger-shaped bruises there tomorrow, and shook her. "Are you fucking insane?" he screamed into her face. "What was that display all about?"

"I saw you talking to that soccer mom cunt in there, and I lost it."

With a growl, Keith shoved her away from him. She slammed into the cement wall of the store, knocking her head against the bricks, and slid to the pavement. Keith advanced on her, looking so much like Roy Vance in that moment that she almost thought she was hallucinating. Before he reached her, however, he suddenly veered to the right. The store was fronted by several stone columns, and he stopped before one and started banging his head against it. Once, twice, three times. Lily could see that his forehead was bleeding but he remained with his head pressed against the rough stone.

"I try to be calm," he murmured to himself. "I try to keep my cool, but you keep pushing me."

"A real man wouldn't let himself be pushed," she spat.

He turned toward her again but still managed to hold himself back. He started beating at the sides of his face with his fists. He was chewing on his lips again, and they were shredded. Blood dribbled down his chin. "I can feel it building up, and I'm so afraid I'm going to explode. I have to go, find somewhere quiet, somewhere to clear my head before I do something stupid. I can't be around you right now."

He started away from her, and she pushed herself up to her feet, probing at the sore spot on the back of her skull. There was no blood but there was a sizable knot that she pressed with her fingers.

"Run away like a fucking baby," she yelled after Keith, but he didn't stop. He rushed to his car and then peeled out of the grocery store's parking lot.

Lily spotted Keith as soon as he stepped into the bedroom, but she didn't let on. She dug her nails into Roy's ass and urged him deeper inside of her. She arched her back and cried out, loud and exaggerated. "You're the best lover I've ever had, Roy. No one can give it to me like you can. I haven't been satisfied since we broke up."

Roy seemed oblivious to the fact that they were no longer alone. He continued to thrust into her hard and brutal, as if his dick was a battering ram. He was so focused on the task at hand he didn't even hear Keith as he let loose with a ferocious roar.

He was across the room in a flash, grabbing Roy by the hair and dragging him off the bed. Still holding him by the hair, Keith punched Roy in the face three times in rapid succession. Blood flew through the air in a spray, along with two teeth. Keith then tossed Roy to the floor. As Lily's ex struggled to get up on his hands and knees, Keith delivered a swift kick to the man's jaw. Roy crawled for the door and Keith followed.

Lily bolted up from the bed and grabbed Keith's arm, tugging on it. "Stop it right this minute. You're going to—"

Keith spun around and delivered a punch to Lily's gut that made her feel as if she were going to vomit everything she'd ever eaten in her entire life. She staggered back, unable to catch her breath, and he followed up the gut punch with a roundhouse to the left side of her head. She crumpled to the floor, a ringing filling her ears that blocked out all other sounds. She saw Keith's foot swinging toward her and braced herself. He caught her in the ribs, making breathing even harder.

He snatched her up by the arm. It felt as if he was going to pull her shoulder out of the socket, and threw her across the bed. She rolled off and crashed into the vanity, bottles of perfume and lotions raining down on her like hailstones. In her periphery she saw Roy snatching up his pants and scrambling out of the room. Not exactly a shining example of chivalry.

Keith towered over her, cords standing out in his neck as he yelled, "You stupid bitch! I have given you everything, my heart and soul. I treated you like a queen, but all you do is tear me down." He punctuated this with a kick to her hip. "Why do you do this to me? Why do you make me want to hurt you?"

Keith fell to his knees, placed his face in his hands, and wept.

WHAT SHE NEEDS

Lily lay on the floor, the glass of the broken bottles all around her, digging into her palms as she tried to push herself up. A long, shuddering moan escaped her as her entire body quaked. Dully, she watched her blood dripping onto the floor.

"I'm so sorry," Keith said over and over, his words muffled by his hands. "God, I'm so sorry. I'm a monster. I promise I'll never lay a hand on you again, I swear on my fucking life."

Still shaking uncontrollably, Lily turned her head away from Keith, facing the wall.

"I'll never do it again," Keith said, this becoming his new mantra. "Never do it again, never do it again, never do it again."

Lily adjusted her body, feeling the dampness between her legs from the orgasm that had swept through her. She moaned again and licked her lips as she was overcome with an aftershock of pleasure. Grinding her hands into the broken glass, her eyelids fluttered and her eyes rolled back in her head.

Behind her Keith was still crying, still promising never to hurt her again, but she knew that he would. She would make sure of it. All the time and effort invested in him was finally paying off.

She was molding him into the kind of man who could give her what she needed.

WELCOME BACK

HEN STEVE CAME down from the attic, he paused in the second floor hallway. He stood by the window and looked out over the street below. Nothing moved this morning. The world was still and deserted—a post-apocalyptic landscape devoid of life. But Steve knew that somewhere out there life did indeed go on. People led their normal lives, going about their regular routines, with no idea of the otherworldly happenings going on right under their noses. Steve envied them their ignorance.

He sighed and placed his hands in the pockets of the oversized jeans he wore, cinched tight with a leather belt to keep them from falling to his knees. He headed down the curving staircase. A thick layer of dust coated the banister, but Steve was not motivated to clean it. This wasn't his house, after all, no matter how many years he'd spent here, and he wasn't going to lift a finger in maintenance of it.

Steve found Al in the living room, reclining on the sofa by the bay window, wearing a pair of sweatpants and a too-tight T-shirt, reading a worn paperback copy of Grisham's *The Firm*. Steve stood on the threshold between the foyer and living room, leaning against the archway, but Al did not acknowledge his presence.

"Isn't this about the third time you've read that book?" Steve finally asked.

Al looked up, annoyance stamped on his face like a tattoo. "Well, considering that most of the shelves in the library are bare and there are only about a dozen books in the house, it's either reread them over and over or read nothing at all. Unless you plan to give up that stupid journal of yours and write some new novels for me to read. Is that what you're planning?"

"Forget I even said anything."

"Gladly," Al said, returning to the book.

Steve turned away and headed down the hall. Things had been strained between him and Al for some time now. Sometimes he thought their relationship started to disintegrate the second they stepped through the door to this house. For the past six months, they had barely been able to stay in the same room without sniping and arguing. They had long since stopped sharing a bed, Steve having moved into one of the guest bedrooms. The love they had felt for one another dried up over the years, until not even the memory of it existed. He was pretty sure Al hated him, in some way blaming Steve for the situation in which they found themselves. As for Steve, he didn't hate Al; he felt nothing for the man. And yet they were stuck here together, incapable of separating any farther than a few rooms.

Steve went into the library and sat down at the roll-top secretary's desk. He opened the bottom right drawer and pulled out a small ledger with a faded red cover.

He had happened across a stash of ledgers and notebooks in the main bedroom's closet about a week after their initial arrival at the house. He couldn't believe that none of the other occupants had ever written in them, but perhaps they had *appeared*, like the food in the refrigerator and cabinets.

Opening the ledger to the first fresh page, about a third of the way through, he grabbed a pen from the penholder. He didn't write in the journal every day. Some months he only made one or two entries, others almost a dozen. Al made fun of him for keeping the journal, and Steve had to admit he wasn't sure why he did it. He just figured there should be some type of record of what was happening here, a memorial to the events that had led them to be in this house.

Steve put the date, his best estimate, in the upper right corner, the pen point making a pleasant *scritch-scritch* on the thick paper. It had been almost a month since his last entry in the journal. It was hard to come up with new things to write when everyday was a variation of the one before it, but writing to some unknown reader, a reader that only existed in his imagination, made Steve feel he had some tenuous connection with the world outside.

Bending over the ledger, Steve started his latest entry.

Al and I have been here for approximately five years now, stuck in this house. Trapped. Prisoners. Since the day our car broke down across the street and we came to the door of

this house, seeking assistance. Sometimes it seems like it happened only yesterday, that the past five years have sped by so quickly. Other times it feels like we've been here forever, that we should have long white beards by now. Today it feels like the latter. When I try to think of what my life was before I came here, before these walls became a tomb for the living, all I can get are wisps of memories, insubstantial pieces that are jumbled and fuzzy. That other life no longer seems real.

For the first year I believed that the house could be beaten, that there must be some loophole, and if I only searched diligently enough, I would find the way out. But what the previous occupants—prisoners—of the house told us proved to be true.

The house will not let us go.

The windows will not break, not even after I spent hours banging on them. The thresholds of the front and back doors cannot be crossed; an invisible barrier preventing exit. Even when I see people outside, passing by on the street, I am invisible to them. I stand at the open door, screaming until my lungs burn. I wave my hands to get their attention until my arms feel like they might fall off. But it is as if I'm not even there. No one seems to hear or see me.

The second year, my quest for escape became more sporadic. Months would pass in complacency, then for weeks I would systematically test the house for weaknesses.

After I had exhausted myself in futile attempts at freedom, I would sink once again into apathy.

By the third year, I stopped trying altogether.

Al's reaction to the situation surprised me. He drew into himself immediately, taking on a fatalistic attitude. He would watch as I tried to penetrate the house's confines, not bothering to offer any help, and tell me it was hopeless and that I was wasting my time. I couldn't understand how he could give up so completely without at least trying. Maybe it was because he was such a fan of horror movies. He accepted the supernatural component of our predicament more easily. In any case, he recognized the truth long before I did.

There is only one way out of this house. Someone has to take our place.

The people before us had been trapped in the house for two and a half years before Al and I showed up on the doorstep. Once we walked inside, they were freed and we were imprisoned. Our only hope is for someone to come to the door and step over the threshold of his or her free will. That would release us and ensnare whoever was unlucky enough to happen across this hell house.

The idea of condemning someone to the torment I now know is unthinkable, but is it as unthinkable as spending the rest of my life in this house?

I'm not sure.

Steve was in the kitchen when the doorbell rang.

Al had gone up to take a nap an hour before and Steve decided to make a sandwich and possibly write some more in his journal. With no television, stereo, video games, or computer, there was a distinct lack of ways to pass the time. On the top shelf of a hall closet were a dozen or so board games, but Al and Steve couldn't stand to be around one another long enough to play a full game anymore. Steve sat at the counter, his half-eaten roast beef sandwich in his hand as he contemplated a new hobby to fill up the endless hours. The doorbell rang, an unfamiliar *ding-dong* that did not compute after the persistent silence. *Ding-dong*. By the second ring, he sprung to his feet quickly, the barstool clattering on the floor. Several minutes passed like tiny eternities, and he was beginning to believe that he had in fact imagined it when the doorbell rang a third time.

Steve was out of the kitchen and headed down the hall before he even realized he was moving. The implications of the doorbell were not lost on him, but they were simply too great for his mind to encompass at the moment. This could be his very freedom at the door, but he couldn't think about that. His body acted on pure instinct, operating on autopilot as he came into the foyer and pulled open the front door. He stared straight ahead, when his eyesight adjusted, he dropped his gaze down.

A young boy stood on the doorstep, surely no older than twelve years old, holding a box of chocolate bars.

"Hi," he said, wearing a bright smile. "My name's Evan. I'm going around the neighborhood selling candy bars. All the money goes to buy new uniforms for my little league team."

Steve didn't say anything, *couldn't* say anything. His mind was in a fog, unable to fight through it to form a coherent thought.

The boy shifted uncomfortably outside the door. He glanced over his shoulder at the street then back at Steve. "They're a dollar a piece. Do you want any?"

"Um, how much are they?"

"A dollar a piece," the boy said again. "Maybe this is a bad time."

"Maybe," Steve said softly, his voice without inflection. "Maybe you ought to go now."

"What's going on?" Al asked, coming down the staircase. He paused halfway to the bottom, his jaw going slack upon seeing the boy on the doorstep. He recovered from his shock quickly, faster than Steve, and hurried the rest of the way down the stairs. "Do we have a visitor?"

"He was just leaving."

"What? Don't be silly. What have you got there, boy? Candy?"

"Yes, sir. I'm selling them to raise money for new uniforms for my little league team."

Al peered into the box in the boy's hands. He was certainly playing it cool. Steve had to admire his level-headedness. He knew that Al must be dying to get the boy to walk over the threshold, but he was maintaining his composure to keep from frightening the boy away.

"I could certainly go for some chocolate right about

now," Al said. "I'll tell you what, how about if I take about ten or so of those bars off your hands."

The boy's eyes widened. "Ten? That would be awesome, mister. The kid who sells the most candy bars gets a brand new baseball mitt."

"Really? In that case, maybe I should buy fifteen."

"Oh man, I'd really appreciate that."

"Well, I have to get my money. Why don't you come on in and—"

"Wait!" Steve said suddenly, the fog finally lifting from his brain as he realized what was about to happen. "Al, can I talk to you for a minute?"

Al shot Steve such a sharp look that Steve was surprised it didn't draw blood. "Can't it wait?"

"No, it can't." Without waiting for further argument, Steve grabbed Al by the arm and dragged him through the archway into the living room, leaving the boy standing on the doorstep.

"What the hell's the matter with you?" Al hissed, keeping his voice low.

"We can't do this."

"Do what? Get the hell out of here? Of course we can. It's what we've been hoping for every single day for the last five years."

"Al, he's a kid."

"So? Are you saying we somehow *deserve* to be here and he doesn't?"

"No, that's not what I'm saying. It's just that—"

"I'm sick of being here," Al said with such vehemence that his entire body trembled. "And I know you are, too. This is it, our 'Get out of Jail Free' card. We have to take it."

"I understand how you feel, I really do, but he's a

kid. We can't leave a kid trapped in this house by himself. It wouldn't be right."

"Nothing about this situation is right. Nothing about this is fair."

"Could you really live with yourself if you walked away and left the kid here?"

"Yes."

Steve looked into the other man's eyes and realized he meant it. Al had become a stranger, and it frightened him.

"You can play the martyr if you want," Al said, "but I'm taking this opportunity and getting the fuck out of this house. This may be the last chance we have."

"Al, please, listen to me for a—"

"Excuse me, are you guys gonna buy any candy bars or what?"

Steve and Al turned to find the boy standing in the foyer, outside the archway. While they had been arguing, the boy had walked into the house, dooming himself. Steve felt his heart shudder in his chest and hot tears filled his eyes.

Al let out a whoop of laughter, pushed roughly past the boy and stood before the open door. He reached out a hand, slowly, cautiously. He seemed to hesitate then plunged his arm through the doorway. It passed through easily and unobstructed. A sob erupted from his throat like a belch. Al followed his arm through the doorway until he was standing outside on the stoop. He sagged against the outside wall of the house, a mixture of laughter and tears tearing through him.

Steve stepped up to the doorway. He wanted to reach through it as Al had done, but he resisted the urge.

"Steve, come on," Al said, taking an uncertain step away from the house, as if he didn't quite trust his newfound freedom. "Come with me. Hurry. The barrier may only be gone for a short time."

Steve stood where he was, just inside the doorway. He wanted to go, he wanted to leap outside and run hand-in-hand with Al down the street. He wanted to find other people, touch them, talk to them. But he couldn't.

"I'm staying," Steve said in a quavering voice.

Al sputtered a laugh. "You're shitting me, right?"

"No, I'm serious. I can't leave, not with the boy here. He will need someone to take care of him."

"He's not an infant. He's practically a teenager. He'll be fine."

"You were right," Steve said. "Nothing about this is right or fair. I won't leave him here alone. I would never be able to forgive myself."

Al's jaw clenched and his expression turned steely. "So what are you saying? That I'm a terrible person?"

"We all do what we have to do, Al."

"Well, if only I could be as evolved as you, Steve. Suit yourself. You want to stay here and play mommy to some brat who will only grow to hate you for what you've done to him, go right ahead. Me, I'm doing the smart thing and getting as far away from here as possible."

Without another word or so much as a goodbye, Al turned and ran down the curved drive to the street. He did not look back as he sprinted away from the house, finally disappearing around a twist in the road.

Steve turned and found the boy staring at him, his expression suggesting that he thought he had stepped into a den of lunatics. If he only knew the half of it.

"Mister, if you're not going to buy any candy bars, I really need to get going."

Steve smiled. "What did you say your name was again?"

"Evan."

"Okay, Evan. My name is Steve. We have some stuff we need to talk about."

With one final glance outside, Steve sighed and closed the door.

KINDRED SPIRIT
(Co-authored with Shane Nelson)

VANESSA SMALL LOOKED up from the computer screen and said, "Who's M. Hunter?"

Her husband Richard was at one of the bookcases in the corner, trying to make room on the already overburdened shelves for the new books he'd purchased earlier in the day. He slid a paperback into a space he'd created—it was a tight fit, but he managed to squeeze it in—and said, "What?"

"There's an email here from mhunter@coolmail.com."

"Oh, that's for me. Save it and I'll read it when you're done."

Vanessa frowned at the screen. She and her husband shared an email account, and she was familiar with the email addresses of all Richard's friends and co-workers. This one was new to her. "Who's it from?"

"A new friend."

"A new friend? Where'd you meet him . . . or her?"

Richard smiled at his wife, coming over to kiss her. "No need to get jealous. It's a *him*. His name's Mace Hunter, I met him online."

"Oh, I see?" Vanessa said with a raise of her eyebrows. "My husband is meeting men on the internet. That certainly makes me feel better. What's next, I'm going to catch you watching *Cabaret*?"

"Ha-ha, very funny, Ness. I met him on that book message board I post on. We seemed to have similar taste in fiction so we started chatting. Turns out he's a writer, too."

"Oh, really? Published?"

"About like me. Some limited success in smaller markets, but most of the big publications still thinks he sucks."

"Where's he from?"

"Washington."

"State or D.C.?"

Richard frowned and pushed his glasses up his nose with a forefinger. "You know, I'm not sure. We haven't talked much about our personal lives, mostly books and writing."

"Have you read any of his work?"

"Yeah, we've traded a few short stories."

"Is he any good?"

"Honestly, he's a hell of a lot more talented than I am."

"I'll take that with a grain of salt."

"What do you mean by that?"

"You're your own harshest critic, Rich. You're much too hard on yourself."

"Well, Mace has given me some very positive feedback on the pieces I've sent him, which makes me feel good."

"I've always told you your stuff is great."

"Oh, I know, I'm not discounting your opinion or

anything, but it's nice to hear from someone else who's serious about writing, who's also pursuing it as a career."

"Sounds nice," Vanessa said, turning back to the computer, checking through her emails. "Did I tell you I finally sold the McKenzie's a house? We close next Thursday."

"That's great, Ness. The one on Magnolia Street?"

"No," Vanessa said with a sigh. "They settled on a two-story Victorian on Scottsdale Avenue."

"You don't sound too thrilled about it."

"That house is listed with Heathcliff Realty, which means I'll have to split the commission with Margie Crews."

"Well, half a commission is better than none."

"Okay, all done here," Vanessa said, pushing away from the desk. She left the email account open. "You can read your message from your boyfriend now."

"You're a riot," Richard said, swatting Vanessa on the butt as she passed him on her way out of the office. Richard sat down at the desk and clicked on the message from Mace.

TO: thesmalls@gmail.com

FROM: mhunter@coolmail.com

SUBJECT: Feedback

Richard, I read the story you sent me, 'And This Too Shall Pass.' I think this piece has a lot of potential. You create an ominous atmosphere right from the beginning, and an escalating sense of dread throughout the narrative. I do, however, have a couple of suggestions on how you could make this story stronger. The character of Aunt Ursula comes across as a tad schizophrenic. She is portrayed at alternate times as a senile old woman, a wise sage, a busybody, and comedic relief. A little more consistency of character is needed, I feel. Also, the implausibly happy ending seems tacked on to me. I almost feel like you were going for something darker then decided to pull your punches at the last minute. The ending as it now stands undercuts the power of the whole piece. My advice would be to not introduce the dues ex machina at the end and allow the couple to remain apart with their lives fucked up. I do think the story was very well written, with a tight, fast pace, and I definitely recommend you submit this one.

For that matter, you should be doing much more submitting than you presently are. You're a damned fine writer, and if you had a little more confidence in your own ability and would get your work out there, I think you'd be quite successful.

And what about that novel idea you mentioned in your last email, the thing about the shape shifters . . . have you started it yet? It sounds intriguing, and I'd love to read whatever you've got written. Well, I'm going to get back to work. I should finish up this new story tonight and I'll send it your way.

Mace

KINDRED SPIRIT

TO: mhunter@coolmail.com

FROM: thesmalls@gmail.com

SUBJECT: Unproductive

Hey Mace, good to hear from you. Thanks for the feedback on 'And This Too Shall Pass.' You really picked up on some of the story's weaknesses. The reason Aunt Ursula seems so all-over-the-place is because she is actually a composite of several characters I excised from the piece. As usual with my stuff, the story started to get a bit unwieldy and bloated, so I removed two characters and gave some of their traits and dialogue to Aunt Ursula, creating the multiple personality effect. As for the ending, the original version was much darker with Peter actually murdering Fiona instead of letting her live without him, but Ness hated that ending. So I went back and added the discovery of the letter Ursula had written before her death and the subsequent tearful reunion.

Ness liked that ending a lot better, but truthfully it bothers me, too. Maybe I'll send you the original version to see what you think of it. I'm afraid I haven't had a chance to start on the novel, or even any new short stories for that matter.

It's been a busy time at the paper. The other guy in my department quit, so for the moment I'm the only one writing obituaries for *The Granger Gazette*. At least I get to work mostly from home, but it doesn't leave me with as much time to write as I'd like.

Then again, I remember reading stories of how King would work long hours in an industrial laundry then write in the basement at night. Maybe I'm not dedicated enough. I mean, I'm 35 years old; by the time King was my age, he was already a best-selling author. What have I done? Sold a handful of stories to publications that don't even pay professional rates. I better stop before I depress myself. If all these old people in town will stop dying—ha-ha—then maybe I'll be able to start something new. And this weekend I'm going to take some time to polish up some of my stuff and get it out there, as you said. Thanks for the encouragement.

'Til later.

Rich

P.S. Are you in Washington State or D.C?

Early evening twilight filtered through the office windows when Ness got home. Richard barely heard the muffled sound of the door closing. His fingers tapped eagerly at the computer keys, eyes tracking the words he wrote. His face seemed bleached in the glow of the computer screen. Ness arrived in the office doorway, a briefcase in one hand. She had to call Richard's name twice before he reluctantly drew back from the computer.

"Hey," Richard said, leaning back in his chair and smiling at his wife. "Didn't hear you come in."

"You must've forgotten I was coming home," Ness said, irritation edging into her voice. "No supper tonight?"

"Oh, damn!" Richard said. He removed his glasses and began to clean them with his shirt. When he put them back on, he looked at the clock. Seven-fifteen. "God, babe, I lost track of time."

He got to his feet and quickly crossed to where Ness stood, impatiently tapping one foot. He took the briefcase from her hand and set it aside. "Tell you what, I'll order in Chinese. You can eat then take a nice hot bath." He stroked her jaw, pushing back her hair.

She smiled. "And a foot rub?"

Richard grinned. "Of course."

"I'll take that bath now." Ness sighed. "Delivery will take at least forty minutes."

"Great," Richard said. Cradling the back of his wife's neck, he gave her a lingering kiss. She blinked in surprise.

"My, my," she said. "What's gotten into you?"

Richard kissed her again and said, "I feel inspired."

"Food's on the way," Richard said.

Vanessa had submerged herself in a tub full of white suds, her head laid back upon the end of the bathtub. Her eyes were closed, dark sooty lashes against her cheeks. She moved slightly, the water rippling, and sighed.

"Wonderful," she said.

Richard sat on the edge of the tub and listened while Ness told him about her day. It had been hectic, with three clients who insisted on seeing everything in the city. Richard listened attentively, waiting for his wife to run out of steam. Ordinarily she didn't ask about his day and he didn't offer—Richard found that trying to talk writing with anyone who wasn't a writer was akin to banging your head against a wall. Today, however, he was bursting with enthusiasm.

"I'm sorry about supper," he said. "I got so caught up in my writing that I lost track of time."

Ness made an inarticulate sound of acknowledgement—*hmm mmm*—and Richard continued.

"You remember that story I wrote, 'And This Too Shall Pass'? Well, Mace had some terrific feedback and I made a few changes today. I really feel like I've got a winner now. And I started two more stories today—*two*—and I usually have trouble keeping one on the go. I haven't felt this inspired since I was a kid. Back then it seemed like writing was *it*, you know? I love that feeling."

Richard had hoped Ness would open her eyes and express her pleasure at his happiness. Instead she gently waved a hand in the water, making soft splashes, and said, "That's nice."

Richard sighed.

Ness opened her eyes and looked at him. "What?"

"Nothing," Richard said. He got to his feet, knees popping. Suddenly the computer in his office seemed to beckon. "I think I'll do a bit more writing before the food gets here."

"Hold on," Ness said, sitting up in the tub. "Something's wrong. What is it?"

Richard breathed another sigh. "It's just that . . . " He found himself stumbling again, as he always did when he tried to discuss his writing with Vanessa. She couldn't understand the fear, frustration and passion. That was what made Mace so great.

"Just that what?"

"I feel like you don't understand my writing and how I feel about it," Richard said. "I know I'm not that good at making it easy to understand, but I wish you got it a bit more. You know . . . the passion I feel."

"I get it, Richard. Really, I do. I mean, I'm not a writer so I can't really relate, but I know how much you love it. It's great that you had a good day and got carried away with your stories. I only wish you hadn't gotten carried through supper."

"That's the thing," Richard said. He crouched by the tub again and reached into the warm water, touching Ness's shoulder, seeking connection. "*Passion* does that. It makes you forget about the world around you. I haven't felt that for my writing in *so* long. I was so happy, and I wanted to share it with you."

"I'm glad," Ness said.

"Writing is all I've ever wanted to do," Richard explained. Ness was listening now. "For as long as I can remember. Didn't you ever have a real, honest-to-God passion?"

"Well," Ness said, "I love you. That's passion."

"I don't mean that. I mean, isn't there a part of you, independent of everything else, that *defines* you? Something you've always felt, loved and known about?"

"I don't know what you mean."

Richard drew his hands out of the water and stood. As he dried his hands, he said, "Okay. Real Estate. It's what you do, right? But have you always wanted to do it? Did you dream about it as a kid?"

Ness laughed. "Of course not."

"That's the difference. Writing . . . I dreamed about that. It isn't what I do, but who I am."

Ness's face was still red and dreamy from her bath and Richard had no idea if she understood what he was saying. He meant to say more, to make it clear how important it was to put passion above everything else, when the downstairs doorbell chimed. Richard's mouth hung open, words about to be spoken.

"That's the food," Ness said.

"Right," Richard said, heading for the bathroom door. Behind him, Ness closed her eyes and submerged herself deep into the warm water.

Richard was hunkered down in front of his computer screen, soft lamplight spilling over one shoulder. He and Ness had finished supper a few hours earlier. After the leftovers were put into the fridge and the containers into the trash, Richard came upstairs to continue with his writing. Now Ness had found him, calling his name and drawing him out of his make-believe world.

"Hey, babe," Richard said, spinning around in his chair and pushing his glasses up on the bridge of his nose.

Ness wore a silk negligee that highlighted her figure. Her hair fell loose around her shoulders.

"You've been in here forever," she said. "I thought I might get that foot rub before bed." She smiled teasingly.

"I want to wrap up what I'm doing. Okay?"

Ness came over to the computer and peered over Richard's shoulder. He felt a twinge of annoyance, as if his privacy were being intruded upon. It passed, however, when Ness put a hand on his shoulder and said, "Wow! You really have been working."

"That's what I told you."

She read a few lines. "This is really good. Is it new?"

Richard tapped his fingers absently on the keyboard. "Uh huh."

She stepped away from the computer. "Well, I'm glad you've had such a productive day. But . . . it's getting late. Will you come to bed soon?"

Richard nodded. "Right away. Promise."

Ness leaned down and kissed him. "I'll be waiting."

After she'd gone, Richard swung his chair around again. The words on the screen glowed. In the past, even the slightest interruption had been an excuse to stop writing. Now, however, he easily slipped back into his story, finding the rhythm without so much as a missed step.

The next time he leaned back in his chair and glanced at the clock, he was shocked to see that it was almost two a.m. Ness would be fast asleep by now. Richard felt a moment of guilt—he'd promised her that he would be coming to bed right away. Still, the guilt was assuaged by his sense of success and joy. God! It had been so long since the writing had been this good.

He saved his work for the night and reached out to turn off the computer. After a moment, he reconsidered and opened up his email program.

TO: <u>mhunter@coolmail.com</u>

FROM: <u>thesmalls@gmail.com</u>

SUBJECT: What a day!

Hey Mace, how's it going?

I just wrapped up the most incredible day of writing and I wanted to share it with someone. I finished up the revisions on 'And This Too Shall Pass.' I think that you were on the money with your suggestions. I'll send you a copy and you can let me know what you think. I want to submit this one soon, as I feel good about it. And, believe it or not, I started two more stories today! This is coming from the guy who used to spend two weeks on one story. I think I have your influence to thank for the great output. I haven't finished either of them yet, but when I do I'm going to share them with you (if you want to read them, that is). But . . . the point is, this was a pretty productive day. I don't know how things are going to go tomorrow. I've got a lot on my plate with the *Gazette* and I know that it's going to eat up most of my potential writing time. I guess that's the curse of the working class. Maybe I'll get lucky and they'll bring someone else in to shoulder some of the load. As I said before, at least I work from home.

Thanks for the support and kind words regarding my writing. I try hard and I know I have the skills . . . but I need to focus now on discipline and dedication. As long as I have you standing in my shadow (or is it the other way around, ha-ha?), keeping me on track, things will work out. Also, it's nice to have someone to talk to about all of this. I tried to explain my feelings to Ness tonight, but she doesn't get it. She wants to, and I think she thinks she does, but she can't fully understand. I think it's only something us hacks can get, right? You're a writer like me and I think you really get where I'm coming from. It helps to have someone to share things with.

Anyhow, I should get to bed. Ness is already fast asleep (and she'll likely be pretty upset at my late hours). I have to get up to work in the morning. In a perfect world, I could get up and go right back to my writing. But, I guess the only truly perfect worlds are the ones we make up.

I'll talk to you again tomorrow.

Rich

TO: thesmalls@gmail.com

FROM: mhunter@coolmail.com

SUBJECT: Different Angle of Attack

Rich, it's great to hear that you kicked some major ass today! I knew you had it in you if you got yourself on the right (or is that write?) track. You'll have to send me the revised version of, 'And This Too Shall Pass.' I think that if you did it the way I think you should have, I know of a great magazine where it might find a home. Send me the other two whenever you get the chance. I've only read a bit of your writing, but I'm already a die-hard fan, and I think you know that.

Sorry to hear that your wife doesn't get how you feel about writing. Believe me, I haven't found a single person who can relate. They seem to look at me with this blank, expectant expression, as if I am either fucking nuts, or talking another language. It's probably even harder with a wife, who should know you inside and out. Oh well, you can't have everything in common with someone, even a spouse. But thanks for sharing with me. If you ever have something that's sticking in your brain, feel free to dump it on me. We might only know one another online, but I feel a real connection between us, Rich. Hell, I don't have many close friends in the 'real' world . . . why not find someone in cyberspace.

And man, do I know about work interfering with what I'm meant to be doing. Half the time I am kicking my own ass to keep things moving, and the rest of the time someone else seems to be kicking it for me. You know what I'd recommend? Another angle of attack. Instead of letting your job work against you, let it work *for* you. I mean . . . you work at home, right? Hammering out obits for a bunch of dead folks? Hell, push that stuff aside when you can and focus on your writing. The other stuff will get done. I say put what's important first. Fuck the rest. What's the worst they can do? Fire you from a job that sucks?

I've sent along my latest story. It's a bit more violent

than I had planned, but I think the ending makes it work. Let me know what you think, as I value your advice.

All right, I'll talk to you again later. Keep writing!

Mace

Vanessa awoke gradually, rolling over and reaching out an arm for Rich. His side of the bed was empty. Empty and cold. In the darkness, her eyes sought out the digital alarm clock on the dresser. It was past midnight. She had come to bed before ten, leaving Rich in the computer room. For the fifth night in a row, he had promised to follow her to bed shortly, but she'd fallen asleep alone. Again.

With a grunt of irritation, she kicked the covers aside and swung her legs out of bed. The uncarpeted floor was cold against her bare feet, and she rummaged around under the bed until she came out with her slippers. Navigating the dark room like a blind person, she stumbled out into the hall and headed for the computer room at the opposite end. The door was closed, which was unusual, but light seeped out from underneath.

Ness tried to remain calm, but this was getting ridiculous. She knew that Richard liked to write, and she supported that—hell, she'd bought extra copies of all the little rinky-dink magazines that published his stories over the years and sent them to her parents in Ohio—but this was starting to border on obsession. Even when they'd first met in college, when Richard had boasted dreams of being the next Stephen King, dreams that had been considerably downsized since then, he had never been this compulsive about his writing. It was silly, but she felt neglected, as if he were having an affair with his fictional characters. And it could all be traced back to when he'd started corresponding with that damn Mace Hunter.

Vanessa opened the door without knocking, but Richard didn't even notice. He was stooped over the computer, his face too close to the glowing screen, his fingers flying across the keys like tap-dancing spiders. For a fleeting moment she wondered if he was looking up internet porn, but she could clearly see the screen and the word processing program was opened and half-filled with text. In a weird way, she'd almost prefer to discover him wanking off to dirty pictures online. At least that would be something she could understand.

"Richard," she said, her voice not penetrating her husband's trance at all. "Rich!" she said more loudly.

Rich jerked and let out a startled squeak, looking around with a guilty expression that quickly turned into anger. "Damn it, Ness, what are you doing in my office?"

"*Your* office? Excuse me, but last I checked this was *our* computer room, a computer we share and which I paid half of."

The anger remained on Richard's face for another few seconds, but it faded in the heat of Ness's own anger. "I'm sorry," he said with a weary sigh, raking a hand over his face. "It's just, you know, a man needs a place to work. Some place all his own where he can have a little privacy and solitude."

"Like Superman's Fortress of Solitude, you mean?" Vanessa asked, smiling, using the joke as a peace offering.

Rich's lopsided smile, the one she had fallen in love with, surfaced. "Yeah, something like that. What are you doing up so late?"

"I could certainly ask you the same question. These late nights are beginning to become a habit. If you're not careful, I'm going to get used to having that big old bed all to myself."

"God, I hope not," Rich said, holding out a hand to his wife. When she took it, he pulled her into his lap and kissed her. "I'm sorry if you're feeling lonely, but I'm on a hot streak lately. I think I'm finally ready to start that novel I've been talking about for the past year and a half."

"Is that what you're working on now?" Vanessa asked, glancing at the computer.

"Oh, uh, no. This is actually for the paper."

"For the *Gazette*? Why are you working on this stuff so late?"

"Gus needs these three obits first thing in the morning so he can get them ready for the Wednesday edition."

Ness glanced back at the computer screen then frowned at her husband. "I thought you were going to finish up those obituaries this afternoon while I was working the Phelner's open house."

"I was, but . . . "

"But what?"

"Well, I got this email from Mace—"

"Here we go again with Mace."

"— and he sent me a new story of his, and it was so

good that it kind of got me inspired. I started on another new story, which will make it the third one I've written this week, and time sort of got away from me and I didn't get to the obits."

"Rich," Vanessa said, bolting out of his lap and pacing around the room. "What is the matter with you?"

"Nothing's the matter with me, Ness. I simply decided to spend the afternoon working, that's all."

"No, Rich, that's the point. You *weren't* working. You were writing your little stories *instead of* working."

"My writing is my work," Richard said, his mouth set in a hard line. "I know you don't understand that—"

"Your writing doesn't put food on the table, Richard. Your job at the *Gazette* does. Do you want to get fired?"

"No one's going to get fired, quit being such a goddamn drama queen," Richard growled. "The obits aren't due 'til the morning, and they'll be done by then."

"And you'll have to stay up all night to get them finished. You know I'm taking tomorrow off, and I hoped we could spend some time together. Instead, you'll be sleeping the day away. I feel like we're becoming strangers, Rich. I never get to see you anymore."

"You see me all the time."

"I see you, but we don't interact. You're always planted in front of that computer."

Richard breathed deeply through his nostrils, the air pushing out in a loud gust. "I'm sorry if it upsets you that I've gotten back in touch with the writer in me. I was stupid enough to hope that you would be happy that I was finally excited about my work again. And even though you don't see it, my writing *is* my work. The job at the paper is just what I do to make ends meet while I try to get my writing career off the ground."

"Your writing *career*?" Ness laughed cruelly. She felt herself on the verge of saying things she knew she'd regret later, but she was past the point of censoring herself. "How much money have you made off your writing in the past year, Rich? A couple hundred dollars? Yeah, some career."

"It would be all about the money with you, wouldn't it? A woman with no passion. A woman who picked her career simply for the financial rewards. You don't understand the passion I feel for my—"

"Great, here we go again with this talk about *passion*. Come on, Richard, you're a writer; certainly you can come up with another word. Want me to get you a thesaurus?"

Richard's face turned a deep shade of red, almost purple. Then Rich's face crumpled, sagging as if it were melting wax, and he buried his face in his hands and started to cry. Not discreet weeping, either, but big snotty sobs.

Vanessa's anger evaporated instantly. Shame took its place. She'd never seen Richard cry before, not even at his father's funeral. She knelt next to her husband, her hand hovering above his shoulder, wanting to touch him but not sure if she should.

"I'm so sorry, Richard," she said softly, tears of her own spilling down her cheeks. "I didn't mean to get so upset. Please forgive me."

Richard looked up at his wife, and in that moment he seemed like a child, lost in a busy shopping mall and crying for his mother. "I don't mean to make you feel like I'm neglecting you, Ness. Really, I don't. I forgot how good writing could make me feel, how much I needed it. I was slowly dying without it."

"I know, I know, honey. It's okay. I realize now how much this means to you."

"It means the world to me, Ness," Richard said, grabbing Vanessa's hands with a frightening desperation. "I *need* this. I haven't been myself without it. And I want to share it with you, I do. If you'll bear with me for a bit, allow me to find my rhythm, it will all work itself out. I promise."

"Okay, Rich, I believe you. Are you okay?"

"Yeah," Richard said with a sputtering, embarrassed laugh. "Sorry for the outburst. I'm tired, but I really have to finish this before the morning."

"What if I go make a pot of coffee?"

"That would be great, babe. Thanks."

Vanessa kissed Rich, wiping a few stray tears from his face, and left the room to go make the coffee. Halfway down the stairs, she heard the computer room door shut and latch. Seeing Richard in such a state had scared her and she vowed to try to be more sympathetic toward him. But something nagged at the back of her mind. Richard had said that he *needed* this newly reawakened infatuation with writing. That he hadn't been himself without it. She couldn't help but wonder, if he hadn't been himself without it, who had she been married to for the past fourteen years?

TO: <u>mhunter@coolmail.com</u>

FROM: <u>thesmalls@gmail.com</u>

SUBJECT: Big blow up

Hey Mace, I really loved the story you sent me yesterday. It is the kind of fiction that exhilarates me while at the same time eating me up with envy. I only wish I could create something as impressive. Your use of language is astounding, and I continue to be amazed by your talent at creating settings so real that I can see them in every detail. I feel so many of my stories take place in a generic void, but you create a sense of place that is vivid and believable. If you can't find a home for this story, then there is no hope for the rest of us.

I started a new story after reading yours. It's kind of a nasty little horror piece called, 'The Thorn House.' Reminds me of the type of stuff I used to write in college. Lately all I've been doing are those slice-of-life vignettes, but I have missed the horror genre. I can thank you for returning me to my first love. I was feeling pretty good today, until . . .

Well, Ness and I had a huge fight. She said some pretty hurtful things, but I probably wasn't too kind myself. She seems to resent my writing, which I find baffling. She treats it as a hobby or a past-time; she doesn't understand that it's a necessity for me, as much as breathing or eating. I've tried to explain it until I'm blue in the face, and I don't have the energy anymore. We made up, smoothed things over, but I feel like there is this gulf opening between us. Writing is my greatest joy in life, I hate that it is causing problems in my marriage. I'm hoping that things will get better as she sees how much happier I am now that I've rediscovered my passion for the craft. It seems impossible that I've never asked, but are you married? If so, is she supportive of your writing?

By the way, I submitted 'And This Too Shall Pass' to the publication you suggested. I'm eager to hear back. Thanks to your suggestions and recommendations, I feel good about that piece, and I think it stands a good chance at acceptance. Normally, I wouldn't submit to a magazine as prestigious as *Dark Corner of the Mind*; I mean, they publish big-named authors who've sold millions of books; what would they want with a story from a nobody like me? But you've really helped boost my confidence, so why not give it a shot? Well, I'm exhausted. I stayed up quite late writing obits, so I'm going to take a nap. Ness wants to go see a movie tonight, and I don't want to disappoint her.

Rich

TO: thesmalls@gmail.com

FROM: mhunter@coolmail.com

SUBJECT: Single and carefree

Hey Rich, sorry to hear about your row with your

wife. I was married once, but I ended it a while back. She didn't understand me at all, wanted me to give up writing and do something that made more money. A real bitch, my ex was. Still is, I'm sure, but I no longer have to put up with it. It's hard living with someone who doesn't understand you. The way I see it, writing is too important to me to spend my life with someone who couldn't appreciate how vital it is. If she didn't love my writing, then she didn't love me because there is no separation between my art and the man I am.

I think you stand a good shot at getting 'And This Too Shall Pass' accepted. *Dark Corner of the Mind* was the first publication to give me a substantial paycheck a few years back. I'm still not where I want to be, but I know that if I persevere, I will find the success I know I deserve. And so will you, you have to stick to your guns and WORK WORK WORK! Don't let anything—or *anyone*—stand in your way. If you ever need anyone to talk to, I'm here for you. I will always have an understanding shoulder to lean on and I'll give you the straight dope, as they say.

Don't forget about that novel. The longer you put it off, the harder it will be to start. The idea sounds like a winner. You have at least one person here who wants to read it. I know life gets busy and shit comes up, but you know what I say. FUCK IT! The story comes first, everything else is secondary. Keep me posted on 'And This Too Shall Pass,' and I'll be in touch.

Mace

The email from *Dark Corner of the Mind* came at two in the afternoon, as Richard was about to start doing his work for the *Gazette*. An early afternoon rain pattered against the office windows in a reluctant rhythm. Richard saw the message sitting in his inbox, docile and benign, and felt his stomach drop and his heart speed up.

Setting aside his cold beer—it was early for a beer, but hell, it was past five somewhere—Richard opened the message. It was from Brian Chance, editor. The email was brief and to the point. The part of it that really struck Richard was the line: *We would be very pleased to publish your story, 'And This Too Shall Pass,' in our upcoming winter issue.* Below that line were a few pleasantries and some suggested revisions. *Minor* revisions.

Richard beamed. He felt light-headed and giddy, the twenty-eight year old Richard who had sold his first short story. He'd picked that acceptance up at the post office and walked in a daze all the way home. Back then he had been elated by his first sale, even if it was for nothing more than a publishing credit and two contributor's copies.

This sale meant even more. It was a foot in the proverbial door. *Dark Corner of the Mind* paid professional rates. Doing a rough calculation, Richard estimated he would be paid somewhere in the neighborhood of seven hundred dollars for this story.

"Holy shit," he said aloud.

He read the email for a third time. Grinning, he

pushed away from his desk and stood. The office, lined with bookcases, suddenly seemed too small. Richard wanted to *dance*. He left the room, carrying his beer with him. Beer isn't enough. No, this needs something really fucking great. He put the beer in the fridge and grabbed a bottle of single-malt scotch from the cabinet. Pouring a drink, he did a quick shuffle-step in front of the sink.

"I've made it!" he said. "I've finally fucking made it!"

He returned to his office. Sure, he might be getting ahead of himself—one professional sale didn't really constitute *making it*, but what the hell? He earned the right to be happy. Sitting down at his desk, he glanced at the phone. He should call Ness. She would be as happy.

He reached for the receiver, but paused. Yes, Ness would be happy, but she wouldn't feel the same sense of unreal ecstasy. That was something only a kindred spirit could understand.

Mace.

Richard opened his mail program. He would tell Ness, as soon as he had written to Mace to share the great news.

He took a hard swallow of his drink and laughed. Then, fingers flying, he sent Mace an email to share the news.

Ness arrived home early, surprised to find Richard in his office with the music blaring.

He had his feet up on his desk, the keyboard in his

lap. There was a bottle of scotch on the desk near his elbow. When he saw her, he smiled.

"Ness, babe, guess what?"

She nodded at the scotch. "It's New Year's and I forgot?"

Richard jumped to his feet. "Nope!" He took Ness in his arms and swung her around. She laughed, though somewhat reluctantly. "That's a celebratory drink."

"I really prefer champagne," she said. "But thanks! You got my email?"

Richard's smile faltered. "Email?"

"Sure," Ness said. "I sent you a 'Big News' message this afternoon. I thought that's what this was about."

"Uh, no," Richard admitted. "I haven't checked my email in the past few hours. I was kind of . . . " He paused, seeing the expression on Ness's face. "Why, what is your big news?"

Now it was her turn to smile. "Well," she said, setting her briefcase aside and removing the dark blazer she had worn to the office that morning. "I finally did it! I sold the DeBurgh house!"

Richard was *very* familiar with the DeBurgh house. To Ness and himself it was known as 'The Pit' simply because it sucked in every realtor's time. No one had been able to move it. It was too big, too gaudy and too expensive. No one wanted it. Until now.

"That's terrific," Richard said.

"It's almost twenty thousand dollars terrific," Ness said.

"That's your commission?"

Ness nodded. "Give or take."

"That is a reason to celebrate."

"It is," Ness agreed, "but you have something else. What is it?"

There was an overstuffed reading chair in the corner of the office. Sitting in it, Richard took a sip of his scotch. He had poured a few drinks during the afternoon and felt almost drunk. It kept the smile on his face almost constantly.

"Just a story sale," he said. "To *Dark Corner of the Mind*."

The name meant little to Ness. "That's great."

"No, it isn't," Richard replied. "It's fucking unbelievable!" He finished his drink and set the glass aside. "Come here and sit, babe." He patted his thigh.

Ness sat on his lap, slinging an arm around his shoulders. "Okay," she said. "What's so great?"

"*Dark Corner of the Mind* is a *big* magazine. National. And they pay pro rates. This is my first big breakthrough, Ness. A story in a national publication!"

She hugged him and said, "Congratulations, darling." A pause. Then: "How much are they paying?"

"I don't have an exact figure yet, but I'd estimate about seven hundred."

"Seven hundred dollars?" Ness wore a look of genuine surprise. "That much?"

"That much."

Ness kissed Richard and then got up from his lap. "I guess I can excuse the afternoon celebration, then. Even if you smell like a brewery."

Lounging in the chair, Richard wore a goofball grin. "Distillery," he said. "I smell like a distillery."

Ness took a place at the desk, behind the computer. "Whatever," she said. "But if you want to celebrate, let's get some champagne. I think we both had amazing days."

Richard bounced to his feet. "You're right. Let me take care of it. We'll order supper and I'll get us a bottle—hell, two bottles—of something expensive. On me, the literary lion."

Ness tapped the computer keys. "Sounds good," she said.

Richard disappeared from the office, going to the kitchen to order food. There was also a liquor store that delivered, so he ordered three bottles of champagne and a bottle of Wild Turkey. Fuck the cost—he was in the red. When he got back to the office, he found Ness sitting at the computer, frowning.

"What's up, babe?" he asked.

"What's with this message from the *Gazette*?"

Richard leaned over his wife's shoulder. He stared down at an email from Gus Thomson, his supervisor at the newspaper. The day's obituaries were late and the deadline couldn't be extended. Gus' words were irate.

Richard was also irate, but with Ness. "Why are you reading my messages?"

Ness looked up at Richard, surprised to see the dark thunderheads on his brow. "Don't get mad at me," she said. "I opened it accidentally. Seems a good thing I did. You spent the afternoon celebrating and forgot about work?"

Richard groaned. "Come on, this was a big deal for me. A huge deal! So, I pushed aside a few obits. So what? Gus can get anyone to write them if I miss a day."

"That's not the point," Ness said. "It's about responsibility. You have a job and you aren't doing it."

Richard bit his lower lip. He could respond quickly, without consideration, and propel them both into an argument. But why bother? It would be easy to tell Ness that with her big commission and high salary that his piddling job at the *Gazette* wasn't worth having, but she wouldn't get it. And right now, Richard didn't want to fight.

"I'm sorry," he said. "I got excited and carried away. Let's not fight. I'll email Gus and make good. Okay?"

Ness nodded. "Okay." She glanced at the screen again. "And there's another message from Mace. *Congrats on the Sale!* You already told him?"

Was that jealousy in her voice?

"He's a writer, like me, so I had to. Besides, he suggested I send 'And This Too Shall Pass' to *Dark Corner of the Mind*. If it hadn't been for his suggestions and revisions, I probably wouldn't have sold it."

"That's the story you sold? The one I read and helped you with?"

Richard nodded. "Yeah, but I changed a few things back. You know, to the way they were."

Ness wrinkled her nose. "I thought my suggestions were good ones."

"Oh, they were, but the story, well, it needed a bit more punch. I went with my original ideas, and added a few new ones from Mace."

If Ness was hurt, she didn't let on. She closed the email application and stood. "If we're going to celebrate, I want to get cleaned up first."

Richard slipped past her and sat down at his desk. "Okay," he said. "I want to do a few quick things."

"Sending a love letter to Mace?" Ness asked, smiling.

Richard slapped her on the butt. "Fuckin' A, babe," he said. "Now get that hot bod in the shower. I might join you."

Ness left the room, surprised at Richard's behavior. She didn't know if the surprise was pleasant or not.

✖ ✖

TO: thesmalls@gmail.com

FROM: mhunter@coolmail.com

SUBJECT: Kickin' Ass and Takin' Names

Richie!

I knew you could do it. From the get-go, I knew it. Congratulations again on the big sale. I told you that 'And This Too Shall Pass' was solid, didn't I? You have to start listening to me. Pretend I'm your conscience or something. Your personal shadow that sees and knows all!

Has this sale helped broaden your outlook on things a little bit? I say that because I think you are selling yourself short, working for some crappy little paper writing shitty copy (obits, of all things. Talk about a dead-end job!). This sale could be the first in a series of real successes, *major* fucking successes. There's no sense in stifling brilliance if you don't have to and you don't, do you? What I mean is, that wife of yours has a real money-making job, doesn't she? Have you ever considered broaching the subject with her, about writing full-time? It isn't going to make or break you, but it might do something for your writing career. And like I said before, writing is like breathing. You have to do it or you'll die!

Anyhow, I guess I got all serious on you here. I want to help you along, Rich, 'cause I know you've got real talent in you. Speaking of talent, I used a bit of my own today and sold a story to an online magazine called *Last Rites*. It pays shit, but it's a published story and that's what counts.

I should wrap this up, but before I do, let me repeat. *Writing is like breathing*, man. Don't let someone smother you! Talk to Ness . . . that's my advice. If she's a loving wife, she'll understand. How could she want to stand in the way of you achieving your dream?

She *won't*. Not if she loves you.

Mace

TO: mhunter@coolmail.com

FROM: thesmalls@gmail.com

SUBJECT: What to do?

Hey Mace, thanks for all the congratulations. But if it wasn't for you, that story would be sitting in a drawer (or on my computer) wasting away. I owe you big time for your suggestions and your insight. You really know me well!

This was a great day and Ness really seemed to 'get

it', you know? Of course, she still doesn't see the big picture. This is a real start for me and I have this feeling that there are bigger and better things to come. I mean, this is a big sale and only more of them can follow, right? I think I finally have the capital-fucking-C confidence that I needed! Of course, Ness might not see it the same way.

I don't know about the whole 'full time writer' thing. Ness would never go for it. Sure, she makes good money, but she also thinks that sitting around all day, writing, is akin to pecking on a keyboard. Perhaps if I put it to her with real heart, framed in my recent success, she might see differently. But the way she reacted to an email I got from my boss today tells me otherwise. (Aand that really pissed me off, too. She opened up my mail as if it were her own. I don't care that much, I'm not hiding a second life or something, but still . . . invasion of privacy.). My boss was also a bit of a prick, making it seem as if writing up the obituary for some old geezer who'd kicked off was the literary equivalent of *The Tell Tale Heart*.

Anyhow, I'm rambling. I'll think about what you said. I do agree with you. Perhaps Ness is smothering me a bit. Right now, though, I'm too goddamn happy to care!

Rich

Vanessa pulled into the driveway after two in the afternoon. She'd had an appointment to show the

Feldmans several properties, but they had called and cancelled at the last minute. She was actually glad. The Feldmans had been looking for a house for the past six months and they were never satisfied with anything she showed them. It was the husband more than the wife; he found fault with everything. He'd rejected one house because he said the air smelled like his grandmother's makeup.

With her afternoon now free, Vanessa left the office, gone by the supermarket to pick up a few items, and headed home. She planned to make some chicken parmesan for dinner, so she and Richard could have a nice romantic dinner. Things had been very strained between the two of them lately. She decided it was time she extended an olive branch.

Taking the bags from the backseat, she hurried into the house and put the groceries up in the kitchen. She half-expected Richard to come down and help her, or at least to see why she was home so early, but as she placed the last of the items in the cupboard, she was still alone. The house was eerily quiet. If she hadn't seen Richard's car in the garage, she'd have thought he had gone out somewhere. She went up the stairs and straight to the computer room. It was where Rich spent all of his time these days, even taking his meals there more often than not.

Vanessa reached for the doorknob but hesitated with her hand inches from it. Richard tended to get ill these days if she walked in unannounced. This upset her more than a bit; this was her house as well, damn it! As a compromise, she knocked lightly on the jamb as she opened the door and stepped inside. Much to her surprise, the room was empty. The computer was on, but for once Rich wasn't sitting there pecking away at the keys. Beer cans littered the desktop and the floor around the chair, eliciting an annoyed frown from Vanessa. Richard had never been much of a drinker, but over the past two months he had really been indulging. Ever since Mace Hunter had come into his life.

It seemed preposterous that someone her husband had never even met in person could have had such a profound effect on him, but it was undeniable. Richard was almost like a different man since he'd starting corresponding with the other writer, and Ness didn't much care for this new man with whom she shared her home.

Vanessa walked back down the hallway to the bedroom, pushing open the door to find Rich lying in bed on his back, an arm thrown across his eyes, resonating snores filling the room. His mouth hung open, and drool had dampened the pillow next to his head. He'd probably stayed up all night, writing and drinking, and he'd be passed out until the evening. Ness closed the door, shaking her head in distaste. She and her husband were headed for one hell of a confrontation, and she was tempted to wake him and get it over with. But she'd wait, she wanted Richard's mind clear when she took him to task for his recent behavior.

She returned to the computer room and opened their email account. There were three new messages in the inbox, one from her sister in Ohio, one from her friend Judy, and one from Mace. The subject line of this last email was: *Loved the Chapters You Sent.* So Richard was letting Mace read what he'd written on the novel he was working on. He hadn't offered to let Vanessa read any of it. Granted, she hadn't asked to read it, but she usually didn't have to ask. He was typically shoving his stuff at her like a drug pusher. Suddenly she wasn't good enough to read his work now that he had his precious Mace.

Vanessa read her messages, replied to them, then exited the internet. She started to stand but then plopped back into the chair, casting a glance at the door. The file for Richard's novel-in-progress, *Subtle Changes*, was right there on the computer's desktop. All she'd have to do was double-click then take a peek. She cast another guilty glance at the door, but there was no reason she should feel guilty. Or so she told herself. She was simply taking an interest in her husband's work. Hell, it was what he'd been badgering her about for months now.

Giving herself no time to change her mind, Ness opened the file. She scrolled past the title page to the first full page of text. She quickly skimmed over the seven-page prologue. By the time she reached the first chapter, she felt queasy. The prologue had started out with a group of preternatural creatures engaging in a wild, hedonistic orgy. The language was coarse and explicit, the sexual acts increasingly depraved and sadomasochistic. The whole thing had been more disturbing than titillating, but what was truly disturbing was what came after. The orgy had eventually devolved into a massacre, violent and vile, bloody and gruesome. What really troubled Vanessa wasn't the violence, but the *joy* of the violence. Her husband had depicted the slaughter as something fun and enjoyable and it left her feeling dirty, like she needed a scalding shower to wash away a residue of filth and slime.

Ness closed the file without reading any more. Richard typically wrote meditative pieces about modern life, ruminations on society and the human condition. They could at times become longwinded and, if she were being completely honest, a bit boring, but she much preferred them to this almost pornographic smut. Perhaps she was being prudish, it was *fiction*, after all, but it seemed as if her husband had delighted in describing the depraved acts, as if he had taken real pleasure in them.

Vanessa wrapped her arms around herself and shivered. She stared at the desktop, chewing on her lower lip. There was a file in the bottom left corner labeled *Rich's Short Stories*, and above it another labeled *Mace's Short Stories*. After another glance at the doorway, she opened up *Rich's Short Stories*. A window opened with a list of about fifty or so story titles. Many of them were older stories she'd already read, but several of them she was unfamiliar with. She clicked on one titled 'The Thorn House.'

The story was twenty-eight pages long, but Ness only made it through page ten before turning away from the screen in disgust. The story was about a ten-year-old girl who had created her own little playland under the thick branches of a large, wild rosebush. At first Vanessa had been charmed by the girl, her boundless imagination, the elaborate otherworld she had created under the rosebush. Then the story had taken a sudden, violent turn. An escaped mental patient discovered the girl under the rosebush one afternoon and held her captive, brutally raping her repeatedly. The way the story was written, it was almost as if Richard were trying to put the reader's sympathies with the mental patient instead of the little girl. Rich spared no detail, depicting the rapes with graphic relish. Vanessa closed the file, feeling that she might vomit at any moment.

She tried to tell herself she was being histrionic, but her husband's writing had left her shaken. There was such darkness in his recent work. *Soulless* was the word that came to mind. It actually put her in mind of some of the more twisted stuff Richard had written in their college years, back when he'd thought it was cool to shock people just for the sake of shocking them. Vanessa had thought he'd outgrown that type of splatterpunk writing, but apparently not.

Vanessa suddenly experienced that mental tip-of-the-tongue sensation she often got when a thought hovered on the edge of memory. Something about Richard's college writing, coupled with the pieces he was producing now, there was a connection she felt was waiting to be made, but then she lost it. Shrugging, she let it go.

She clicked on the file *Mace's Short Stories*. She wanted to read some of the work by the man her husband couldn't stop raving about, the man who had becomeing more important to Rich than his own wife. There were about twenty stories in the file, and she picked one at random. A story entitled 'Coming in For a Landing.'

The story wasn't especially long, fifteen pages. It was a science fiction piece set in the distant future, where a group of space explorers land on a distant planet in search of intelligent life. What they find is a race of vicious creatures that enslave the explorers, using them as both sexual toys and servants. At first the explorers resist, but they eventually grow to love the abuse and degradation, ultimately sending word to Earth that the planet is a paradise so that more potential slaves will be sent. The story was sick, making victimizers into heroes, and she suddenly knew what had reawakened her husband's interest in dark horror. Or she should say *who* had awakened her husband's interest in dark horror. There were several parallels between Mace's story and what she'd read of her husband's recent work. It was almost as if Rich had adopted the other writer's style. Not copying, exactly, nothing so blatant, but the influence was unmistakable. Vanessa hated to sound so mom-ish, but Mace certainly seemed to be a bad influence on her husband.

No longer in the mood to fix a romantic pasta dinner, no longer with much of an appetite at all, Vanessa left the office, making sure to close the door behind her, and retreated down the hall. She paused at the bedroom door then hurried downstairs.

She was suddenly in no hurry for her husband to wake up.

Richard stumbled downstairs at a quarter past eight that evening. Vanessa sat in the living room, eating a sandwich with the TV playing softly across the room. She wasn't really watching the inane reality show, but she kept her eyes glued to it as her husband came into the room, refusing to acknowledge him.

He stood there for a few minutes, his hair sticking up in wild corkscrews, scratching himself and staring at his wife, as if waiting for her to say something. When she continued to ignore him, he finally cleared his throat and said, "Hey," in a husky croak.

Finally turning her eyes toward her husband, she said, "The sun sets and the creature arise."

"What's that supposed to mean?"

"Nothing. You tend to keep vampire hours these days. Do you even remember what the sun looks like?"

"Big yellow ball of fire, right?" Rich said, yawning into his hand. Looking at his wife's half-eaten sandwich, he said, "Did you fix anything for me?"

Vanessa leveled such a heated glare at her husband that he held up his hands and backed away, as if she had aimed a gun at him.

"Never mind," he said. "I'll go fix something myself. Then I have to head upstairs and get to work. I gotta finish a half dozen obits by morning."

"Another all-nighter, huh? You didn't used to get so behind."

"I know," Richard said, rubbing at his temples. Vanessa suspected he was hungover as well as tired. "This job is getting to be a real burden. I wish I could quit."

"Well, you can't."

Rich stood by the sofa for a moment, rocking on his feet, fiddling with the tail of the T-shirt he'd slept in. Finally he looked sheepishly at his wife and said, "Why not?"

"Why not what?"

"Why can't I quit?"

Vanessa paused with the sandwich halfway to her mouth and stared at her husband as if he'd lost his mind. She suspected he had. "Please tell me you're not serious."

"Hear me out," Richard said, sitting next to her. "You've been selling houses left and right lately, and that has really padded our bank account. I've sold another two stories to publications that pay pro rates. I'm really on a roll now."

"Three stories, none of which you've been paid for yet, hardly constitutes a roll," Vanessa said coolly.

"I'm telling you, Ness, this is the beginning. Big things are around the corner, I can feel it. And the new novel I'm working on is going tremendously well."

"Your novel," Vanessa said with a sneer, before she cut herself off. She wasn't sure why, but it felt important not to let Rich know she'd read some of his work.

"Yes, I really think I'll be able to find a publisher when I'm finished, but I need to focus, and the job at the *Gazette* is a distraction I don't need right now."

"Need I remind you that when you first got the job at the paper, you were ecstatic. 'Finally, a job that utilizes my skills as a writer,' you told me."

"So-and-so passed away last night, and is survived by a wife and two kids," Richard said mockingly. "Not exactly Nobel material. I really feel that I'm on the precipice of a major breakthrough in my writing career. I need to devote more time to it."

"How is that possible?" Vanessa asked. "How could you possibly devote *more* time to your writing? You already spend every waking second at it, neglecting everything else. Your job, the house, your wife. The only way you could spend more time at it would be to add extra hours to the day."

"Ness, please, listen to what I'm—"

"No, Rich. No! Right now I'm doing well at my job, but real estate is a fickle business. If the market were to go south, my commissions would dry up and we'd be in quite a bind. If you're looking for me to tell you it's okay with me if you quit your job, you're out of luck."

Richard stood, his mouth puckered as if he'd tasted something sour. Vanessa noticed a tick in his left cheek, causing his eye to twitch. "I don't know why I bother trying to talk to you," he said. "You never understand."

"Well, maybe if you started talking sense, I'd understand."

"You're a fucking philistine."

Vanessa tossed her unfinished sandwich in the wastebasket then turned to leave the room. "I'm not in the mood for this. I'm going to turn in early. I have a long day ahead of me tomorrow."

Without a "good night" or a kiss, Vanessa walked past her husband and out of the room. Only after she was safely behind the closed door of the bedroom did she allow the tears to flow. Something was very wrong with her husband and she didn't know what to do about it. After changing into her nightgown, she crawled under the covers of the big, empty bed, still warm from Richard's body, and wept softly into the pillow until she fell asleep.

TO: <u>thesmalls@gmail.com</u>

FROM: <u>mhunter@coolmail.com</u>

SUBJECT: Loved the Chapters You Sent

You've nailed it, Richie!

I am totally fucking hooked on *Subtle Changes*. I need another fix, so hurry up and send me some more chapters. I can tell you've finally stopped holding back and are letting the muse flow through you. No more safe, dull stories for you; from here on out, it's all a trip down the rabbit hole into a world of insanity and depravity. I think you're finally learning that nothing makes an impression like the extreme. I like to think I've played at least a small part in helping you tap into the dark power that you're showing in this novel. If it keeps going this well, I'll bet you'll have agents beating down your goddamn door to represent you, and there will probably be a bidding war among all the big publishers. I'm not blowing smoke up your ass, either; I am truly impressed.

So is the wife still being a bitch about all this? I don't mean to badmouth the missus or anything, but from what you've told me, she sounds like a really insecure woman. Maybe she's jealous of your talent, bitter because she doesn't have a gift like yours. In any case, sounds like she's really trying to stand in your way. It's a shame some people have to be like that, a hindrance instead of a help. A truly devoted wife would bend over backwards for you, do whatever the fuck she could to make your life easier so you could focus on your writing. Your wife sounds like she wants *you* to make *her* life easier. This is what happens when all this women's lib shit gets taken too far. You end up with women who think they're men, women who want their husbands to play the housewife. You're wife sounds like she needs a wakeup call, something to let her know you're the man of the house, and she can either support you or get the hell out of your way.

You know, Rich, I've been thinking about this, and perhaps it's time you and I met face-to-face. I mean, I feel a kinship with you that I've never felt with anyone else. It's like we've known each other for years, like we really understand how one another's brains work. I'll be traveling in your neck of the woods to visit some family in the near future; maybe I could swing by and we could spend some time together. Perhaps together we could persuade your wife to be a little more understanding. Let me know what you think.

Mace

TO: mhunter@coolmail.com

FROM: thesmalls@gmail.com

SUBJECT: Pain in My Ass

Hey Mace, I broached the subject of quitting my job with Ness earlier tonight. She reacted predictably, which is to say like a real cunt. She has pretty much forbidden me to quit the paper. Like she wears the pants in the family or something. With the money she makes at her job and the money I know will start coming in now that I'm having some success with the bigger magazines, there's no reason I should keep that lousy shitty job at the *Gazette*. Crazy as it sounds, I think she resents the fact that writing makes me so happy, and I swear she is out to spite me. She's really changed in the past couple of months; it's like her mission in life to make me miserable. I don't know what her problem is, but she needs to get over it right fucking quick. I mean, I haven't been able to get any decent writing done tonight, she put me in such a bad mood. And I simply cannot allow anything or anyone, not even my wife, to interfere with my writing. That is unacceptable. She is in need of a serious attitude adjustment.

You know I'd love to meet you, Mace, but the idea also makes me a little nervous. I mean, it would be like meeting an idol. Your work is so fan-fucking-tastic, I am afraid I would feel totally inadequate in your presence. Let me give it a little more thought, and I'll get back to you.

Well, I was supposed to finish up a bunch of obits to send off to my supervisor in the morning, but I think I'm going to take some of your advice and say FUCK IT! I would rather spend the time working on *Subtle Changes*, and it's not like those folks will be any less dead if I don't write their obituaries. I'm going to try to get some work done so that I'll have some more chapters to send you by the weekend.

'Til later.

Rich

Vanessa could remember a time when she found absolute pleasure in coming home after a day in the trenches. Nine times out of ten she would find Rich in the kitchen, tending to something on the stove or in the oven. Often he had something romantic waiting— a rose in a vase, soft music on the stereo. Even in the early years of their marriage, when he worked at temporary labor jobs while she studied to pass the realtor's exam, he found the time to be romantic. Now she stepped into the house with a ball of dread knotted in her stomach. The door closed behind her with a muffled thump and she stood in the foyer, listening.

She could hear the steady, bass *thud* of music from the upstairs office. The room that had become Richard's domain.

Ness moved through the house, putting her briefcase and jacket down in the dining room. The house was dim, the blinds in the same half-drawn position they had been when she'd left that morning. The breakfast dishes were heaped in the sink, unwashed. The anger that Ness wanted to feel— righteous anger at her husband's sudden dismissal of everything in his life outside of his writing and his friendship with Mace—was dampened by fear.

Are you really afraid of Richard? Afraid of your own husband?

To be honest, Ness thought she was. She never imagined there might come a day when Richard could frighten her, but here she was, standing at the bottom of the stairs, listening to the heavy notes of music that came from behind the closed office door. That closed door seemed to represent everything that had come between them in the past months. It was a barrier that had never existed before.

Drawing up her courage—and some of her anger—Ness mounted the stairs. She meant to have it out with Richard now, for better or for worse. She couldn't continue living with him if he was going to treat her like something secondary. She wouldn't be afraid or upset by him any longer.

She paused outside the office door, the floor vibrating underfoot. She could smell smoke. It wasn't the bitter smoke of a fire or something burnt, but rather the acrid aroma of tobacco. Ness was immediately taken back a dozen years, to a time when Richard still smoked. That had been his one true vice when they'd first married. He used to smoke like a chimney, in fact, until Ness squeezed it out of him and made him quit. Now, it seemed, he'd gone back to his old habits.

Ness put a hand on the doorknob and turned. Part of her, that same frightened, saddened part, half-expected the door to be locked, but it wasn't. The knob turned and the door swung open. With the barrier removed, the blasting beat of the music rushed around her like a hot summer wind.

Richard sat at his computer, chair leaned back and feet on the corner of the desk. He held a half-smoked cigarette between his lips and stared at the computer screen through a haze of smoke. On the desk, by his elbow, was a bottle of Jim Beam and a tumbler, half-filled with amber liquid. Richard scrolled down the screen with his mouse, lips moving slightly as he read the text.

"Rich?" Ness said. She wanted to speak sharply, with anger and authority, but the word came out in a stifled croak. Richard didn't hear her. He continued to read the words on the screen, cigarette smoldering.

Ness drew a quivering breath and said, "Richard!"

His feet dropped off the desk and he swung around, his face bearing an expression that was one-half surprise and one-half anger. The cigarette bobbed in his mouth.

"Ness," he said, lifting his voice above the music. "You're home already?"

"Of course," Ness said. "It's past six."

"What?"

"Jesus, Richard, turn that racket down so we can talk!"

Richard reached over and dialed down the volume on the stereo. The music faded away like an echo of thunder. Setting his cigarette down in an ashtray, Richard said, "There."

They regarded one another in a long stretch of silence. Ness didn't like the expectation she saw in Richard's eyes. He knew that she had come here to confront him, and there was almost a childlike glee in his expression. He was *waiting* for her to say something.

"You're smoking?"

Richard picked up the cigarette and tapped the ashes into the ashtray. "Yep," he said.

"I thought you quit."

"I did, but only because you wanted me to."

"That's not true," Ness said.

"It is," Richard replied. "Hell, Ness, I've done a lot of things in my life because you wanted me to do them.

I quit smoking, moved out here to the suburbs, got a job at the *Gazette* . . . "

Ness raised her eyebrows. She had never suggested that Richard write obituaries for the *Gazette*. He found that job himself and gone out of his way to obtain it. He thought it was going to be a lead-in to something better, a way to get a full-time writing position.

"So," Richard went on, drawing contentedly on his cigarette, "I decided to reconsider a few things. I figured it was time I did things for myself. Like this, for example." He waggled the cigarette at her and smiled.

"Richard, I never said . . . when you decided to get the job at the *Gazette*, it wasn't me who . . . "

She realized that the conversation distracted her. She hadn't come here to defend herself against Richard's accusations. She came here to confront him about his behavior. Gritting her teeth, she struggled to regain focus. She crossed the room and took up a spot in front of her husband. "Richard, what the hell is going on with you?"

"Going on?" Richard asked, exhaling plumes of smoke. "I don't know what—"

"Damn it Richard, put that cigarette out and talk to me! And turn this *off*!" She reached around her husband and switched the stereo off completely. The music evaporated, leaving behind the strained silence of the room.

With slow, deliberate motions, Rich butted out his cigarette. Then, leaning back in his chair and crossing his arms, he said, "You've obviously got something to say, so say it."

Ness began speaking quickly, before she could

think about what she was saying and change her mind. "I *do* have something to say. You aren't acting like yourself at all. Smoking. Drinking. The late nights. The moods you get in. I don't even feel like I know who you are anymore. You barely have time for me and when you do, you scare me."

"What?" Richard said. "That's crazy."

"You're acting crazy. You have to see it."

"I don't," Richard said. His eyes flickered.

"You spend every waking hour in here at the computer. I never see you anymore."

"I'm working," Richard said.

"Really? I never see you working. Everything you do for the *Gazette* is done late or not at all. And when you—"

"I'm *writing!*" Richard shouted. Ness jumped. "*That's* my work! Not that fucking bullshit I do for the *Gazette*. Jesus Christ, that was a distraction, a fucking measly paycheck. If you ever thought of that as my work then you're the crazy one, Ness. Not me!"

Tears rose in her eyes. She tried to choke them back. "That's what I mean," she gasped. "You're ignoring your work for your writing and—"

Richard came out of his chair quickly. Ness backpedaled, terrified for a single moment that her husband was going to strike her. Instead he slammed a hand on the desk and grabbed for a pack of cigarettes.

"My writing is my work," he said. "Why don't you get that? You don't understand. The *Gazette* was nothing. *Nothing!* I quit that fucking job a week ago. Christ, if it wasn't for Mace I wouldn't have anyone who understood."

"You quit your job?"

Richard shook a cigarette out of the package. "I did." He pinched the cigarette between his lips. "That job was a dead weight on me, Ness. Don't you understand that? It was holding me back. Now I can focus on what's important. It's like Mace says, nothing can get in my way. I have to keep my eyes on what matters. My writing. I sold another story today, did you know that?"

Ness blinked. "No, but Richard, please, you quit? Without talking to me?"

"You see?" Richard said, lighting the cigarette and exhaling a curl of smoke. "I told you I sold a story and all you can do is harp about that job. No congratulations for the story. Nothing."

"There are bigger things going on right now," Ness said.

"For me, my writing is the big thing. I've made more money with my writing in the past month than I have before. And right now I'm working on a novel and it's going to be—"

Before she could stop herself, Ness said, "It's ugly! It's vile and disgusting, that's what it is." As the words spilled out of her, her strength collapsed. Tears coursed down her cheeks.

"What?" Richard said.

Ness didn't reply. She closed her hands over her face and sobbed. She felt lost, adrift, and longing for someone to help her.

Richard grabbed her shoulders and squeezed. "You read my novel without asking?"

Ness lowered her hands and stared into her husband's face. It wasn't the Richard she knew. She didn't recognize this man at all. The man she knew should have taken her into his arms to comfort her, not accuse her.

"I read it," Ness said. "Because you shut me out. You didn't ask me to read your stuff anymore, because of Mace."

Richard lowered his hands. "What?"

"Mace!" Ness screamed. "Your precious goddamn Mace. That's all I hear. Mace this and Mace that! You practically worship a man you've never even met."

Richard spun on a heel and sat back down at his desk. For a few moments he stared at the computer screen. Then, carefully saving his work, he turned to face his wife. "Well, don't worry. That's going to change."

"What is?"

"I'm going to meet Mace. He and I were discussing it via email. I actually said I wanted to wait—to make sure. Maybe talk to you. But I don't think I need to wait. I'm going to invite him for a visit. He said he'd be glad to come."

"Here?"

"Of course here," Richard snorted. "Where the fuck else would he go?"

"But you don't even *know* him. You know nothing about him! You can't invite a stranger to our house."

Richard blew a stream of smoke out of the corner of his mouth. "He isn't a stranger."

Ness swallowed tightly. She watched while Richard set his cigarette aside and picked up the glass of whiskey. He took a lingering sip.

"God, Richard," she whispered. "What's happening?"

Richard set his drink aside. "Things are changing around here. I've put up with you stifling me long enough. I'm a writer, Ness. An artist. I create. It's what I do, and it's what I'm *going* to do. I'm going to write my novel and it's going to sell. Big! Before you know it, you'll be asking *me* to let you quit your job."

"Richard, please listen to me."

"I'm through listening," Richard said. "Mace is coming here for a visit. End of story. And I'm going to be writing full-time. No more shitty *Gazette* gigs. Big things are coming, babe. This is all for the best. Trust me."

Ness drew a hitching breath. "I don't know if I can."

Richard rolled his shoulders in a slow shrug. "That's up to you," he said. He turned back to his computer and added, "Close the door on your way out, okay? I've got to get back to work."

Ness opened her mouth to speak, to utter something, a single word that might repair whatever damage had been done, but no sound came out. A moment later Richard turned the stereo on and dialed up the volume.

Ness backed out of the office, something cold lodged in her chest. She drew the door closed behind her.

TO: mhunter@coolmail.com

FROM: thesmalls@gmail.com

SUBJECT: Invitation

Hey Mace, I wanted to send you a quick message to extend an invitation. You are formally invited to Casa de Small (or the Small House, or whatever the fuck you want to call it, ha-ha). I was going to pass the idea by the wife tonight, but I decided to make a unilateral decision. Don't worry, though, Ness is fine with it. She's a bit cold to the idea of having someone she's never met before in the house, but I know she'll feel differently as soon as I introduce the two of you.

And there's even more good news, Mace! I dumped that shitty *Gazette* job and I'm going to focus on my writing full-time. That's something Ness was REALLY going to throw a bitch-fit about, but I didn't let her. I put my foot down, as you've suggested (better than having to break it off in her ass, huh?). She has to realize that I'm the man in this marriage and I call the shots. I know she'll come around. Right now these changes are all really overwhelming for her—hell, they're overwhelming for me—but I feel great about *Subtle Changes* and I know it's going to give me the break I deserve. When I sign a six-figure book deal, she'll be living the high life and she'll thank me for taking the reins (and she's going to thank you for being the driving force behind me).

Speaking of that . . . how is the writing going on your end? You're a helluva great writer—better than I am—so I expect you and I will be co-chairing a few professional writing conferences in the future (not to mentioning book signings, right?). I'm going to send you the new chapters right away, but you have to send me something. I'm jonesing for a hit of Mace Hunter right about now!

Anyhow, I should go and make sure the wife is calmed down. Maybe I'll take the evening off, reassure her. Give her a lay . . . that kind of thing (wink-wink). Get back to me soon, Mace!

Rich

TO: thesmalls@gmail.com

FROM: mhunter@coolmail.com

SUBJECT: Thanks for the invite

Richard,

Thanks so much for the invitation. I will be packing my bags and scheduling my life so I can get out to see you as soon as possible. I'm glad you started to approach things in a more aggressive fashion. First with your writing (the new chapters on *Subtle Changes* blew me out of the fucking water, my man! I didn't know whether to be turned on or terrified. You have a real knack for pure, visceral horror), and now with your personal and professional life. I think you're right about Ness: she's going to be reluctant to accept the changes at first, as anyone would be. She'd gotten too used to running the show. It's time you put her in her place.

As for me, well, I placed a couple of short stories, but nothing as good as what you've done. I feel as if you've got me beat, Rich. The student has become the teacher and all of that, right? Actually, reading your novel has inspired me to possibly write a novel of my own, but now I'll be coming to you to get some advice.

Let me know when you want me to come out there. My life is pretty open, so you say the word and I'll be there. Don't worry about preparing anything special on my behalf, either. I think we're enough alike that I can get by at your place. All I need is a place to lay my head (and a nice bottle of whiskey to fog the same fucking head).

I'm really excited about meeting you. Nervous, too, you know? I feel as if I have to make my 'real' first impression. I know that we've talked online over and over again, but this feels like a big leap forward. A revelation, you know? Maybe I'm being dramatic.

Talk to you soon.

Mace

Vanessa was waiting in the computer room when Richard awoke the next night.

After a stop at the bathroom, he came into the office then halted abruptly when he saw Ness standing by the desk. She stood rigidly, her facial muscles pulled taut. As her husband stared at her, she felt her body tremble but she forced herself to be still.

"What are you doing in here?" Richard asked.

"I was using the computer."

"What for?" Rich said, and the suspicion dripped from his words like sap.

"I was doing a little research online."

"*Ten Ways to be an even Bigger Bitch*?"

Vanessa snorted, not exactly a laugh but in the same family. "You think you're pretty funny, don't you?"

"No, I think I'm fed up. Now, I've got work to do, so if you don't mind."

"And what if I do?" Vanessa said, refusing to back down. She still felt the fear, but she would not give in to it. She was a strong woman whose own mother had taught her to stand up for herself. "What if I do mind? This is my computer, too. What if I want to stay up all night in the *Grey's Anatomy* chatroom?"

Rich crossed to the desk, shook a cigarette out of a near-empty pack, and lit up. Having him this close, looking at her with that gleam of contempt, made her knees feel weak, but Vanessa locked them in place and stood her ground.

"What is it?" Richard said, blowing a foul cloud of smoke directly into his wife's face. "You obviously want to talk about something, so let's get it over with so I can get you the fuck out of my hair. What do you want to talk about now?"

"Mace Hunter."

Richard flinched, the cigarette drooping in his lips for a second, then said, "What about him?"

"Is that his real name?"

"Of course it's his real name." Richard seemed flustered all of a sudden, as if this line of questioning had thrown him off track. "What kind of stupid question is that?"

"Well, is that the name he publishes under or does he use a pseudonym?"

"Where are you going with this, Ness?"

Vanessa took a deep breath and said, "I decided to look Mace up on the Internet, see what I could find out about him, and I—"

"You did what?" Richard shouted, his sudden nervousness evaporating in the heat of rage. "You snooping little whore, what gives you the right to go sticking your nose in where it doesn't belong?"

"What gives me the right?" Vanessa countered, stoking the fires of her own rage. "You are inviting a stranger into this house, and you think I don't have the right to find out everything I can about him? Well, excuse me, but if I'm going to have that man under our roof, I want to know as much as I can."

"He's my friend; that's all you need to know."

"Richard, listen to me. Whoever this Mace Hunter is, he's a phony."

"Get out of here," Richard said, sitting down in front of the computer and opening the file for his novel. "I don't want to look at your face right now."

"Richard, please listen. He told you he had been published in *Dark Corner of the Mind*, but I went to their website and looked up the contents of every issue for the past four years. They have never published any story by a Mace Hunter. I also looked up some of the smaller publications you told me he'd been published in—*Shadows, Out of the Deep, Galaxy Explorer, Shaman, Last Rites*—and I couldn't find anything by Mace Hunter. I went back years."

Richard put his hands over his ears as if trying to block out his wife's words. "Stop it! Why are you doing this?"

"Richard, you have to hear this," Vanessa said,

grabbing her husband's hands and prying them away from the sides of his head. "Mace has been lying to you all this time. I don't know what game he's playing, but he's not who he claims to be."

"Shut up!" Richard said, shooting to his feet. He knocked the chair back and it clattered to the floor. He grabbed Vanessa by the arms, squeezing hard, and shook her like a maraca. "Don't talk about Mace that way, don't you dare say one more fucking thing against him! I won't have you badmouthing him. He's all I've got."

Vanessa looked pleadingly into her husband's eyes, searching for some sign that the man she'd fallen in love with was still in there somewhere. "Rich," she said, trying to pull out of his grip, "he's not all you've got."

"Oh yeah? What else do I have?"

"You have me."

For a second, Ness saw the old Richard resurface. She was sure of it, but then he roared and shoved her to the side. She collided with the side of a large, wooden bookcase and went down on her knees, a few thick hardbacks pelting her as they fell from the shelves.

"I think it's best if I take a walk," Richard said, his voice eerily calm and inflectionless. "I need some time away from you."

"Richard, I'm begging you—"

"I suggest you don't say anymore. You'd do anything to turn me against Mace, but it's not going to work. He's coming for a visit, and he's free to stay as long as he wants. You can either accept it or pack your fucking bags."

Vanessa felt her anger rising back to the surface like a bloated corpse from a watery grave. She grabbed a shelf and pulled herself to her feet. Her gaze had steel in it as she said, "You can't kick me out. This is my house, too. And I don't want that lying son of a bitch here."

"I'll be back later," Richard said, turning away from her. "I'll give you time to come to your senses and we'll talk about it later."

"Do you hear me, Richard? I'm not going to change my mind. I don't want that bastard in this house."

Richard said nothing more, simply left the room. Vanessa heard him go out the front door, and distantly she heard his car crank and drive off down the block. She suddenly felt too weak to stand. She grabbed the edge of the desk to keep from crumpling in a puddle on the floor again. She couldn't deny any more how afraid she was, afraid of her husband and afraid *for* him.

Reaching a decision, she absently wiped the tears from her eyes and righted the toppled chair. She settled down in front of the computer, opened up Internet Explorer. She had to find something concrete, some definite proof that Mace Hunter was a fake, something she could show her husband and he could not deny. Where to start?

A metaphorical light bulb blinked over Vanessa's head and she opened up the 'Favorites,' running down the list of websites she and her husband frequently visited. Richard said he had met Mace on a message board, and there it was. Vanessa clicked on the link, www.bookaholics.com. The site offered many different options for discussing books. There was a reviews section where people could post and read reviews of various books, a message board, and a live chatroom. There were currently three chatters online, according to the site. Vanessa figured this would be her best shot.

She had no idea what Richard's User ID was, so she quickly created her own profile, using the name SmallNess. She entered the chat room and was immediately greeted.

BookMan: Howdy SmallNess.

Literary_Queen: You must be new to the board. I don't recall seeing you here before.

SmallNess: Yes, this is my first time here.

Scout: Well, welcome to our humble little board. We were discussing the latest by Tom Clancy, if you want to join in.

SmallNess: Thanks, but I was actually checking things out. My husband comes on here a lot.

BookMan: Who's your husband?

SmallNess: Richard Small.

Literary_Queen: Doesn't ring a bell. What's his screen name?

SmallNess: I'm actually not sure.

Scout: Well, there are many regulars who come on here.

SmallNess: Do any of you know Mace Hunter?

BookMan: Oh yeah, we certainly know Mace. His handle is WriteStuff.

Scout: He used to come on here all the time, but we haven't seen much of him in the past few months.

Literary_Queen: Which is a blessing, you ask me. I for one can't stand that pretentious asshole.

SmallNess: Yes, that certainly sounds like Mace to me.

BookMan: He can definitely be overbearing. Made quite a few enemies on this board. I think he's on more than a few people's Ignore List, if you know what I mean.

Literary_Queen: Acts like he's better than everyone else. He can't accept that some people don't agree with every single one of his opinions. If someone contradicts him, he gets all adolescent and starts in with the name-calling and insults.

Scout: Well, I'm not the guy's biggest fan either, but you have to admit, he is one hell of a writer.

BookMan: I'll give you that one.

SmallNess: You've read his work?

BookMan: Yeah, he posted a few of his short

stories on here earlier in the year. Said he was desperate for some feedback.

Literary_Queen: I was rather fond of that one story he wrote about the married couple, 'And This Too Shall Pass.'

Vanessa leaned back in the chair, staring at the words on the screen as if they were in a foreign language. 'And This Too Shall Pass' was Richard's story, but apparently Mace Hunter was taking credit for it. Was that the bastard's game? Stealing her husband's work and passing it off as his own? It made sense in a way, but . . .

But wait. BookMan said Mace had posted the story earlier in the year, and Rich and Mace had not started their correspondence until a few months ago. How could he have stolen Richard's story and posted it online before they'd started trading stories? Unless, was it possible that Richard was the plagiarist? That he'd read Mace's story on the board and stolen it? There was a time when Vanessa would have considered that possibility preposterous, but Richard had been behaving so erratically lately that she could no longer discount it.

Exiting the chatroom, Vanessa began exploring the rest of the site. She discovered that she could look up specific member profiles by their User IDs. She typed in 'WriteStuff' and hit enter. She drummed her fingers on the desktop as her request was processed. It took only five seconds, but patience was a virtue no longer in her repertoire. Finally Mace's profile appeared onscreen.

KINDRED SPIRIT

NAME: Mace Hunter
LOCATION: Seattle, Washington
GENDER: Male
AGE: 42
STATS: 6'3", 180 lbs., eyes dark as sin, hair the color of midnight
PROFESSION: Writer
MARITAL STATUS: Divorced (quite happily)
PERSONAL QUOTE: "When life hands you lemons, rub the bitter juice into your scars until you become immune to the pain."

"What kind of personal quote is that?" Vanessa mumbled out loud. It was ridiculously macho, and yet oddly familiar. As was the "eyes dark as sin, hair the color of midnight" reference in his stats. It was like something she may have once read in a—

Vanessa gasped as the connection that had eluded her the other day was finally made. The revelation crashed down on her like a cartoon anvil, but she shook her head as if to deny it. It couldn't be. It didn't make sense. Yet it made perfect sense in a warped sort of way.

She pushed away from the desk and hurried downstairs to the hall closet. It was piled high with boxes, the junk they had no use for but could not bring themselves to throw out. She rummaged around, heedlessly tossing items out into the hallway, until she found the box of Richard's college momentous. She dug through the contents, pushing aside Rich's cap and gown, yearbooks, playbills, and there in the bottom she found a stack of magazines. *Reflections*, the school's literary journal.

Vanessa sat Indian-style on the floor, flipping quickly through the magazines, looking for Richard's work. Halfway through the third one, she found what she was searching for. It was a short story of Richard's that she had forgotten about, entitled 'Hunter's Prey.' The main character was Mace Hunter, a 42-year-old writer from Seattle, Washington. In the first paragraph he was described as having "eyes dark as sin, hair the color of midnight." Near the end of the first page, he tells his ex-wife, "When life hands you lemons, rub the bitter juice into your scars until you become immune to the pain."

Vanessa's mind was a chaotic whirlpool of confusion. Mace Hunter, her husband's new best friend and confidant, was a product of Richard's own imagination. He had been thought up over a decade and a half ago.

But that was impossible. Mace Hunter had to be real; Richard had been exchanging emails with him for months now. If Mace didn't exist, that would mean Rich had been handling both sides of the correspondence, writing back and forth to himself as if he were two different people. Why would he do something like that? Was he so desperate for encouragement and understanding that he'd invented a source for it, convincing himself this other person was real?

Clutching the magazine in her hands, Ness hurried back upstairs to the computer room. She typed in www.coolmail.com and was directed to the Log In page. For User ID she put "mhunter" then tabbed down to the password. The cursor blinked on and off at her like a winking eye. She thought for a moment then typed in "August5," her and Richard's wedding anniversary and the password for their shared email account. An angry red message appeared, informing her that the password was incorrect.

Vanessa tried everything she could think of—Rich's mother's maiden name, his birth date, her birth date, his social security number, the name of his first pet—all to no avail. Running out of ideas, Vanessa leaned back and tried to clear her mind, hoping the obvious would come to her if she made room for it. Her eyes wandered to the literary journal, lying crumpled beside the keyboard.

She reached out and pecked out the word 'Reflections' then hit enter. The screen went white for a moment, and then Mace Hunter's inbox popped up. Vanessa had not expected success, and it took her overwrought brain a moment to realize she had, in fact, succeeded. She leaned forward, not wanting to admit what this meant, not wanting to think about the implications.

There was only one new message waiting in Mace's inbox, and it was from her husband. With trembling fingers, Vanessa opened the email.

TO: mhunter@coolmail.com

FROM: thesmalls@gmail.com

SUBJECT: Two Halves of the Same Whole

Mace, I simply cannot wait until you get here.

You understand me like no one ever has, and having you here will mean so much to me. I know it may be a bit presumptuous, but perhaps you could even extend your visit indefinitely. I need someone like you in my life.

I have come to realize that I've been kidding myself by thinking Ness will ever be able to understand me. She doesn't get it, and she never will. All she does is throw up obstacles, and I don't foresee her changing. I think you are right. I don't need that kind of negativity. It is time that I got rid of her. I think I have known that for some time now, but I didn't want to face it. But when you are here, standing by my side, together we will have the strength to do what needs to be done. I won't have any use for her once you are here.

We'll take care of her, then we can live happily ever after.

Rich

Vanessa bolted up as if she'd received an electrical shock. The chair rolled away on its wheels, stopping only when it banged into a glass-fronted bookcase. Vanessa stared down at the email, her breath sounding loud and ragged in her own ears, her hands clammy and cold. Richard needed help, serious professional help. She had to admit to herself that he was quite possibly dangerous. She needed to get out of the house, and quickly.

Vanessa turned toward the door and froze, a tiny squeak leaving her lips. It sounded like a rubber-soled shoe skidding on a freshly waxed floor. Richard stood in the threshold, blocking the way out, staring at his wife. He did not move. He did not blink. His expression was blank and utterly unreadable.

"Richard," Vanessa said, trying to make her voice firm but failing. When her husband did not respond, she said, "Rich?"

Still Richard did not move. He barely seemed to be breathing. Vanessa looked into his eyes and saw nothing but a stranger.

Backing away from the door, realizing that there was nowhere for her to go, Vanessa looked at the man in the doorway, a man who looked like her husband but wasn't, and said in a quavering voice, "Mace . . . ?"

THE END?

Not at all.

If you enjoyed this book, I'm sure you'll also like the following titles:

The Outsiders Lovecraftian shared-world anthology—They'll do anything to protect their way of life. Anything. Welcome to Priory, a small gated community in the UK, where the only thing worse than an ancient monster is the group worshipping it. Is that which slithers below true evil, or does evil reside in the people of Priory? Includes stories by Stephen Bacon, James Everington, Rosanne Rabinowitz, V.H. Leslie, and Gary Fry.

Tales from The Lake Vol.1 anthology—Remember those dark and scary nights spent telling ghost stories and other campfire stories? With the *Tales from The Lake* horror anthologies, you can relive some of those memories by reading the best Dark Fiction stories around. Includes Dark Fiction stories and poems by horror greats such as Graham Masterton, Bev Vincent, Tim Curran, Tim Waggoner, Elizabeth Massie, and many more. Be sure to check out our website for future *Tales from The Lake* volumes.

Through a Mirror, Darkly by Kevin Lucia—Are there truths within the books we read? What if the book delves into the lives of the very town you live in?

People you know? Or thought you knew. These are the questions a bookstore owner face when a mysterious book shows up.

Where You Live by Gary McMahon—Horror is everywhere, in the shadows and in the light. It takes on every shape, comes in every conceivable size. But most of all it's right where you live. With the WHERE YOU LIVE short story collection, Gary McMahon delves into the depths of dark and brooding horror in every day events, objects, and the ghost of human nature.

Samurai and Other Stories by William Meikle—No one can handle Scottish folklore with elements of the darkest horror, science fiction and fantasy, suspense and adventure like William Meikle.

Stuck On You and Other Prime Cuts by Jasper Bark—A word of caution gentle reader, these tales will take you places you've never been before and may never dare revisit. They'll whisper truths so twisted you can only face them in the darkest hours of the night. They'll unlock desires so decadent you'll never wash their taint from your flesh.

Tricks, Mischief and Mayhem by Daniel I. Russell—Tricks, Mischief and Mayhem. These are not just some of the themes lurking in this tome of horror, but the names of three mischievous carnival clowns. Along with them you'll meet some of Australia's most popular monsters and legends, along with a popular cast of ghosts, demons, and zombies. Hell, there are more than a few stories portraying nature fighting back.

If you ever thought of becoming an author, I'd also like to recommend these non-fiction titles:

Horror 101: The Way Forward—a comprehensive overview of the Horror fiction genre and career opportunities available to established and aspiring authors, including Jack Ketchum, Graham Masterton, Edward Lee, Lisa Morton, Ellen Datlow, Ramsey Campbell, and many more.

Modern Mythmakers: 35 interviews with Horror and Science Fiction Writers and Filmmakers by Michael McCarty—Ever wanted to hang out with legends like Ray Bradbury, Richard Matheson, and Dean Koontz? *Modern Mythmakers* is your chance to hear fun anecdotes and career advice from authors and filmmakers like Forrest J. Ackerman, Ray Bradbury, Ramsey Campbell, John Carpenter, Dan Curtis, Elvira, Neil Gaiman, Mick Garris, Laurell K. Hamilton, Jack Ketchum, Dean Koontz, Graham Masterton, Richard Matheson, John Russo, William F. Nolan, John Saul, Peter Straub, and many more.

Writers On Writing: An Author's Guide—Your favorite authors share their secrets in the ultimate guide to becoming and being and author. With your support, *Writers On Writing* will become an ongoing eBook series with original 'On Writing' essays by writing professionals. A new edition will be launched every few months, featuring four or five essays per edition, so be sure to check out the webpage regularly for updates.

Or check out other Crystal Lake Publishing book for your Dark Fiction, Horror, Suspense, and Thriller needs.

BIOGRAPHY

Mark Allan Gunnells loves to tell stories. He has since he was a kid, penning one-page tales that were Twilight Zone knockoffs. He likes to think he has gotten a little better since then. He has been lucky enough to work with some wonderful publishers such as Apex Publishing, Bad Moon Books, Journalstone, Evil Jester Press, Etopia, Sideshow Press, Sinister Grin, Great Old Ones, Crystal Lake Publishing, and Gallows Press. He loves reader feedback, and above all he loves telling stories. He lives in Greer, SC, with his fiancé Craig A. Metcalf.

Connect with Crystal Lake Publishing

Website (be sure to sign up for our newsletter):
www.crystallakepub.com
Facebook:
www.facebook.com/Crystallakepublishing
Twitter:
https://twitter.com/crystallakepub

With unmatched success since 2012, Crystal Lake Publishing has quickly become one of the world's leading indie publishers of Mystery, Thriller, and Suspense books with a Dark Fiction edge.

Crystal Lake Publishing puts integrity, honor and respect at the forefront of our operations.

We strive for each book and outreach program that's launched to not only entertain and touch or comment on issues that affect our readers, but also to strengthen and support the Dark Fiction field and its authors.

Not only do we publish authors who are legends in the field and as hardworking as us, but we look for men and women who care about their readers and fellow human beings. We only publish the very best Dark Fiction, and look forward to launching many new careers.

We strive to know each and every one of our readers, while building personal relationships with our authors, reviewers, bloggers, pod-casters, bookstores and libraries.

Crystal Lake Publishing is and will always be a beacon of what passion and dedication, combined with overwhelming teamwork and respect, can accomplish: Unique fiction you can't find anywhere else.

We do not just publish books, we present you worlds within your world, doors within your mind, from talented authors who sacrifice so much for a moment of your time.

This is what we believe in. What we stand for. This will be our legacy.

Welcome to Crystal Lake Publishing.

We hope you enjoyed this title. If so, we'd be grateful if you could leave a review on your blog or any of the other websites and outlets open to book reviews. Reviews are like gold to writers and publishers, since word-of-mouth is and will always be the best way to market a great book. And remember to keep an eye out for more of our books.

www.ingramcontent.com/pod-product-compliance
Lightning Source LLC
Chambersburg PA
CBHW060946120726
47910CB00002B/511